C000214714

THE MIDNIGHT MAN

THE MIDNIGHT MAN

CAROLINE MITCHELL

embla
books

First published in Great Britain in 2021 by

embla
books

Bonnier Books UK Limited
4th Floor, Victoria House, Bloomsbury Square, London, WC1B 4DA
Owned by Bonnier Books
Sveavägen 56, Stockholm, Sweden

A CIP catalogue record for this book is available from the British Library.

1

ISBN: 9781471415425

This book is typeset using Atomik ePublisher.

Printed and bound in Great Britain by Clays Ltd, Elcograf S.p.A.

Embla Books is an imprint of Bonnier Books UK.
www.bonnierbooks.co.uk

Praise for Caroline Mitchell

'Whenever I pick up a Caroline Mitchell book I always feel safe in the knowledge that she is going to take me on a tense, thrilling, twisty ride'
Angela Marsons

'Caroline Mitchell is one of my favourite authors . . . she takes the reader on a journey to a dark place where monsters hide in plain sight'
The Book Review Café

'With her police officer experience, Caroline Mitchell knows how to deliver on plot, character and most importantly, emotion, in any book she writes'
My Weekly

Also by Caroline Mitchell

To Jane Snelgrove,
for bringing magic to my words

If you open your door to the Midnight Man,
Hide with a candle wherever you can.
Try not to scream as he draws near,
Because one of you won't be leaving here . . .

Prologue

Monday, 31st October 1994

Blackhall Manor

I remember the day I died quite clearly. It began as a nothing day, just like many nothing days before it. Back then, I didn't understand the important things in life. It wasn't about pop stars, or clothes, or boys, or any of that stuff I thought I couldn't live without. It was about family. But you don't appreciate the people who matter until they're gone.

I didn't know what dread was until we moved into Blackhall Manor. Sometimes I'd wake in the middle of the night, my sheets damp from sweat as apprehension swallowed me whole. What frightened me the most was not being able to put a name to these feelings, or explain them away. I think my grandmother sensed something was wrong because she took my brother and me out as much as she could. It was her idea to take us trick-or-treating, and I remember being jolted in my seat that night as she swerved to avoid a pothole in the road. I hated that pothole because it meant we were almost home.

The comforting glow of the street lights was behind us, and I winced at the sound of the brambles clawing the side of the car as we drove down the winding dirt track. Dead fingernails clawing for attention. I was nothing if not imaginative. I glanced back at my younger brother as we passed through the wrought iron gates, wondering if he, too, was consumed by a similar sense of dread. But Robin was too busy calling out 'Black Jacks! Fruit salads!' and 'Flying saucers!' like some sweet-obsessed four-year-old with Tourette's. 'Swap you a white mouse for a cola bottle,' he said, extending his chubby hand.

I peered through the gloom at the blob of white chocolate melting on his palm. 'No thanks,' I said, turning back to draw a sad face on the condensation-streaked glass with my finger.

There were ten years between my brother and I, who had been deemed a 'happy accident' when he arrived in the world. I adored everything about him, but since hitting my teenage years I preferred to spend time with my friends.

Trick-or-treating was for babies, I decided, and this would be the last year Robin and I would go. I was far too grown up to suffer the indignities of traipsing from house to house with a less than spooky grandmother and a mini Batman in tow. I remembered when we lived in town, Mummy and Daddy had a party and invited the whole street. Daddy dressed up as Dracula, and everyone said how brilliant he was.

My spirits sank as Blackhall Manor came into view. The dilapidated building was perched in solitude on its hilltop, surrounded by a thick white mist which rolled in off the fields. It wasn't the lifeless trees standing sentry that gave me the creeps as we navigated the winding path. Nor was it the ravens perched on the barbed wire fence. It wasn't the sound of the wind howling through the galvanised outbuildings, or the creatures scurrying

2

in the thick undergrowth. All those things would have frightened me once, but they paled in comparison to the tall brick building looming ahead. It came with a history fit for any ghost story. None of my friends visited. Neither would I, given a choice. In Blackhall Manor, it was Halloween all year long. Daddy said that living with Granny and Grandad would be fun. But after five long years of helping them with the farm, even he didn't believe that anymore.

We parked up next to Uncle John's BMW, which was facing out on the gravel drive. *Ready for a quick getaway,* I thought. Mummy once described him as a mediator, and by the look on his face as he exited the house, his visit had not gone well. Clutching my bag of sweets, I took slow, reluctant steps through the open front door, leaving Granny to exchange words with Uncle John.

A cold wind chased me as I walked inside. The air was thick with negativity and it was clear by the look on Mum's face that an argument had taken place. Grandad stood at the base of the wide stairwell; his bushy brows knitted in a frown as he helped Robin with his wellington boots. 'Look, Mummy!' Robin squeaked, showing off his bag of sweets as she approached. 'I got loads!' Robin did not notice that Mummy's eyes were red-rimmed from crying, but I did, and my heart sank even more. I followed them into the kitchen. 'Where's Daddy?' I asked, undoing the button of my witch's cloak. At least it was warm in the kitchen. Grandad kept the Aga fed with timber cut from our private woodlands, and the sweet smell of moss-covered cedar hung in the air.

'Come along, young man,' Grandad said as Robin downed a glass of milk. 'Up to bed with you.'

I always found it strange how Grandad idolised my little brother, yet fought with Daddy all the time.

'Brush your teeth,' Mummy said. 'I'll be up in a minute to read you a story.' But her words were hollow, her smile forced.

I walked towards the doorway, lingering as Mummy and Granny spoke. 'Did you sort anything out?' Granny said, her voice low.

But Mummy shook her head.

'Give it time,' Granny replied with a sigh.

Rarely a day passed without an argument of some kind. There were kids in my school whose parents were divorced. I didn't want that happening to us.

'Where is he now?' Granny said.

'In his study.'

I straightened as Mummy caught me standing at the door. 'What are you doing there? Up to bed.' The sadness I sensed in her took my breath away. I ran towards her like a little child, inhaling the scent of lavender as I wrapped my arms around her.

'Love you,' I said, feeling her relax in my embrace.

'And we love you too,' she said, too swept up in her own concerns to see mine. 'Now go on, bed.'

I turned left on the landing, to Daddy's study, instead. Peeping through the crack in the door, I watched him clean his shotgun. Methodically, he inspected each piece, a throwback to his army days before he gave it all up to help Grandad with the farm. His face was vacant, his eyes flicking towards the door as a floorboard creaked beneath my foot. Tentatively, I pushed it open, gauging his reaction as I stepped inside.

'Hey wicked witch, what are you doing up?' He lay the barrel of the gun on the mahogany desk before turning to face me. He looked tired but raised his arm to draw me in for a hug. 'It's late;

you should be in bed,' he said, his short beard tickling my forehead as he kissed me goodnight.

The sparse light of the moon only added to the coldness of my bedroom as I lay awake in bed that night. No number of posters or fairy lights could cheer the space up. Pulling my blanket to my chin, I squeezed my eyes shut and prayed for sleep.

At first, I thought the sudden boom was thunder. Rubbing my eyes, I tried to focus as I sat up in bed. *What time is it?* I flicked on my bedside light, but the room remained in darkness. The electricity had gone again. But why hadn't the generator kicked in? I squinted at the digital clock as it ticked the seconds past midnight on my dresser. The air was too chilled for thunder tonight. *Fireworks?* I wondered, half asleep as I slid out of bed. The floorboards felt like ice beneath my feet as I tiptoed towards my bedroom door. I froze as I heard my mother's footsteps rapidly hitting each stair. I wanted to call out for her, but the words locked in my throat as she screamed Robin's name. My hands rushed to my mouth as I heard my mother's guttural howls. Grandad called out from downstairs. Where was Daddy? Nothing made sense. Heavy footsteps thumped across the landing towards my bedroom door.

'Nigel!' Mummy's voice echoed throughout the house, but no response came. 'Not her. Please, not my little girl!'

Why was she calling Daddy? I thought, feeling weak and confused. Jumping into bed, I pulled the blanket to my chest as a struggle took place outside my door. As Mummy's screams evolved into bargaining, my thoughts went to my brother. *Where's Robin?* I watched in horror as my door-knob twisted, left, then right, before finally engaging in the mechanism. It opened with a click. I drew my knees to my chest. My heart was hammering hard, a rush of blood pulsating in my ears.

'What's going on up there?' Grandad's voice rose from downstairs for a second time. The movement behind my door stilled and the door was pressed shut. It was followed by the *thump, thump, thump* of a steady descent down the stairs.

'He's got a gun!' Mummy screamed, and I pinched my arm hard. This had to be a nightmare. It couldn't be real. But this wasn't a nightmare I woke up *from*. It was a nightmare I woke up *to*.

The rational part of my mind remembered that Daddy had been cleaning his shotgun. Maybe Mummy was upset because it went off by accident. But where? In Robin's room? *Not my little girl,* she had screamed. My teeth were chattering now, a sudden sob erupting in my throat as realisation dawned. Daddy didn't have accidents when it came to his gun. Climbing out of bed, I forced one foot in front of the other as I returned to the door and pressed my ear against the wood. I recoiled as another crack of gunfire shook the walls of the house. Downstairs, Granny screamed something about calling the police. Her words were killed by another deafening crack. Thunder. It was relentless. My legs weakened as my world collapsed around me. Then silence.

No, I squeaked. My eyes were blurry with tears, every instinct telling me to hide. But I needed to get to Robin before Daddy did. My hands felt like jelly as I twisted the door-knob. The door opened a crack, and I shrieked as I was met with Mummy's tear-stained face.

'Shhh.' Her breath trembled as she placed a hand on my mouth. Her skin was cold, her face ashen. I nodded in understanding and she released her grip. 'Hurry,' she whispered, guiding me by the elbow. I craned my neck as we padded past Robin's room. His door was open an inch, but I couldn't see all the way in. Part of me didn't want to.

'Here,' Mummy whispered, leading me to the antique wardrobe in the corner of her bedroom. 'Hide in here and don't make a sound, do you hear me? No matter who calls.' Her hands trembled as she pushed my hair off my face. 'Wait for the police. They're on their way.'

'I can't do it,' I cried. 'I can't . . . Please. Mummy . . . don't leave me.'

'Listen to me, you can, and you will. You're my special girl.' Gently, Mummy steered me inside, her quick, panicked breath against my face as she kissed my cheek. The stairwell creaked.

'Not a sound,' Mummy reiterated, her face ravaged by fear. As I stood at the back of the wardrobe, she gently closed the door. I peered through a crack in the wood as the key turned in the lock. There was a soft click as the key was extracted, and in the dark, I made out my mother's outline as she left the room. But what about Robin? I bit on my knuckles to stop the scream erupting from my throat. I already knew the answer. Robin was dead.

Leaden feet climbed the stairs. My mother's screams were cut dead as another shot ripped through the night. As each door on the landing was flung open, I counted the shots so far. The first shot had been for Robin. Then Grandad. Then Granny. Then Mummy . . . and now he was coming for me. The thought was too horrific for my young mind to contemplate. The light left the room as the moon dipped behind a cloud, and I struggled to make out my father's form as he entered. His footsteps were steady and methodical. Every instinct told me to call out to him. Daddy wouldn't hurt me. He would keep me safe. But my mother's warning lingered. The gun hanging from his arm, he grunted as he checked beneath the bed. The metal hangers jingled above me as I recoiled from his presence. It seemed like the loudest sound in the world as Daddy's footsteps stilled.

His voice seemed different as he called my name; robotic, void of emotion. A sob escaped my throat, betraying my presence in the room. I flattened myself against the sides of the wardrobe as a strong hand rattled the door. I held my breath. Silence. Police sirens screamed in the distance. A tiny flicker of hope. But as I peered through the crack in the wardrobe, all hope died. My view was consumed by the barrel of his gun. I remember the floorboard creaking. There was a sudden, blinding flash. I was swallowed by the dark.

That was the day I died, and I haven't left Blackhall Manor since.

1

Sarah chased her peas around her plate with her fork, wondering if fish fingers and chips were more nutritious than the ready meals she had been eating all week. The air fryer was marginally better than the microwave – wasn't it? She prodded the limp fish finger. To think, some poor creature gave up its life to end up like this.

'Fancy it?' she dangled the soggy offering before her ginger cat. His eyes narrowed in silent protest of her presence on the sofa. Most evenings, Sherlock preferred to watch *Pointless* re-runs on his own. 'Alaska,' Sarah blurted, as the quiz show host asked for US states ending with an 'a'. She plopped her fish finger back onto her plate before rising to empty the remnants into the recycling caddy in the kitchen.

'How about a nice juicy chicken leg?' she shouted, her head in her fridge.

'Don't give him that, he'll choke on it.'

Sarah's lips thinned at the sound of David, her husband. He shouldn't even be here. She told herself not to respond.

'There you go, Sher, knock yourself out,' she said, as the chicken landed with a bump on the living-room rug. She sensed her husband's disapproval and she liked it. Sherlock's tail gave a

9

couple of thumps against the sofa cushion before he pounced on the chicken leg. The soft swish of the cat flap followed as he disappeared with it into the night. One day he'd find somewhere more deserving of his nobility and never come back.

Sarah glanced around her drab bungalow, wishing she had the energy to clean the place up. It wasn't as if she'd been busy this last twelve months. Busy eating, maybe. The sofa made a scrunching noise when you sat on it, because of all the sweet wrappers shoved down the sides. Biscuit crumbs littered the creases of the cushions, and she dare not look behind it for fear of the cobwebs lurking there. There was a wine stain in the shape of Italy on her carpet, and the kitchen floor was only clean because she'd used Fairy liquid after she ran out of dishwashing tablets and suds had spilt onto the lino. At least she'd had the presence of mind to get her suit dry-cleaned for tomorrow. The sharp ring of her landline almost made her jump out of her skin. It was so seldom that anyone called that it took her a second to figure out what it was. Even the cold callers didn't bother because she kept them on the line so long. She reckoned they had put her on a blacklist of some sort.

'Hello?' she said, into the heavy, old-fashioned handset.

'It's Gabby,' a voice replied in a no-nonsense tone. Sarah straightened at the sound of her voice, her hand automatically going to her forehead and tugging on her fringe. It was a nervous tic that she was barely aware of anymore.

'Oh . . . h . . . hello, Sarge,' Sarah stuttered, wishing she'd been pre-warned about the call. Then she could have given herself a pep talk, worked out what she was going to say.

'Just checking you're still up for tomorrow, everything OK?'

'Yes,' Sarah said, still fiddling with her fringe. 'Looking forward to it.'

'Good. Don't let me down.'

A dead ringtone followed before Sarah could reply.

'Are you sure about this?'

Sarah glowered as her husband spoke. She should bill him for Botox because he had aged her horrendously – she felt a hell of a lot older than her forty years.

'I mean . . . are you sure you're ready?' he continued. 'Look what happened last time.'

'That was down to you.' Sarah ground her teeth as she broke her vow of silence. David knew how to push her buttons when it came to work. Heading back into the living room, she almost tripped over an empty pizza box. She really should clean this place up.

'It's long hours,' David continued in a patronising tone. 'You'll get no thanks for it.'

'I'm on restricted duties,' Sarah snapped. 'I won't be doing much.' It was a shitty way to resume her new role. But it did mean regular hours and not taking on more than she could handle until she was cleared. Her husband knew all of this, given his years of experience in the police. Such jobs were fine for the boys, not for the little missus at home. She sighed. Perhaps he was right.

'The world's a dangerous place,' he continued, determined to drive his point home.

'You think I don't know that?' Exasperated, Sarah threw her hands in the air. 'I know what the world is, and I know what *you* are. You made this happen and now I'm paying the price. So, do me a favour and keep your bloody opinions to yourself.'

It was true. She'd lost the respect of her colleagues before she'd even begun. Marching down the hall, she walked into her bedroom and slammed the door. This was the one space in the house where David left her alone. Their marriage had long since broken down, but he still popped in on occasion to tell her what to do. Despite her best efforts, she let him. What was wrong with her?

The bed bounced as she sat, making a rusty ew-aw noise. Its springs were the old-fashioned sort, which groaned loudly when she turned in the night. Buying a new bed was also on her checklist of things to do. She slid open the top drawer of her bedside table and fetched a deep sigh. Picking up her ID card, she rubbed her thumb against the picture that had been taken when she was a recruit. She was the oldest person in her intake, and right now, she felt like the least confident. David was simply vocalising what had been in her head all along.

She pulled open the second drawer, her gaze falling on the glorious stash of tablets within. Enough to send a horse to meet his maker. Each small white tablet a promise she could hold in her hand. A promise that could make everything go away. Because if she couldn't make things work on the outside world, there was no point in going on.

2

Libby kicked a stone as she walked down the old dirt track. If their parents could see them now; a group of Catholic schoolgirls sneaking out to the most out of bounds building in Upper Slayton. The invite had been exclusive. Only a few people from her school were 'chosen' to attend as they broke up for half-term. She turned over the stiff black card which had been placed in a small envelope and shoved inside her schoolbag. It read:

You are cordially invited to play
The Midnight Game
Blackhall Manor
31st October 2019
00.00

On the back of the card in a tiny font were the words 'If you tell, you'll go to hell'. Nobody had admitted to it yet, but they all guessed that Angelica was responsible. She was the most theatrical in the group, and this year she had upped her game. It certainly wasn't twins Bethany and Isobel, who lacked the imagination and flair. Then there was Jahmelia, the youngest among them. She was even more frightened than Libby. The waxing crescent moon was a thumbnail in the sky as they crept down the jagged path.

'So, which of you losers hasn't had their first kiss yet?' Angelica said, Tesco bag in one hand, cigarette in the other. Angelica was the first person in their group to smoke. She was also the first to French kiss. At fifteen, she was a year older than the others, because she'd had to repeat a school year. She had lots of older friends, which made it all the more surprising that she was spending Halloween with Libby and the gang.

'It's Jahmelia for sure,' Bethany said, matching Angelica's mocking tones. Libby rolled her eyes. Bethany was the biggest suck-up in the group. Her parents were what Libby's would call 'social climbers', and they brown-nosed Angelica's mum and dad every chance they got. But Angelica's parents were bigots according to Libby's parents.

Libby was meant to be sleeping in a tent down at the bottom of Jahmelia's garden tonight. That was as scary as things were meant to get.

'I like kissing my baby brother,' Jahmelia said in a quiet voice, small plumes of white breath filling the freezing air around her. 'He has soft cheeks, and he smells nice.'

Jahmelia was the youngest in the group, at barely thirteen years of age. Her intelligence had propelled her forward in class, but she had little in the way of street smarts.

'"*I like kissing my baby brother*,"' Angelica imitated Jahmelia's voice in a high-pitched squeak. 'That statement is wrong on *so* many levels.'

'Leave her alone.' Libby linked Jahmelia's arm. 'If the security guy hears us, we'll be in deep shit.'

Angelica shot her a thunderbolt of a look. 'He's not due for hours.'

It had been Angelica's job to work out the security rota, and he came twice a night, checking the perimeter under torchlight before moving on. The house was far from the gate so he wouldn't be able to see them once they were inside. Bethany and Isobel were tasked with bringing the props and it was Libby's job to find a way in. There was no way they could get through the thick black brambles, and the iron gate was padlocked. But she had found a place near the back of the outhouses where a barbed wire fence had fallen down.

Under the light of her phone torch, Libby led them to the gap in the fence.

'Are you sure you want to do this?' she said, her feet numb as they sank into the cold, wet earth.

'Go home then, if you're scared.' Gripping her carrier bag, Angelica ducked under the wire. 'I'll do it by myself.' Libby believed that she would. Angelica had an underlying current of darkness. She wasn't just foolhardy, she was angry at life. As if to prove the point, she slipped a baggy from the pocket of her jeans and dangled it before them. 'For later.'

That was the point where Libby should have gone home. But instead, she held up the wire to allow everyone through. 'Whatever happens . . .' She became breathless as they trudged towards the house. 'Stick to the cover story, alright?'

'Yada yada, whatever,' Angelica said, her steps quickening. 'Hurry up. It's ten to.'

Already, Libby felt suffocated by the house before her. She kept her head down, watching her footing on the jagged ground. Her hair was damp with dew and a thick mist curled around the Manor – a protective barrier which only the foolhardy would pass through. She didn't want to think about the family who died here. Of the man who shot his own children with a gun. Libby inhaled a sharp breath at the crunch of glass breaking underfoot. 'I hope we don't have to climb in through the window,' she said, flashing her torch over the broken pane.

'No need,' Angelica whispered as the front door swung open. She pulled down the hood of her coat and looked them all squarely in the eye. 'Alright, spill your guts. Who organised this?' But as Angelica handed each girl a candle, she was met with blank stares.

'We thought it was you,' Bethany whispered, bug-eyed with fear. But Angelica shook her head. Her smile only faltered for a moment as another thought occurred.

'It must be Jason. He's been wanting to get me on my own for ages.'

Isobel and Bethany shook their heads in tandem at the mention of their big brother. 'No, he hasn't,' said Isobel. 'Jason's gone to Dublin for the half-term.'

Their voices faded as they followed Angelica inside, their shadows dancing behind their flickering candles as they lit each one in turn. They turned to survey the grand entrance hall – a ghoulish museum to the mass murders of exactly twenty-five years ago. The furniture was decaying, the pipes leaking through the walls, and each doorway was framed with ragged cobwebs loaded with dust. Libby fought a shudder. The house may be dying, but it still carried a sense of something moving to and fro.

'We should go,' Jahmelia groaned, hugging herself. If her shoulders rose any higher, they would be touching her ears.

'Bunch of wusses,' Angelica muttered as she checked her watch. 'It's nearly time.'

She bent to take the last chunky candle from her carrier bag. 'Think how cool we'll be at school when we tell everyone—'

Her words were cut short by sudden, frantic flapping. A black cloud of bats exploded from the rafters and swooped past them before flitting out through the open door. A cacophony of screams erupted as the girls clung to each other. The screams turned to laughter, which dissolved into tears as the last bat flew out.

'Oh my God, your faces,' Angelica laughed, one hand on her chest.

'Yeah . . . I think a little bit of pee came out!' Libby laughed, wiping a tear from the corner of her eye. It was good to feel part of a group. To feel like she belonged.

Dipping her hand into the carrier bag, Libby pulled out some cards and handed them around with a pen. Each one of them scribbled their names, wincing as they pricked their finger with a needle and added a spot of blood. The temperature had dipped since they entered, and the last of Libby's confidence began to evaporate. They had only just arrived but already, she felt a creeping sense of being watched. She looked beyond the cobwebs and the creaking floorboards. Shadows from the past were coming to life.

'What do we do next?' Bethany said nervously, as they followed Angelica back out to the front door. Her face was flushed, despite the cold.

Isobel's gaze darted around as she knelt to place the candle at the doorstep, on top of the bloodstained cards with their names. She was the mirror image of her twin sister and seemed every bit as scared. 'Quench your candles but leave the one on the step lit. Knock twenty-two times but time it so the last knock lands on the stroke of midnight. Then blow the last candle out.' She delivered the instructions with confidence. The game was an urban legend. The details weren't hard to find online.

Angelica made a fist, preparing to invite the Midnight Man in. The girls huddled together as each ominous thud broke twenty-five years of silence. To think that a family once lived here. Once cried and laughed within these walls . . . Knock . . . knock . . . knock . . . Libby counted each thud as they echoed in the darkness. *Eighteen, nineteen, twenty, twenty-one* . . . She shuddered as a cool breeze curled around the back of her neck.

With one eye on her watch, Angelica knocked for the last time. There was no going back now.

The girls stood in quiet reverence as Angelica explained the rest of the game which was played only by the bravest of teenagers in Slayton every Halloween. They were to wander around the house in silence, avoiding capture until 3.33 a.m. It was a simple concept, but players had reported experiences from hallucinations to full-blown paranormal encounters. That's if they could be believed. As nervous as Libby was about coming here, she wasn't so sure that the stories were all true.

Solemnly, Jahmelia blew out the flame. Flicking her lighter, Angelica relit it. As per the rules of the game, they each had a candle to guide their way.

'Remember,' Libby said, her stomach churning with anticipation. 'If your candle goes out, it means the Midnight Man is near. Either relight it or step inside a salt circle for protection – but you've got to be quick.'

'OK, freaks,' Angelica said. 'I'm off to explore.'

'Don't leave me!' Isobel called out, almost extinguishing her candle as she trotted after her in the dark. Bethany looked from Libby and Jahmelia back to Angelica before chasing after her twin.

'Eww.' Jahmelia pointed at a dead rat in the corner of the room. A splatter of blood rose up the skirting board. Its neck was snapped in a trap. 'Do you really want to do this?'

'You know what Angelica's like.' Libby picked at a piece of wax on her candle. 'We'll never live it down if we don't.'

'But if Angelica didn't shove those invites in our bag, then who did?'

'It's her. She's trying to frighten us, that's all. I bet they're laughing their heads off, wondering if we've fallen for it.'

'Yeah,' Jahmelia said, relaxing a little. 'Where did she get the weed from?'

'Her mum's herb rack,' Libby snorted. 'She's probably at home now, wondering where her rosemary has gone.'

Libby was glad she was able to put Jahmelia's mind at rest. They had bonded through study group. The two of them had some of the highest IQs in the school, but Angelica's grades were slipping. It wouldn't have surprised her if she *had* brought drugs to the house. Libby wouldn't have any part of it, but neither would she tell. A floorboard creaked from overhead and Libby held her breath.

'They must be in the bedroom,' Jahmelia said, inching a little closer to her. 'That's where it started, isn't it? With the little boy.'

Libby nodded grimly. She didn't want to think about the family that died here. She wanted to get to 3.33 a.m. and leave. But the darkness beyond her candle felt alive. A low, whistling sound echoed throughout the building as a rush of icy wind shot past.

'You know what the worst part is?' Jahmelia nervously cupped the pale flame. 'We can't turn on the lights. I mean, I know we're not meant to but . . . what happens if our candles go out? We won't be able to see.'

'Then don't blow out your candle,' Libby said, as they entered the kitchen. A scratching noise from the corner of the room made her jump, the candle wax burning her fingers.

'It's a mouse,' Jahmelia said. 'I hate mice. But we're in a house where a family were murdered, on Halloween night. I'm barely scared of that sucker.'

All the same, they edged out of the kitchen, huddling over their candles as they entered each room. The air was sour with mould; damp spores blossoming up every wall. Their voices low, they talked and joked, occasionally hearing murmurs from upstairs.

'Is it OK to eat?' Jahmelia said, sliding a Twix from her jacket pocket. Libby waved it away as she offered her half.

'Not my little girl . . .'

'What did you say?' Libby said, as she walked towards the window.

'I asked if you wanted some chocolate.'

'No, after that.' Libby frowned. 'You whispered something about a girl.'

Jahmelia shook her head. 'Wasn't me.'

'C'mon, keep moving.' Goosebumps prickled on Libby's skin as they shuffled out of the room. Jahmelia felt as tense as a mousetrap as they linked arms and made their way to the hall.

'Not my little girl . . .'

'Did you hear that?' Libby said, her throat tight. She glanced around the room. The mist seemed to have followed them in.

'Hear what?' Jahmelia spluttered, her mouth full. Libby was about to respond when a scream rose from upstairs. It was Isobel.

Libby stared up at the expansive stairwell. She did not want to climb those stairs. A flicker of candlelight illuminated sudden movement on the landing as Bethany and Isobel flew out of one of the rooms.

'I've only got ten seconds, I've only got ten seconds!' Isobel whimpered from the top of the stairs as she tried to light her candle. She rasped the flint lighter, the flame flickering in her shaking hands.

'What happened?' Libby watched Isobel and her twin descend, their eyes wide with fear.

'There's someone up there,' Isobel panted. 'I swear, I saw a man next to the bed.'

'I heard whispering!' Bethany piped up. 'And there're huge white moths flapping everywhere!'

Libby remained silent. They had two hours to go before they could leave. She wasn't going to chicken out first.

'Where's Angelica?'

'We lost her.' Bethany looked as if she was about to burst into tears.

'Maybe she gave up playing and went home,' Isobel added.

'You're kidding,' Jahmelia's voice echoed in wonderment. 'I didn't see her leave.'

'Must have been when we were in the kitchen.' Libby's grip on her candle tightened. If she could make it through the next couple of hours, then she could lord this over Angelica for years. She smiled. There would be no more smart remarks about being a loser, or taunting of Jahmelia. Angelica would answer to her.

'What are we doing? Are we going home?' Jahmelia said

hopefully. All eyes were on Libby as they awaited a response. She licked the dryness from her lips. Set her jaw firm.

'Make a circle with some salt. We'll sit back-to-back.' She gazed at the pallid faces before her. 'We came here to play a game. I'm not leaving until we win.'

3

Maggie rubbed her arms as she slid out of bed. It wasn't the cold which had awoken her, nor the rattle of the pipes in the walls. It was instinct. She grabbed her cardigan off the corner of the metal bedstead. If fear had a smell, she would reek of it right now. Standing at her bedroom door, she tried to muster up enough courage to leave her room. Her fingers tightened around the cold metal door-knob, and she willed herself to turn it. But it was the memory which bloomed that held her prisoner, still as fresh and painful as when it happened three years ago. Her four-year-old son, Elliott, pale in the moonlight, his eyes full dark.

'I don't like Auntie Emily's plait,' he'd said, sitting bolt upright in bed. His voice had been so flat and emotionless that it had taken precious seconds to process his words.

'Sorry, love? What was that?' she'd said, fetching an extra blanket as a chill descended in the room. She must have misheard. Her sister's hair was long, but she always wore it loose.

'The plait,' he'd said again. 'I don't like it. It makes her face all funny.'

Back then, Maggie was yet to familiarise herself with the night terrors that would take hold. Elliott's eyes slipped shut, before

23

rolling open again. Only this time, his gaze was focused on her. An uncomfortable creeping sensation raised goosebumps on her skin.

'You're dreaming,' she'd said, guiding him back to his pillow. 'Go back to sleep.'

'Make her take it off,' Elliott had insisted, placing his hands around his neck. His words were raspy, as if he were being choked.

'It's just a dream,' Maggie whispered, her smile frozen. But her words felt like the most dreadful lie. 'Go back to sleep.' She could barely remember tucking Elliott in before leaving his room. But when the door clicked closed, she'd sprinted down the hall to grab her phone. Her hands shaking, she muttered beneath her breath as she dialled her sister's number. 'It's ridiculous. It's just a nightmare. It's . . .'

Maggie blinked away a tear as she recalled the day her sister took her own life. It took her an hour to drive to her house, to find the police outside her door. But they wouldn't allow her inside. Why? Because they'd had to wait for the inspector before they could cut her body free from the noose. The 'plait' Elliott had referred to had been a thick brown rope. As they took her sister away in a body bag, Maggie had turned away from the scene. And now, she was creeping down the corridor to her son's room, scared of what she might find.

Oh, Elliott. Her spirits sank as she saw him at his bedroom window, his face pressed so close against it that his breath was fogging the pane. She opened her mouth to speak, her hand hovering mid-air. She should tell him that he was dreaming, but she was rooted to the floor. Because when the night terrors came, the words which left Elliott's mouth were not those of a seven-year-old child.

Maybe he's sleepwalking, she thought, taking another slow step towards her son.

Despite the floorboard creaking, he didn't move an inch. Rigid and unblinking, he was lost in the night world. Fear tempered Maggie's movements as she forced herself to approach. She could barely describe the sense that woke her when Elliott was like this. An invisible thread, powerful enough to pull her from sleep. Not that she welcomed it. That was a hard fact to admit. She checked her watch. It was just gone half one. Taking a deep breath, she approached him, gently placing a hand on his shoulder.

'Elliott?' she said. 'It's Mummy . . .' But her words were cut short as his scream tore through the air.

'Get off me!' he raged, kicking, scratching, tearing at her skin. Her jaw set tight, Maggie locked her arms around him in a bear hug, squeezing her eyes shut as she took the blows. Elliott may have been small for his age, but he was getting strong. Too strong for her to do this without getting hurt. She wished her husband was here. He would know what to do. Being an army wife brought its own set of challenges, but since Lewis was admitted to hospital last year, she'd felt totally isolated and alone.

'Baby, it's Mummy,' she said, crying out as he sank his teeth into her arm. She repeated the words. Mummy was here. He was dreaming. He was safe. Slowly, he came back to her. His limbs relaxed. His breathing slowed. She released her grip. He batted his long black lashes, a string of drool hanging lazily from the corner of his mouth. Staring at her in confusion, he emerged as if from a trance, the moon casting his skin in a blue hue.

'Mummy?' His breath shuddered from exertion.

'It's OK,' she smiled, wiping his chin with the corner of her cardigan before guiding him back to bed. 'You're sleepwalking, that's all.' It was the most reassuring way of describing what he was going through.

She hugged him tightly, feeling warmth from the damp patch in his pyjamas where he had wet himself. She would bathe him in the morning, but right now, she needed to get him back to sleep. Offering quiet reassurance, she changed him into clean, dry pyjamas before tucking him into bed. A glint of silver caught her eye and she picked up the object from the floor. Elliott couldn't sleep without his medal. His father had been awarded the Queen's Gallantry Medal for fearlessly running towards a helicopter crash and saving many lives. Perhaps Elliott hoped his daddy's bravery would rub off on him. Slipping it beneath the pillow, she smoothed over Elliott's hair, just as she did when he was a baby. A soft trickle of blood oozed from the bitemark on her forearm as she waited for the sound of his gentle snores. She shuddered as a draught caressed her skin.

He had never been this bad before. She could have asked him what he was dreaming about while it was fresh in his mind. Like the time he foresaw that awful train crash in Bristol, or when a school bus in Romford had lost control in the snow and three people had died.

She recalled the grim-faced police officer asking how she knew her sister had taken her own life. 'Instinct,' she'd replied. Because instinct, people could deal with. Premonitions they could not. Tonight, her son had seen something truly terrifying, and to her shame, she didn't want to know.

4

The sun broke in ribbons between the trees, casting Blackhall Manor in a sepia tone. Standing on the hill I gazed at the building, my mind a blackish flies' nest of thoughts.

Dawn was approaching and my life had taken a surreal turn. Bracing myself against the biting wind, I replayed last night's events. The build-up, the anticipation. The careful attention to detail. A part of me couldn't believe that I had gone through with it. Then again, this had been no random murder. There had been months of preparation, and the house guests were willing participants in my game. But when it came to Angelica's final moments, I was rash and impetuous. The knife had cut through her flesh like butter. I had underestimated my own strength.

I sucked cold air between my teeth as I relived each moment: the smell of the woodlands, her chest hitching, wrists taut against rope. Then the sudden spray of blood. Spitting at the taste of warm iron. I'd watched the true crime dramas, where presenters talked about the 'mind of a killer'. I was no psychopath, but when it came to Angelica's last moments, all I felt was numb. There was much more to this than ridding the world of some silly little teenager who was out to impress her friends. She would have hated to know it, but Angelica was nothing but a pawn.

I craned my neck upwards, taking in every facet of the gothic ruin.

I'd heard the rumours about how Blackhall Manor was a cursed house in an equally cursed town. Had it spoken in a whisper that only Mr Middleton could hear? In the end, the man had lost his mind and turned his gun on himself. But not me. It was my turn and I would play the game to completion.

I took the scrub path towards the dilapidated house, despite every instinct urging me to leave. Soon the place would be infested with police, but I was in its magnetic pull. I was not the only one drawn here; the place was teeming with life, from the rooks perching on the guttering to the insects burrowing in the wood.

The air felt heavier in the hall, thick with the stench of bat droppings. The devil's songbirds, my mother called them. They hung from the rotting rafters, seeking shelter in the shadows from the unforgiving chill of the November winds. I lifted my sleeve to check my watch. I shouldn't be here. But so what, if the police came? I knew the crawlspaces; the network of veins running through Blackhall's fractured skeleton. Slowly, over the course of my visits, the Manor had revealed itself to me. Then it gave me the gift of the Midnight Game, and the schoolgirls who were gullible enough to accept my invitation. And so, I stepped into the shoes of the Midnight Man.

I approached the grand entrance and rested my hand on the banister. Dragging my feet up the stairs, I passed through the veils of time as I retraced Middleton's steps. Had he planned the attack? Or was he lost to the force of Blackhall, turned inward like a cowering child? Newspapers reported that he spent time in his study that night, methodically cleaning his gun. Given his years in the army, he was a good shot.

Taking a left on the grand landing, I approached the old study door, loose on its hinges. In my mind's eye I caught a glimpse of a long-buried past. Middleton's daughter standing in a witch's costume. Her father telling her to go to bed. The hairs stood sentry on the back of my neck each time I was greeted with this vision. Was it an echo of the past – a residue of violence, or simply my imagination? I didn't know. But as I stepped through the door, I saw him sitting at the decaying mahogany bureau.

The house was a museum, every piece of its story left where it should be. Upstairs, the air was sweet from patches of mould which patterned the walls. I turned back down the hall, to where Middleton took his first shot. The door to Robin's room groaned in defiance as I pushed it aside. The frame of Robin's small single bed was still in the middle of the room. I stood in quiet solemnity. I could see Mrs Middleton, her eyes bulging in horror. I'd replayed this in my mind so many times. Middleton's father was found slumped downstairs, one arm through his bloodied dressing gown. His mother had been shot between the eyes while she phoned for help. As I turned towards the master bedroom, the door slammed shut in my face.

'Not my little girl,' a woman's faint voice carried in the mildewed air. I had heard it before. I'd heard lots of things in this godforsaken place.

I gripped the door-knob and was met with resistance. Grunting, I forced it to turn. There was a sense of surrender as the rusted mechanism came free. Had Middleton gone straight to the wardrobe, or searched the room for his daughter? Had he looked behind the door? Pushed aside the long limp velvet drapes that touched the floor? The wardrobe did not survive the shot. The room was deathly quiet, an echo chamber for my pulsing heart. Dropping to my knees, I traced *the stain of blood ingrained on the wooden floor. It had to be hers. The key to the wardrobe door was found by police in Middleton's wife's pocket. A last, desperate act to save her child. Then the last shot of gunfire, ripping through the silence as Middleton turned the gun on himself. I lay on the floor, staring up at the ceiling, in the same position he had been found. It was a pleasure to resurrect the Midnight Man.*

5

'It'll be OK. Relax. You'll get through this.' The voice was that of Sarah's husband. She didn't want to hear it. Not today. 'Did you hear me? I said you'll get through . . .'

'Leave me alone!' She raised her hands to her head, as if swatting away an errant fly. She would be fine. She had to be. Besides, it was just one day. One day to get her bearings, then the weekend off and she'd begin properly on Monday. She had her DI to thank for that. A bloom of guilt rose. She shouldn't have allowed him to mollycoddle her but today, she was grateful for it. 'Sherlock. Here, puss, where are you? Mummy's off now.' Her marmalade moggy was stretched out on the sofa, regarding her with disdain. 'Be a good boy, I'll be back before you know it.' She reached out to pet him, withdrawing her hand sharply as he hissed. He had always been David's cat. But apart from her DI, he was the only friend she had. 'Right,' she said, checking the mirror in the hall. She tugged at the waistband of her trousers before smoothing back her hair. Was that a pimple breaking out on her chin? 'Oh, God,' she groaned. 'I'm a mess.'

'You look fine.'

Sarah rolled her eyes. 'Not one bloody word from you, you hear me? Not one fucking word!' Grabbing her keys from the hall table, she traipsed out the front door. She had so many things to remember. Rule one: Don't talk to yourself. Rule two: Don't talk to him. Rule three: Don't take any crap. Rule four: Don't talk about what happened. Rule five: Act normal. Rule six . . . She sighed. She couldn't remember rule six.

Sarah inhaled. After gearing up to this day for months, she was already falling apart at the seams.

She rammed her Mini Cooper into gear as she reversed off her front drive. 'Sorry,' she said, as the gears ground. She swore beneath her breath. She had broken rule one *and* five and she wasn't even out of her drive.

It felt good to be out and about, and Sarah was looking forward to reacquainting herself with the town she had spent the last twelve months hiding from. The roads seemed busier these days as people were drawn to Slayton, despite the chilly November weather.

As they drove the incline towards town, visitors were treated to a breathtaking view of the lake. Further up was Blackhall Manor, perched high on its hilltop with the woodlands as its backdrop. It overlooked the residents of Upper Slayton and the crop of newbuilds and gated communities that were popping up. Town was centred around one long, tree-lined street with a mixture of chain and independent stores, set back on broad pavements. The train tracks running through the centre acted as a divide between the classes, and every hour, the electric gates rose and fell. Properties on the upper side could fetch tens of thousands of pounds more than their counterparts on the other side of the gates. So while Upper Slayton residents frequented the bistros with their striped awnings and artisan coffee shops, people from

Lower Slayton preferred the cheap and cheerful cafés, and livelier music bars.

But one building was the great leveller. Sarah stared up at the police station, a newly refurbished concrete monstrosity which loomed over Slayton High Street, not far from the train tracks. The station flag billowed at the front of the building, above the steps. Sarah drove around to the back and parked in the rear car park, her rusted Mini painfully out of place. The bumped and battered little red car didn't help her image, but each dent held a memory and she couldn't bear to part with it. David had always hated it, but to Sarah it was a familiar friend in a chaotic world.

Head up, chest out, she thought, as she slammed the car door. This could either be the best or worst morning she'd have this year. *You'll win them round.* She breathed in a lungful of air so crisp it could have been a spring day.

As she gazed up at the four floors of windows, her mouth was bone dry. The last time she was in this building she was escorted out through the back entrance. She gathered up all her reserves before passing through reception. Her arms felt empty, but everything she needed was inside. Everything except for her self-confidence, that was. She needed to bring that herself.

Her first stop was with her old DI, Bernard Lee. She had considered going straight to her office, to rip the plaster off, but Bernard had helped her so much in her career and was the tonic she needed right now. Saint Bernard, they called him. Sarah liked to believe the nickname was down to his good nature, rather than his jowls. It was hard to believe he came from running his family's slaughterhouse to joining the police. He had a penchant for hopeless cases, which is perhaps where she came in.

Bernard was sitting behind his desk, a broad-shouldered man no stranger to physical work. His office was situated just across the hall from CID. His workspace was littered with files and folders, and photographs of children and grandchildren took pride of place on a back wall shelf.

'Take the weight off,' he said as she entered, gesturing for her to sit down. 'How are you doing? Chomping at the bit?' Bernard's use of idioms was known by all.

'It's good to be back,' she said, wondering if she should tell him she was quaking in her boots instead.

'Coffee?'

'No thanks.' Her stomach was in knots as it was. The pot behind Bernard's desk was always brewing, despite being against health and safety regulations. It seemed that police could be trusted with everything except a coffee pot.

'I've spoken to the team.' He glanced over the rim of his coffee cup. 'I know you won't want any fuss, so I've told them to carry on as normal. They're looking forward to working with you again.'

Sarah gave him a look to say that she knew better. 'Are you sure? Because the last time I saw them, things didn't go well.' That was the understatement of the year. It made her cringe to think about it.

Bernard rested his cup on his desk. 'Don't be so hard on yourself. I'm as much to blame as anyone, I should have noticed something was wrong.' He gave her a knowing look. Bernard was one of the only people in the station who knew everything about her.

'If anyone is to blame it's . . .' But the words died on her tongue. She could not bear to say his name aloud. It had taken a year of therapy to stem the anger she felt inside.

'I know.' Bernard delivered a reassuring smile. 'Old news now.'

But it wasn't old news. As long as she was around, it never would be. 'Thank you. For everything. I know you were instrumental in having me back.'

'You're a good egg, why wouldn't I?' Bernard's voice took on a serious tone. 'Are you . . .' He tapped his forehead. 'All ship-shape?' He was asking about her mental health in his own unique way. Occupational health had given her the all clear, but she knew he had to ask.

'All ship-shape,' she agreed, pressing her knees tightly together as she forced a cheery smile.

'Champion,' he said. 'We'll ease you in gently, just statement taking for now. No pressure.'

Sarah nodded gratefully. Work had been sympathetic but they were desperate to fill her post. She was lucky to have her job. But was it a job she was strong enough to return to?

6

'Christian! Christiannnnnnn!' Elsie's voice echoed around the three-bedroom semi. 'What's a gal gotta do to get some fried chicken around here?'

Elsie was lying in the living room, the only place big enough to house her reinforced bed. The air smelled of toffee-flavoured popcorn, one of many snacks within reach. There was movement on the bed as two sausages – one black, one ginger – shifted off her feet. Felix exposed his teeth in a yawn, his pink tongue curling as he exhaled the stink of burped Whiskas. He turned his yellow eyes upon her, his paws working the duvet before settling in contentment by her side.

Toni, her ginger feline, rolled onto her back and emitted a soft hungry mew. As for the rest of her brood . . . Gregory and Officer Dibble were out on the hunt while Boo Boo and T.C. were curled up in a basket on the floor next to her bed. Elsie wriggled her toes as pins and needles spiked. Her circulation was abysmal these days.

'Christian?' she called again. No answer. 'Fine.' She muttered beneath her breath. 'You know what happens when you ignore your mom.' Leaning to one side, she flicked off the switch to the BT broadband. The response was instant.

'Ah, Mom!' Her son's anguished voice rang out from upstairs. 'I was almost finished with my game!' Throwing open his bedroom door, he came down the stairs.

Elsie floundered as she tried to launch herself into an upright position. 'You know the rules. Don't ignore your momma. Or do you want to lose another hour?' The Wi-Fi was her only tug on the leash when he stepped outside the boundaries or ignored her calls for help. God knows she had no physical way of controlling him. Red-faced and sweating, she tried to raise her 400lb frame. 'Pillow,' she gasped, grabbing for the handle dangling from above the bed.

Sulking, Christian wedged the pillow behind her back. She caught his disapproving glare but chose to ignore it. A waft of stale sweat and dried urine rose and Elsie watched as he turned his head away. She knew what he was thinking. Sometimes, Elsie wished he'd come out and say it: that her illness was self-inflicted, and she had nobody to blame but herself. Watching her son, she felt the bitter edge of her own self-disgust.

Her gaze followed her son as he dragged his feet to the American-style fridge-freezer, the door jingling with bottles as he opened it wide. Her bed was next to the living-room windows, but if she craned her neck, she could see into the kitchen, her favourite room in the house.

'Here puss, puss,' Christian called, filling up a cat bowl with milk. A chorus of miaows ensued as her felines joined him in the kitchen and lapped at the bowl.

Elsie watched him bend to stroke each of them in turn. He was a good boy, really. He just needed to be kept in line. She observed him grab the bucket of KFC, one of two he had brought home for her last night. What she *wanted* and what she *needed* were two entirely different things. The bucket of chicken would serve as breakfast before he went to work. Opening the freezer door, he grabbed a packet of frozen éclairs, enough to keep her going until he made it home for lunch.

'About time,' she said, grabbing the food from his outstretched hands. 'Now remember what I said. And no swearing. I didn't raise you to have a potty mouth.'

'I didn't swear.' Christian wiped his hands on the back of his trousers.

'Bull spit,' she replied, before sinking her teeth into a chicken wing. 'You were just about to. And where's my chocolate milk?'

'I'm getting it.' Christian's head hung low as he turned back to the kitchen. 'I'm twenty-five, Mom,' he mumbled. 'Stop treating me like a kid.' Elsie frowned as she watched him walk the worn path from the bed to the fridge.

'Who licked the red from your ice lolly? You're in a right ol' stinky mood today,' she said, as he returned with a two-litre carton of chocolate milk. Glasses were just a formality. It saved on the washing up when she consumed things directly from the pack. She did her bit for the environment.

'Sorry,' he sighed, his shoulders slumped. 'I'm whacked. I've been putting in some long hours in the office, then there's all the housework . . .'

'You act like a kid, you get treated like one,' Elsie said, before he changed the subject and started guilt-tripping her for not helping out. *You eat like a pig and you look like one.* Her father's taunt reared its head, one of many in his repertoire. They slipped into her mind at the oddest of moments, a reminder that she could never truly escape. His bones may be dust and dirt, but the taunts lived on.

Grabbing a slice of kitchen roll, she wiped away the chicken grease that was sliding down her chin.

She watched Christian cast his eyes over the Kit-Cat novelty clock, its eyes flicking left to right as it relayed the time. The clock was one of many ornaments she had imported from the States.

'I'm gonna be late for work,' he said, picking up some empty crisp packets from the floor.

'Have you emptied the litter trays?'

Christian exhaled a weary sigh. 'No time. I'll do it when I get home.'

'You said that yesterday,' Elsie tutted. 'Have you fed the cats? Milk ain't enough to keep them going all day.' She would do it herself, but her back hurt like the dickens. The painkillers the doctor prescribed weren't cutting it anymore.

Christian retreated into the kitchen, and the rattle of dried cat food hit the metal trays.

'Don't forget to drop my books off at the library,' Elsie called, over the cacophony of miaows. Ripping off a chunk of chicken flesh, she made short work of her food. 'And honey, bring home some decent books this time. Glorified immorality is not my idea of a fun read.' She shooed Felix away as he jumped up on the bed. He knew better than to beg for scraps.

Christian's expression softened as he returned. 'It's a crime thriller, Mom, I thought you'd like it.'

Elsie raised an eyebrow. 'I don't read books by male authors. Too much profanity and sexual content.' She caught her son wincing as she threw the chicken bone into the bucket. 'Besides . . .' she continued, reaching for a book from the pile at the end of the bed. 'This one is *foreign*.' She spoke the word with disgust.

'It's Scandi crime,' Christian took the grease-stained book from her grip. 'It's all the rage.'

'More like scanty,' Elsie replied. 'Given how many times they took their clothes off.' As the daughter of a Presbyterian minister, Elsie was no stranger to vocalising her discontent. 'Get me a nice Mary Cleveland. Her writing's like a warm buttered biscuit, just melts off the page.'

'I'll try.' Christian gathered the stack of books.

'And remember to pick me up a skinny latte.' She vocalised one last order. 'Five squirts of hazelnut syrup with extra cream.'

'Bye, Mom.' Christian kissed her on the forehead. 'Have a good day.'

She gave him a tinkly wave as she watched him leave. His shirt strained across his shoulders. Since when had he got so broad? Sometimes she forgot that he was a man now. It did him good to escape her company, even if it meant working for his uncle Ron. It was a sympathy job, because Christian had been her carer from the tender age of ten, when Elsie's parents passed away in the same year. While relatives felt sorry for them, few were willing to help. She was tired of their pity, but she couldn't seem to find a way out. Right now, the biggest challenge she could face was making it to the restroom on time.

7

Sometimes Libby felt scared, but the stuff that frightened her before was nothing compared to how she felt today. This wasn't in the same realms of worrying about a science test or a spot on her nose. This was grown-up fear. Fear so dark that she wasn't able to get out of bed. 'Time of the month?' her mother had asked, and she had responded with a nod. Now her mum had gone to the shops to buy her paracetamol for her tummy and ice cream to cheer her up. She only hoped she didn't hear about Angelica while she was out. Because unlike her, Angelica hadn't returned home this morning.

Libby slipped her hand beneath her pillowcase and pulled out the stiff black card. *You are cordially invited to play the Midnight Game.* A sense of dread lingered as she turned it over. *If you tell, you'll go to hell.* If Angelica hadn't sent the invites, who had? Where was she now?

Libby jumped as her mobile phone rang, and she quickly shoved the card back under her pillow. It was Jahmelia.

'Have you heard?' she asked, sounding as panicked as Libby felt. 'Angelica's mum has been ringing all her friends asking if they've seen her.' Libby had heard the landline ring after her mum left for the shops. She had also seen the Facebook post by one of Angelica's friends, reporting her missing.

'I know,' Libby said. 'I thought she got bored and went home.'

'We shouldn't have let her leave on her own.'

The hairs on Libby's arms stood to attention. In the cold light of day, Jahmelia's words made sense. They all knew about stranger danger. But things like that didn't happen in Upper Slayton – did they?

'We can't say anything. Mum and Dad will kill me if they find out.' Libby pulled her Paddington teddy bear close. She hadn't slept with her childhood toy in years, but this morning she had dug him out from her old toybox and brought him into her bed. She didn't want to be an adult if this was what it was like. She wished she could turn back the clock.

'But what if she doesn't come back? You don't think . . .' Libby heard Jahmelia's short, sharp breaths as she paused. 'You don't think he's real, do you?'

Libby didn't need to ask who she was talking about. 'Don't be silly,' she mumbled. But her words were hollow. Last night, she hadn't been herself. She would never have stayed in that creepy old house if she had been thinking straight. As scared as she was, her compulsion to complete the game had been stronger than her will to leave. But Angelica didn't finish the game. Angelica lost.

'What did your mum say?' Libby asked, coming back to herself.

'That we slept in the tent with Bethany and Isobel, and you all left at nine this morning.'

'Then stick to that. Have you spoken to Bethany and Isobel?'

'They're pooping their pants,' Jahmelia said. 'Remember the back of the card?'

Libby could hardly forget the warning. *If you tell, you'll go to hell.*

'What if he comes for us next?' Jahmelia's voice reduced to a whine. 'I . . . I can't stop thinking about it. I read that he stays with you . . . watches you. I'm scared.'

Libby's fingers tightened around the handset. 'It's not real. It's just a stupid game.' She didn't like where the conversation was turning. It made her feel sick inside.

'But last night . . . Isobel saw a man in one of the bedrooms . . .'

'And when she blinked, he was gone.' Libby finished her sentence for her. 'It's a trick of the light. It was dark. We had candles. We were bound to see stuff that wasn't there.'

'We can't tell everyone when we go back to school on Monday,' Jahmelia said, which was the whole point in going through with it.

'We can. Just not until Angelica turns up.' The warning on the back of the card flashed in Libby's memory. *If you tell, you'll go to hell.* But that referred to adults as far as she was concerned. Playing the Midnight Game gave you instant kudos in school. Now Angelica had gone and messed it all up. 'She probably staged the whole thing for attention,' she added for good measure.

'I'm scared, Libs,' Jahmelia whined. 'What if Angelica's mum calls the police?'

The mention of the police made Libby hug her teddy tighter. He smelled musty, but it was a comforting smell, and all she wanted was to stay in bed. Thoughts of school and parents and the police made her chest so tight it hurt. 'It'll be fine,' she said, but she didn't believe that any more than Jahmelia did. The words of the game rebounded in her mind. *If you open your door to the Midnight Man, hide with a candle wherever you can. Try not to scream as he draws near. Because one of you won't be leaving here . . .*

The rhyme had come true. They hadn't visited the house of their own accord. Someone invited them to Blackhall Manor – and one of them hadn't left.

8

Almost there, Sarah thought, as she was passed by a crowd of police probationers in the corridor. She'd been standing outside the CID office for five minutes now. If she didn't get a move on, she'd be late. So why weren't her feet going in the direction they needed to go? A distraction. That's what she needed. A quick fix, then she'd just walk straight through. She slid her phone from her pocket and brought out the dictionary app. She couldn't help but smile at the word of the day.

Fantabulous, a slang term meaning excellent, wonderful, is a blend of fantastic and fabulous.

Perfect. Pressing her ID tag against the wall, she waited for the familiar buzz and click then pushed open the door.

The office looked exactly as it did when she'd left it, different mug shots, same crimes. It still housed the same half a dozen desks, basic furniture and creaky swivel chairs. The same drab blinds hung limply from the windows, the functional blue office carpet was littered with a smattering of crumbs. The air was warm and stale given that it was too cold to open the windows at this time of year. Her colleagues barely lifted their heads as she walked past.

She recognised Yvonne Townsend, who she'd always found frosty, and Damien 'Richie' Richardson, who was chatting animatedly as his colleagues hung on his every word. 'So I said, "the short answer is no, and the long answer is fuck no!"'

A burst of laughter followed. Sarah cast an eye over his leather jacket which hung from the coat hook in the corner. He was still a biker then, but he now sported a neatly trimmed black beard. She glanced around the office. It seemed that there had been a fair bit of turnover as she didn't know the remaining officers. She watched them return to their desks, banter over, ready for work. Their sergeant, nicknamed 'The Ballbreaker', had taken over from Sarah's husband. Her eyes flicked up as Sarah stood before her and cleared her throat.

Sergeant Gabrielle – Gabby – Bassett was of African-American and French descent. At fifty, she was ten years Sarah's senior, and wore a permanent expression of vague annoyance. Sarah had met her before when Gabby had conducted a home visit to check on Sarah's welfare. She had not expected a warm welcome. She just wanted to get through the day.

'That's your spot.' Gabby pointed at the coffee-ring-stained desk shoved against the wall. It was only a couple of feet from hers. When Sarah had started this role, she'd had a view out of the window. Her sergeant obviously wanted to keep an eye on her.

'Oh, OK.' Sarah pulled out the swivel chair. Her stomach was swarming with butterflies, like a kid on the first day of school. The kid who had been marked out as unpopular before they'd even begun. She caught the side glances from her colleagues, heard whispers from the back of the room. The atmosphere had taken a nosedive the second she walked in. *I'm in my bubble,* she told herself, as she sat at her desk. It was one of the coping mechanisms her therapist had taught her in the course of the year. But her beautiful rainbow bubble popped at the sound of her sergeant's voice.

'What are you doing?'

'I was going to log on, check my emails.'

Gabby looked at her indignantly. 'You don't need to check your emails. I'm right here in front of you. Come, talk to me.' A low ripple of murmurs rose from the corner of the room. Her head bowed, Sarah approached her sergeant and was handed a folder of paperwork. 'There's lots to do. You can't sit on your backside all day.'

Gabby silenced the whispers with a glare before returning her attention to Sarah. 'Take a job car and start taking statements. You can brush up on the details case by case.'

Sarah's heart sank as she flicked through the paperwork. 'Reports of a prowler,' she said. 'Do we need a statement for these? Last night was Halloween.'

'Are you questioning my authority, *Ms* Noble?' Gabby said, one eyebrow raised.

'No, Sarge.'

'Well, as it happens, I agree with you. But the DI has decreed that the good residents of Upper Slayton need a bit of hand-holding today. It's the perfect job to help you find your feet.'

Sarah nodded, relieved at least that her sergeant had agreed with her. 'Here's your trolley.' She pulled out the small suitcase on wheels. It contained a portable printer and notebook computer as well as pens, paperwork and everything she needed to take statements. 'I don't expect to see you until this evening. We're not exactly in a hurry for these.'

'Um...' Sarah stalled. It seemed a waste to use her as a statement taker when she was a trained detective. She knew she was on restricted duties, but she thought she'd be dealing with more pressing matters than Halloween pranks. These were the words Sarah *wanted* to say, but they failed to materialise.

'Yet despite the look on my face, you are still here.' Gabby drummed a red-varnished nail on her desk. Clearing her throat, Sarah signed out the keys of an unmarked car before turning to leave. Why had her sergeant pushed her out the door the minute she stepped inside?

'Good riddance,' somebody muttered in her wake. It seemed rock bottom had a basement.

It was a relief to reach the car, although she was hit with the stale odour of takeaway food and forbidden cigarettes the second she opened the door of the Ford Focus. Some things never changed. She familiarised herself with the paperwork as she sat behind the steering wheel. The brief was to reassure residents of Slayton who had reported a prowler in the area last night. Sarah sighed. Halloween was the one night of the year in which kids were allowed off the leash.

Slayton was an odd town, fractured by events of twenty-five years ago. After the shootings, children were monitored, doors and windows locked. But why, when the perpetrator of previous monstrosities came from within? Then gated communities began to pop up, along with private security firms which still patrolled the area today. 'Choose safety for your family,' was the slogan on the signage for Upper Slayton, and it appeared the PR spin had worked. The town's population doubled to eight thousand residents. As residents of Lower Slayton struggled with unemployment, drugs and poverty, the walls of Upper Slayton grew and its houses were priced way out of the market for anyone in Lower Slayton to afford. Still, if you had a clean record, you could get a job as a cleaner, housekeeper or gardener – as long as you knew your place. People in Lower Slayton were low in more ways than one.

Sarah hated the hierarchy, but she couldn't see things changing anytime soon. Dubbed as the 'Saviour of Slayton', Simon Irving of Irving Industries was responsible for many of the gated developments. He was an influential man with powerful friends, including their very own Police and Crime Commissioner. So for now, residents of Upper Slayton would take precedence over everyone else.

It was why Sarah decided to go against the grain and prioritise Lower Slayton today. She slid the printout of the incident from the bottom of the pile and placed it on top. Alerting control via her airwaves, she attached her call sign to the job. She looked at her reflection in the mirror, straightening her fringe over her face. Her first stop was to see Maggie Carter and her son.

9

When Elliott woke with blood on the sleeve of his pyjamas, he knew he had done something bad. He stared at his trainers as his feet dangled beneath the kitchen table. The laces had come undone again. He wasn't very good at laces. It was easier to kick them off than to try and work out which bunny ear went where. Today he was too tired to do much of anything. The night stories were back.

'Eat your toast,' Maggie said, before returning her attention to the dishes in the sink.

He had called his mother Maggie for as long as he could remember. He knew she didn't like it, but he couldn't help himself. She was humming the theme tune to *EastEnders*. She always hummed TV soap theme tunes when something was wrong. Since Daddy went to hospital, she hummed them almost every day. But today he was the cause of her worries. He couldn't make her feel worse by telling her what he had seen.

He toyed with the medal pinned to his shirt. His mummy only let him wear it at home. He hoped that one day, Daddy would come back. His daddy was a very brave man.

'Did you know that tortoises smell with their throats?' His tortoise facts always put a smile on Maggie's face.

'I didn't know that,' she said, glancing over her shoulder.

'And they have to empty their lungs before they go into their shell,' he said, encouraged.

'Interesting,' Maggie replied, elbow-deep in suds.

Elliott frowned. He wished he could talk to someone about his nightmares. He wasn't just a watcher. The smells, sounds, and feelings swallowed him up and followed into his days. His brow knitted as the blurry image of the bad man faded. Then poof . . . like blowing out a candle on a birthday cake, it was gone. But the fear had soaked deep into his bones. He winced as his fingernails dug into his palms. He reached for his toast and took a couple of bites before swallowing the dry offering. Maggie had forgotten to butter it. She was standing at the sink, staring out of the window, humming slightly off-kilter, her head tilted to one side. Something inside her had broken. Elliott gulped his tumbler of milk, and rested it back on the fold-up kitchen table. The big house he had lived in before was a fading memory now too. Everything changed after Daddy got sick.

'I'm expecting a visitor soon,' Maggie said, with an almost-smile as she did up the buttons of her cardigan. 'Nothing to worry about.'

Elliott jumped off his chair and wriggled his big toe as it poked through the hole in his sock.

'Here, put your slippers on.' Maggie handed him a pair of Gruffalo faces which were distorted with wear. 'It's a police officer – just popping in for a quick chat.'

'Should I put the good towels out?' he said, in an effort to please her. When they had visitors, they put out the bright yellow towels – the ones without the holes.

A little bit of sadness left Maggie's eyes. 'Yes, good boy. They're in the hot press.'

He turned and bounded down the hall. But with each step he took, a feeling of dread rose. His feet became heavy, as if he were wearing space boots. *Thump . . . thump . . . thump*, the echoes of heavy footsteps against a long wide staircase played in his mind. He wiped his damp palms against his jeans before pushing the feeling away. But the badness in his tummy wouldn't go. He wished he could talk to his friends. Not school friends – he sat alone in the playground – but Libby and Jahmelia. When they babysat, they were always nice to him. Once, he had even tried to tell them about the nightmares, but Libby had looked at him funny and asked if he was feeling OK. Maggie had warned him about sharing secrets. She said people wouldn't understand.

Elliott had just laid the towels on the rack in the bathroom like his mother had shown him when the doorbell rang. He stood behind her in the narrow hallway as the woman was allowed in. She was smaller and broader than Maggie, with dark wavy hair. She smiled at him as she spoke, but Elliott didn't smile back. Just because people looked friendly, it didn't mean they could be trusted.

His mother seemed surprised. 'Sarah, I wasn't expecting . . .' she said, staring but smiling. 'I mean, I didn't know you were back at work.'

The woman was holding a small leather notebook in her hand. 'It's my first day back today.'

'Good for you.' Maggie touched the woman's arm. 'It's great to see you out and about.'

Maggie switched her gaze to Elliott. 'Elliott, do you remember Sarah? She's an old school friend of mine.' Elliott didn't recall the woman before him, but gave her a smile, now she came with his mother's approval. Mummy stopped going out after

Daddy went to hospital. She didn't have any friends around. He followed them into the sitting room, edging around the sofa as his mother took a seat.

'I see you're still painting then.' Sarah pointed at the pictures on the living-room walls. Both Maggie and her sister had been artists. Elliott's favourite picture was the one of a tortoise which hung in his room.

'When I get time,' Maggie replied. 'But you're not here to talk about that.'

Control had already called ahead to let Maggie know that enquiries were being made. 'We've had reports of a prowler last night,' Sarah said, taking the armchair. 'Patrolling officers gave chase, and they cut through your garden as they ran away. It was most likely kids...' She grinned at Elliott. 'Given it was Halloween.'

'Creepers creeping.' Elliott's voice seemed to surprise them, and he caught his mother's warning glance. But the lady with the notebook didn't seem to mind. She had curious eyes, like he was in a story she was trying to read. That's what he did too. People, things, places – they were all part of stories. He could tell if people were happy or sad, just by looking at them. Smiles meant nothing, they were like the jumpers you wore for school. You put them on because you had to. He watched his mother's friend intently; she seemed sad behind her smile.

The Midnight Man is coming...

The words swept over his mind, invoking a shiver. He was so tired of all the black things in his head. He watched Maggie and the lady chat and laugh as she scribbled in her notebook. 'It's been too long. I'll call you soon,' Maggie said, as she rose to leave. 'Have a proper catch-up.'

'I'd like that,' Sarah replied. 'I'm free most evenings.' She meant it, he could tell because her eyes sparkled. She seemed happier than when she first got here. 'How's Lewis?' Sarah said, glancing at a picture of him in his army uniform.

Maggie said he was doing well. Sometimes grown-ups said one thing and meant another. Elliott knew his mum didn't want him to feel sad. Maggie glanced down at him. 'Elliott is minding his medal until he comes home.'

Elliott smiled at his mother as she ruffled his hair. But he'd heard Maggie talking on the phone to the hospital. Daddy wasn't getting better.

Maggie returned her attention to her friend. 'Hang on, let me give you my new mobile number.' Maggie walked out to the kitchen to search for a pen. Elliott had turned inwards. His chest was rising and falling with the speedy beat of his heart. *The Midnight Man is coming* . . . his lips thinned as the words threatened to spill. Insistent knocks on the door of his consciousness. He saw a flash of a bloodstained knife and took a sudden breath.

'Everything OK?' Sarah said, a little crease on her forehead.

The words climbed up his throat and were out before he could stop them. 'The Midnight Man is coming,' he blurted, feeling instant relief. 'The angel is dead.' Sarah stared, the colour draining from her face.

'Wha . . . sorry, what did you say?'

Elliott took two steps backward. He had said too much. The woman fixed a smile as Maggie reappeared, her hand rising to adjust her fringe. Elliott scurried out of the room.

'Elliott? Where are you off to in such a hurry?' his mum said, as he bounded away.

'I think he's shy,' he heard Sarah say, keeping his secret. Had he done the right thing? He *had* to tell, despite what his mother had said. Because this was just the beginning. There was worse to come.

10

Sarah had welcomed her chat with Maggie. It was a shame that they had grown apart, but it brought it home to her that she wasn't alone. Her old friend seemed as lonely as she was. Maggie's once blonde hair now had some slivers of grey, but time had been kind to her, and she was the same warm person Sarah had grown up with. It was tragic, what happened to Lewis. His heroism had made the papers, but it also broke his family apart.

Elliott had surprised her. Elliott, with *those eyes* so dark and deep they spoke more than words could ever convey. The sight of him wearing his father's medal was both sweet and comical as he stood in his Gruffalo slippers and too-small jeans. But his warning came with such a sense of magnitude, his concerns beyond those of a seven-year-old boy. Opening her police-issue notebook, Sarah sliced her finger on the page. 'Bugger,' she whispered, sucking the paper cut. She needed to commit the words to paper before she forgot.

The Midnight Man is coming, she wrote. *The angel is dead.* She stared at the page, stained by a drop of her blood. How did the poem go again? She beckoned it from her memory. It had been around for as long as she could remember and was resurrected by local teenagers every Halloween.

If you open your door to the Midnight Man,

Hide with a candle wherever you can.
Try not to scream as he draws near,
Because one of you won't be leaving here . . .

Wasn't there something about staining paper with your blood? she wondered, as the poem repeated in her mind. 'I guess he's coming for me now,' she said on the breath of a sigh. She didn't believe in silly superstition, but what about Elliott? He had uttered the words as if they were causing him physical pain, then one blink of those full moon eyes and he was gone. It wasn't just his words that concerned her, it was the cuts on his mother's arm, the bruises on her collarbone. They hadn't come from a pet – she had scanned the room for signs. Cats left hairs and Sarah had a good sense of smell. Maggie was more or less a single parent, so it was just her and her son. She mentioned two local girls who babysat for her. Perhaps they had been feeding Elliott creepy stories over Halloween? Sarah exhaled. Of course. Children were like sponges at that age. They were probably messing with him. But the scratches and bruises? She made a mental note to keep an eye on things. She stiffened in her seat as a group of teenagers skateboarded past, whooping and cheering each other on as they raced.

Updating control, she attached her call sign to the address of Elsie Abraham, another school acquaintance she had lost touch with. Elsie had always been an outsider. Her Presbyterian parents had emigrated from America to start up a branch of their church in the UK. Sarah had tried to include her, but her odd turn of phrase and strange dress sense set her apart from the crowd. She first met her parents in Tesco Metro when she was packing bags to raise money for the Girl Guides. Their faces stiff with holiness, they quoted bible passages in between beeps as the checkout girl scanned their Weetabix and potatoes. She shook her head at the memory. She never realised how many oddballs lived in Slayton until that day. Elsie's parents ranked in the top five . . . no, top three of the strangest people she had ever met. Her mother was a skinny, meek woman with a thick southern American accent and Nellie Oleson curls. As for her father . . . an overbearing lump of a man with X-ray eyes. As his gaze roamed over Sarah's body, it felt like he could see right through to her mismatching underwear. The disturbing thing was, he had looked at his daughter in the same way.

She programmed Elsie Abraham's address into the satnav and started the engine for the short drive up the hill. Elsie's abode was on the outskirts of Upper Slayton and had yet to be included in the restoration taking place. There was no proper front garden at Elsie Abraham's terraced home, just a rusty gate off its hinges, a concrete frontage and an overstuffed green wheelie bin. Next to it were recycling tubs filled with empty chocolate milk cartons and cardboard containers that once housed crisp and chocolate multipacks. As a pre-teen, Elsie had eaten for comfort. Now, she either had a huge family, or her eating habits hadn't improved.

Sarah pressed her finger on the stiff plastic doorbell to hear a quirky rendition of 'The Lord is My Shepherd' from inside. 'Just a minute!' a high-pitched voice shrieked from within. Sarah was about to lift the letterbox to check she was OK, when a shadow filled the door pane. It was Elsie – or at least, she thought it was, as she was greeted at the door. Sarah kept her expression fixed, her shock hidden behind the smile she portrayed to the world. Elsie wasn't just overweight now; she was morbidly obese. Sweat-shiny and panting, she could barely stand. Her hair was pulled back into a long thin pigtail, her polyester smock stretched to its limits across her chest.

'I'm DC Sarah . . .' she began to introduce herself, proudly raising her warrant card in the air. It had been years since she'd last seen her. Would Elsie recognise her now?

'Sure, sure, come in and close the door. You're letting all the good air out,' Elsie wheezed, turning left to the living room. As Sarah closed the door she was overwhelmed by the pungent odour of ammonia. Judging by the overfull litter trays, the stench was cat pee. She pinched the top of her nose as she held back a sneeze. She would not stay long. A hospital-style bed took up most of the living room. The surfaces were littered with religious pictures and cat ornaments, old mahogany furniture, cat beds and a variety of books. On every wall hung a mirror, covered in a thin layer of dust.

She watched as Elsie manoeuvred herself onto the bed. She must spend her day there, Sarah realised with a mix of shock and sympathy, thinking of the sweet wrappers in her own sofa at home.

'Christian – he's my son – usually lets people in.' Elsie grunted as she hauled one leg, then two onto the mattress. Her calves were mottled purple, her ankles swallowed up by excess skin. 'Not that we get many visitors.' Elsie tugged on the overhanging handle as she tried to shift her weight. 'Mother of pearl . . .' she groaned, before looking to Sarah for support. 'Can you fix my pillows? I feel like I've been chewed up and spat out today.'

'Sorry for getting you out of bed.' Sarah plumped her pillows, wedging them against the metal bed frame. A trail of sweat bloomed down Elsie's back. The folds in her skin appeared itchy and raw. Judging from the staleness of the bed linen, it hadn't been changed in a while. Elsie scooted back on each buttock as she sat up.

'Don't apologise. It's nice to have visitors at any time of the day. I know you, don't I?' Slicing a square of kitchen tissue paper, she pressed it to her forehead to absorb the sweat.

Sarah nodded in response. 'Yes, we went to school together many moons ago.'

'That's right,' Elsie said, the air between them cooling. 'I remember you. Have you moved back to Slayton or do you just work here?'

Sarah was staring at the empty crisp packets littering the bed. Heat rose to her cheeks as she realised she'd been caught out. 'I live here, I've been here for almost two years.'

'I don't get out anymore,' Elsie explained. 'Are you Upper or Lower?'

'Lower.' The question wasn't about her location, it was to judge her social status. Elsie's terraced row of houses bordered Upper Slayton. They weren't an accepted part of the well-to-do community, but they shared the postcode just the same. Judging by the smile creeping onto Elsie's face, it was something she took pride in. 'Not everyone's lucky enough to live in this part of town.'

As she looked around the room, the last thing Sarah felt was envy.

'Keep off the bed!' Elsie warned as she leaned against it. 'Not unless you want those fancy black pants of yours covered in flea powder.'

Sarah bit back a smile. 'Oh, sorry,' she said, stepping back. 'I didn't realise.' As for her fancy pants – hardly, given an elastic band connected the button to the buttonhole concealed beneath her shirt.

'It's Gregory and Officer Dibble,' Elsie explained. 'Those dirty purdys are out hunting all day long.'

'I'm sure,' Sarah said, presuming the 'dirty purdys' were her cats. 'A clowder of cats,' Sarah mused, pointing to the felines winding their tails around her legs. 'It's the term for the collective,' she continued, in an effort to bond with the woman who had regarded her with suspicion since she had entered the house. 'I'm owned by Sherlock myself, a ginger tom. He doesn't like me very much, but he's company.'

'Uh-huh.' Elsie sat with legs spread wide to accommodate her extra flesh. 'Mine are presents from my son. Christian's got a soft heart. He keeps bringing strays home.' She pointed to a nearby stool. 'Take a pew.' It seemed Sarah's cat had earned her acceptance.

'I bet you were surprised when you saw me. I've grown since we were in school.'

It was a difficult question for Sarah to answer. 'We've all changed a great deal,' she said with a smile. 'It's nice to see you again.' She nodded towards the window as a bread van trundled past. 'The place hasn't changed much, apart from all the gated communities springing up.'

'There's nothing wrong with wanting to feel safe in your bed.' Elsie's cat purred loudly as she rhythmically stroked its fur. 'Christian has been a blessing. It's just the two of us at home since Mom and Pop died. He's an estate agent, y'know. Although he's real good at computer games.' Sarah paused to take her son's details as she updated the police records. Now that she recalled it, this was Elsie's family home. She had never left. Progressing the interview, she asked if Elsie had seen anything suspicious the night before.

'Nope, not a dicky bird.' Elsie glanced at the yellowing window blinds. 'I fell asleep, which is a minor miracle in itself. Christian woke me at midnight. Said there were some teenagers outside, but he scared them away.'

'Which is why you reported the damage to your gate?'

Elsie nodded. 'It's nothing really. Christian will fix it when he gets home.' Sarah made note of her comments. By the look of it, Christian had a lot on his plate.

'Are you sure about the time?' Sarah remarked. A gate off its hinges was hardly the crime of the century, but the elements of her police training still remained: question everything, then question it again.

Elsie pointed to a novelty cat clock on the wall. 'I've had that timekeeper for twenty years and it's never let me down.'

Sarah's eyes roamed to the picture of Elsie's parents, their lined faces glaring in disapproval. Her father was instantly recognisable by the deep cleft in his chin. Her mother's ringlet curls had been replaced by a short grey bob. A string of rosary beads hung limply over the picture frame, which was cloaked in a layer of dust. Elsie followed her gaze. 'The Lord took them both into his bosom. Natural causes. They died just weeks apart.'

'Sorry for your loss,' Sarah said faintly, keen to move things on.

Elsie regarded Sarah thoughtfully. 'I guess it's quite the novelty for you, meeting someone like me.'

'Someone like you?' Sarah asked, genuinely perplexed. 'What do you mean?'

Elsie flushed. 'Do I have to spell it out? Someone of my size. Come on, y'all must be wondering, but you're too polite to ask.'

'It's none of my business, is it?' Sarah clicked the top of her pen. 'It's not my job to sit in judgement.' She knew how it felt to be talked about. She wouldn't wish it on anyone.

Elsie seemed taken aback. 'At least you've made something of your life. A detective, no less.'

'Don't set your standards by me,' Sarah laughed dryly. 'My life is far from perfect as I'm sure you know.' Sarah relaxed on her stool. This may be veering off police business but care in the community was part of it too. 'Have you spoken to your GP? Maybe they could help.'

'Scoot.' Elsie nudged her cat and it darted down to the end of the bed. Almost unconsciously, her hand fell to the box of éclairs which were resting on her bedside table. 'I have to lose weight for the surgery,' she said, tearing open the box. 'But it's an addiction. I can't just stop.' She sank her teeth into the éclair and cream squirted out the sides of her mouth. 'Besides . . .' She licked her lips. 'If I *do* have surgery, I could die under the knife.' She swallowed the éclair before reaching for another. 'So I think about it, and I think about it some more, and then I get scared, so I eat to make myself feel better and . . .'

'You're back to square one,' Sarah finished her sentence.

Elsie shoved the rest of the pastry into her mouth, talking between chews. 'You know, this is the first time I've spoken about it in years. Even the health professionals have given up on me.' She sniffed, grabbing a square of kitchen paper and wiping her mouth. 'I don't even taste it half the time.'

'I'm sure help is there when you're ready for it,' Sarah said. She should be moving on, but she couldn't leave Elsie in this state.

Elsie cleared her throat. 'Seeing you out in the world . . . after everything life has thrown at you . . . Maybe there's hope for me after all.'

'I'm glad I've inspired you,' Sarah said, upon receiving the backhanded compliment. 'Is there anything I can do for you before I go?'

Elsie shook her head, one hand on the box of éclairs. 'I only reported it because Christian told me to. They're hot on the Neighbourhood Watch around here. Good thing we don't get any *real* trouble in these parts.'

'To be fair, we don't have much trouble in the Bronx, I mean, Lower Slayton, either,' Sarah winked.

Elsie chortled at her response. 'Sorry for being a bit of a snooty pants before. Truth is, I wouldn't be living here if my baby daddy hadn't provided for me so well.'

'You weren't,' Sarah said, amused by her turn of phrase. 'I've enjoyed the catch-up. And if there's anything you need in future, you know where I am.' She handed Elsie her card. 'My mobile number is on the back.' She was about to say more when her phone rang. The sight of her sergeant's number ignited a frisson of trepidation.

'How's it going?' her sergeant barked, as soon as Sarah picked up the call. Usually, any instructions would come through her police airwaves, delegated by control. Was she checking up on her?

'I've just finished my second job,' she said, checking her watch. 'About to head to my third.'

'Scrap that, go straight to Simon Irving's address.'

'Irving?' Sarah said. 'What's happened?'

'He's not there, but his wife needs speaking to. She's reported her daughter missing, it's not the first time she's done a bunk.

Fill in the MISPER forms, give reassurance, then do the usual follow-ups . . . Noble, are you there?'

And to think she'd been worried about not having enough to do. 'Yes, Sarge,' she breathed into the phone. She would have to reschedule her other appointments, do a bit of juggling. Sergeant Bassett was still talking. 'I can't spare anyone else right now, and she's insisting on a detective, so pull out all the stops. The kid's name is Angelica. I'm sending through a photo. She went out last night and never came home.'

Sarah powered up her laptop as she sat in the car. The morning's visits to Maggie and Elsie had sucked the energy out of her. She opened her emails, clicked on the attachment and Angelica's image filled the screen. She appeared to be in fancy dress, complete with tinsel halo and wings. With her white-blonde hair and clear blue eyes, she looked like . . . 'An angel,' Sarah whispered. A trail of shivers danced down her spine as Elliott's words came to play . . . *the Midnight Man is coming . . . the angel is dead.*

11

As Sarah approached the gated community of Slayton Crest, she was grateful she was driving the job Ford Focus, instead of her battered red Mini. With their well-kept lawns and perfectly trimmed bushes, these exclusive communities wouldn't look out of place in LA. Some even had swimming pools, dotted with exotic trees. But they could not buy the weather, and Sarah flipped her windscreen wipers as a speckle of rain came down.

Manoeuvring the car up to the red-brick gateposts, Sarah identified herself to the CCTV camera, which was operated remotely. The black electric gates rolled back on their runners, allowing her access. This was a place where every move was monitored, and apart from the occasional domestic incident, police were rarely needed inside. There were standards to be kept and rules written into the deeds of each property. In Slayton Crest, your house was not your own. Despite the hefty price tag, homeowners were expected to keep their properties uniform in design. There were no caravans on the drives of the lavish properties, no exterior home improvements allowed, and pets were limited to one per household. Unlike in Lower Slayton, there were no signs of children or dogs on the streets. People didn't pop next door for a cup of sugar. In Slayton Crest, privacy was everything and the most you could hope for was a wave from across the exclusive street.

She drew up outside the two-million-pound property, the biggest on the close. It was perched at the end with stunning views of the back of the woodlands surrounding Blackhall Manor. This house was the home of local entrepreneur, Simon Irving. He was a bit too flashy white teeth and fake tan for Sarah's liking. Sarah parked next to his manicured front lawn and walked past the expensive-looking Range Rover on their drive. It was most likely a status symbol, used for the school run.

The front door was opened immediately by a woman that Sarah recognised as Mrs Irving, and Sarah was ushered into the family living room. The scent of oranges and jasmine was a distinct improvement on the Febreze that Sarah sprayed on her sofa once a week to chase away the smell of cat. Claudia Irving sat before her, playing with a long gold chain around her neck. Her fingers were dazzling with diamonds, her forehead no stranger to Botox, by the look of it. Not that Sarah was judging. She could do with a few jabs herself.

She had seen pictures of Claudia in the local paper as she attended various business events and charity dos. She obviously didn't know who Sarah was, or what her husband had done. If she did, she probably wouldn't have let her inside the door. Today, Claudia appeared elegant, if a little tired. Claudia gestured for Sarah to sit down. The chairs were velvet with gold trim, and Sarah perched on the edge, her feet crossed beneath her. Claudia sat, resting her hands on her lap before reaching for her necklace again. Sarah worked through the online MISPER forms, gaining as much information as she could.

'Angelica lied about staying overnight at her friend's house, is that right?'

Claudia responded with a nod. 'I usually ring to check where she's staying but I dropped her off at Jennifer's at seven to go trick-or-treating and saw her mum there. When Angelica texted me later to say she was staying over, I had no reason to doubt her.' There was a pause. A flash of self-recrimination. 'I should have checked.'

'You weren't to know,' Sarah said. But as they worked through the online forms, Claudia seemed to shrink into herself.

'So many questions,' she murmured. 'What she was wearing, her last meal . . .' She paused. 'Why do you need to know what she ate?'

Sarah avoided answering the question. Such information was needed in case there was a post-mortem and stomach contents were examined. Not all bodies found were identifiable. She suppressed a shudder as Elliott's words whispered in her thoughts. *The angel is dead.* All morning, it had tugged on her periphery. Why was she letting the words of a seven-year-old child affect her like this? Yet the sense of foreboding would not let up.

Sarah skimmed previous reports as they came through on her laptop. The records consisted of calls from the Irving address, recorded for officers to read and updated by control while the incident remained ongoing. Three incidents were logged on the police system from within the last year, all of them concerning Angelica Irving.

'Has Angelica ever stayed out overnight before?'

'No, she's never stayed out this long. The latest she's come home is one or two in the morning. And I know . . .' Claudia raised a manicured hand, 'it's bad parenting on my behalf. Angelica's only fifteen. But I've done everything in my power to safeguard her . . . apart from locking her in her room.'

Sarah lifted her head from her laptop as Claudia emitted a loud, tearless sob. It was so theatrical, Sarah wondered if it was genuine, then immediately felt guilty. The truth was, if this *did* escalate, Angelica's parents would be of interest to the police. Sometimes accidents happened. Sometimes people died, and *sometimes* people did everything in their power to cover it up.

'I've got a bad feeling.' Claudia snatched a tissue from a box on the coffee table next to her chair. 'I'm her mother . . . I just know something's happened to my girl.'

'It's not unusual for children of Angelica's age to go missing,' Sarah said, trying to offer reassurance. 'Especially during Halloween. Teenagers dare each other to spend the night in graveyards, or they go drinking and sleep in. It could be that she's staying with a friend you don't know about.'

'But why isn't she answering her phone?' Claudia carefully dabbed at her eyes.

'She could have turned it off,' Sarah replied, but her words felt hollow. Claudia had every right to be concerned. She lowered her head as she completed the paperwork. It wouldn't do to worry the mother at this early stage. She checked off the list of friends Claudia had handed her. 'Have you called all these numbers?'

'Yes,' Claudia said. 'It's all over social media too.'

'What about the Find My Friends app, have you got it on your phone?' It was handy for keeping track of family friends and loved ones, although in Sarah's experience, domineering spouses made good use of it too.

'I installed it, but she turned it off on her phone.'

Sarah glanced through her paperwork. 'And there were no family arguments recently . . . she wouldn't have run away?'

Rising from her chair, Claudia walked to the rain-speckled window. 'Never. Her clothes, her purse, and all her things are still in her room. I checked her online banking. Her account hasn't been touched.'

Sarah was aware of that, although it was very early days. She also knew from previous reports that Angelica's grades were slipping. She may have disappeared for attention. Her parents' busy social lives took them away from home a lot. Or it could be that she was vulnerable, picked on by a predator who had gained her trust.

Sarah swallowed. Her throat was as dry as dust. It was coming up to lunchtime and she hadn't eaten a thing. Her stomach rumbled in confirmation. It was quite a shock for her system to go without food for so long and the beginnings of a headache made itself known. At home, cups of tea and toasted Warburtons crumpets had been on tap. Her visit to Elsie might have put an end to that.

'This is meant to be a safe community.' Claudia's voice was thin with worry as she stared out the window. 'So why doesn't anyone know where she is?' But she was asking the wrong person, given that her husband was the one who penned the Upper Slayton slogan 'Choose safety for your family'. In Sarah's experience, complete safety was a promise that nobody could offer. Where was he, anyway?

'Officers are patrolling the area,' Sarah said. 'I'm sure we'll find her soon. In the meantime, we'll speak to her friends in person, see if they know more than they're letting on. We're putting some feelers out in the local community to see if any meetups were arranged last night.' Sometimes kids in the community hung out in abandoned buildings, smoking weed and playing music, and such gatherings were pre-arranged. But they were usually reserved for Lower Slayton's older teens, not Upper Slayton's young Catholic schoolgirls.

Claudia nodded in acknowledgement. 'I've telephoned the hospital, spoken to the local parish priest. Simon's out looking for her too.'

Of course, Sarah thought. *Not all husbands are only out for what they can get.* She hated that her view of men had been tainted in this way. After uploading the completed questionnaire to the system, Sarah updated control. A search was underway, dog units were being called in and police community support officers were checking the playgrounds, school bike sheds, all the local kids' haunts. Weather permitting, the force helicopter would scout the area too.

Angelica's brother, Ryan, wandered in and sat in the corner chair. He was a stocky kid, late teens by the look of it. Folding his arms, he slumped back in his chair and began to examine his phone. Claudia turned to him.

'Any updates on social media?'

He replied with a taut shake of the head. Sarah watched him closely. Concern was etched on his face. But there was something else there too. His eyes met hers before returning to his phone. Another loud rumble of her stomach. Sarah flushed.

'I couldn't trouble you for a glass of water, could I?' She directed the question at Claudia. 'I've been going from job to job.' It wasn't unusual not to be offered refreshments in homes such as these. Usually, the people with the least offered the most. Not that she expected anything. They had more to worry about than her caffeine withdrawal today.

Claudia drifted from the room, leaving Sarah alone with Ryan. The water was as good an excuse as any to garner some alone time. He rose from the chair to follow his mother, but Sarah raised her hand. 'Ryan, have you got a minute?' she said.

Reluctantly, he sat back down.

Sarah tilted her head to one side. 'There's more, isn't there? You need to tell me what you know.'

He drove a hand through his hair, dragging his fringe over his forehead. He seemed barely able to meet her gaze. 'Mum will go ape when she hears about this.' His gaze fell on the door. 'As for Dad . . . he'll kill me.' Rain tapped on the window as Sarah waited for answers. *The angel is dead.*

'Nobody's going to kill anyone,' Sarah said. 'Where's your sister?' she pressed. 'Who's she with?'

Ryan pulled the hood of his sweatshirt up. 'I didn't think she'd go through with it. But Angelica has this rebellious streak and . . . ah man, Dad's going to go mad.'

Leaning forward, Sarah kept her voice even and low. 'Then best you tell me now, before we hear it from anybody else. At least that way, you'll be the one helping us with our enquiries.'

'What's this?' Claudia said, glass of iced water in hand. She thrust it towards Sarah while looking at her son. 'You look worried. What's going on?'

'Ryan's remembered something that might help,' Sarah said, taking the glass from Claudia's extended hand. 'He was just about to tell me.'

'You have?' Claudia stood over him. 'Out with it then, before your dad gets home. Where is she?'

As she sipped the filtered water, Sarah sensed that Mr Irving was not an easy man to live with. From what she'd heard, there was an unsavoury side to him kept firmly from view.

'If I knew where she was I would have told you straight away, Mum.' Ryan exhaled. 'It might be nothing, but—'

'I'll be the judge of that,' Claudia interjected. 'What is it?'

The uncomfortable teenager straightened in his seat. 'She was talking about some Halloween game that kids here play every year. I told her not to be so stupid, but she said it was all planned.'

'What sort of game?' Sarah said, another layer of dread rising. She already knew the answer.

'The Midnight Game,' Ryan continued, confirming her worst fears. 'Some weird pagan thing where you walk around in the dark with a candle and invite "the Midnight Man" in.' He looked from Claudia to Sarah. 'I told you it was dumb.'

Sarah's fingers had tightened around her laptop, and her heart was beating as if the devil had asked her out on a date. She forced herself to blink. *Rule five: Act normal.* 'I take it she was playing with friends.'

'She wouldn't have done it on her own. She's stupid sometimes but not *that* stupid.' Ryan shook his head.

'Your sister is not stupid!' Claudia snapped.

'Then where is she?' Ryan countered, jumping up from his chair. His cheeks were burning. He stood several inches over his mother. This was a boy who didn't like to be contradicted. Perhaps lessons had been learned from his father. It wouldn't surprise her.

'Did she say where she was playing the game?' Sarah said, in an effort to break the tension.

Ryan shrugged. 'She wouldn't have played it at home. You can't be disturbed, and you have to do it in darkness with the front door unlocked. There're loads of stories about it online if you search for it.' He paused as they both watched him, waiting for more. 'If you ask me, there's only one place in Slayton you go to play a game like that.'

'Where?' Claudia asked.

Sarah was rooted to her chair. *No. Not there . . .*

'You already know, Mum. Where's the spookiest place in Slayton?'

'That ugly old asylum on the outskirts of town?' Claudia replied. But Ryan shook his head. 'Somewhere creepier than that. A proper old haunted house.'

'Blackhall Manor,' the words were ghostly on Sarah's lips. This was not good. This was not good at all. For one thing, Blackhall Manor was a death trap. The timbers were rotting, the structure was unstable, the place was falling apart. But there was something else. Blackhall Manor was deadly in more ways than one.

Claudia's voice upped in pitch as she began firing questions. Sarah raised her hand. 'If you bear with me for a minute, I need to relate this back to control. They'll send officers round there, if they haven't already.' A slow sickness washed over Sarah. There was no way she was attending that place and nobody, not her sergeant or her DI, could make her.

12

As predicted, Her Majesty's constabulary were soon crawling all over Blackhall Manor, poking their noses into cupboards, picking up things and laying them down again. How stupid did they think I was? As if I would leave a trace of my actions for them. I hoped they would fall through the stairwell and break their inquisitive necks.

They wouldn't be the first people Blackhall Manor swallowed whole. Every Halloween, the local paper featured a piece on the Manor. Like many old buildings in Slayton, it was erected in Victorian times. It was said that the build had its share of casualties. The erection of the steep mansard roof was the cause of one of three recorded deaths as a labourer snapped his neck after falling off during a gale. The second met his death while creating the ornate flourishes in the corners of the high ceilings at night. The third was found dead in one of the many crawlspaces that Middleton insisted they build. The building was filled with gaps in the walls large enough to accommodate a grown man. The trick wasn't just how to get into them, it was how to get out again afterwards.

No one knew why the crawlspaces were implemented, but they were never included on the plans. Now the place lay in ruins, but I was not ready for its reign to end. It was the perfect backdrop for the Midnight Game.

I learned everything I could about the players I chose. Where they lived, what they ate, their deepest fears and dreams. But it was Libby who piqued my interest the most. Freckled-face Libby who had stayed, despite her friends pressing her to leave. Libby who thought she was strong enough to ward off the Midnight Man.

A vision of Angelica's face returned in a vivid memory. Dots of blood in her pupils. Her lips parting as her jaw grew slack. Cupping her mouth with my hand as I caught her last breath. There would be no knee-jerk reaction the next time. I would be regimented, organised. In control. Freckle Face would never graduate high school. She would never fulfil her dream of becoming a veterinary nurse. She would never marry and have children. I would rob her of that and more.

I didn't feel pity for the fourteen-year-old.

Nobody felt sorry for me.

13

Sarah checked her watch. Five o'clock on the dot. She had been told not to return a minute before, and that in itself pissed her off. Her day had been relatively productive but she needed to reintegrate with the team. The sooner they accepted her, the easier it would be to get on with her work. The team worked a mixture of eight- to ten-hour shifts, with three days on and three days off, covered by the opposite shift. But it was all hands on deck when anything serious came in, and it seemed the overtime budget was a generous one. She passed her DI's office and noticed his empty chair. Bernard may have gone home early but he would still be available should anything come up. Inspectors didn't get paid overtime, and Gabby would call him should any new leads arise. The man was nearing retirement and it seemed his heart wasn't in the job.

As she entered the battleground of the CID office, she was immediately hit by the smell of greasy chips. Someone had done a kebab round but they'd failed to include her. *Deliveroo it is then,* she thought, striding past her colleagues' desks. With telephones ringing and printers spitting out paperwork, it looked like they were in for a long night. Her sergeant was plucking chips from an orange polystyrene box while clicking her mouse.

Sarah rolled her trolley up to her desk. From the corner of her eye, she saw Gabby push up her shirt sleeve to check her watch. 'You can shoot off now, Noble.'

'I'm OK to stay.' Sarah forced a bright smile while pulling out her chair. 'I thought I could follow up on enquiries with Angelica's friends. I'm pretty sure one of them is covering something up.'

'It's all under control, and you're on restricted duties. Off you go.'

'But . . .' Sarah stared at her sergeant.

'Am I speaking in tongues here?' Gabby's voice intensified. 'GO.' Heads rose in their direction, but they did not linger for long.

Sarah's cheeks burned with humiliation. 'Can I have a word in private . . . Sarge?'

Gabby's eyes narrowed as her head rose from her monitor. Sarah stood firm. A beat passed between them as Gabby sized her up.

'Make it quick.' She pointed to the room nicknamed 'the confessional'. It was one of the few places that offered some privacy, and was the DI's office before he moved to the bigger one across the hall. It was easy to understand why. The room was cramped and claustrophobic, with cheap metal shelving filled with box files lining each wall. As Sarah followed her sergeant inside, she summoned every ounce of courage. *Start as you mean to go on.*

'I get the feeling that I'm not wanted here.'

'And?' Gabby surveyed her with cold interest.

'Well, what then . . .' Sarah began to witter. She had expected a denial at the very least. 'What do you want me to do? Leave? Is that it?'

'You don't get to do that.' Gabby raised her finger in a tick-tock motion. 'You don't get to whine and complain after we've kept your job open for a year. What did you expect when you sauntered back in here? Bunting? Champagne?'

Sarah stared at her shoes. She had gone too far. She should have just gone home. 'Sorry,' she said, feeling her throat constrict. *Oh God, don't cry.* 'It's just that . . . I don't think I should be blamed for what my husband did. I didn't know . . .' Her chin wobbled as her emotions built in the back of her throat.

But Gabby just shook her head. 'You don't get it, do you? It's nothing to do with him. There are consequences to having your job unfilled for this long. We couldn't hire a replacement with you claiming sick pay. We've all had to pull *your* weight.'

Sarah bowed her head. She had been so busy blaming David that she hadn't thought of the team struggling in her absence.

'Your ambitions are running ahead of your ability,' Gabby said. 'You've had a good day. You got us a lead – a decent one. But don't expect our heartfelt thanks, because we've been sinking while you've been gone. You should be thanking *us* for covering your arse for so long.'

'I thought everyone hated me because of what he did.'

'And would you blame them? They'd been betrayed by their own sergeant. A man who gave his team a bad name. Isn't there enough hatred towards the police without him proving them right?' She stared at Sarah, unblinking. 'We would have had a lot more respect if you'd faced the music, rather than hiding away.'

'I wasn't well . . .'

'And I appreciate that,' Gabby said. 'I'm not demeaning your mental health issues. But shit, Sarah . . . a whole year? You could have freed up your position in CID. We're a family . . .' She cast an eye through the window over the bunch of officers who were getting on with their work. 'A fucked-up, dysfunctional family, but we work together as a team. All I'm saying is, you could have spared them a thought.'

Sarah felt sick listening to Gabby. She was the one who had forced this conversation, and now she was hearing everything she had been avoiding. All those late nights on the sofa, mindlessly eating crap. She'd been so focused on just getting through each day – hating her husband as if it were a sport, and holding onto the hope of going back to work – that she hadn't thought about the team being an officer down. Truth be told, she hadn't let herself go there.

'Look, it's your first day. Things will get easier. Just keep your head down and get on with your work.'

'Sarge, how can I do that if you're making me go home?'

'You're on restricted duties. Those are the rules. You're limited to an eight-hour shift.'

'Then why have you kept me out of the office all day?'

'So you could pull your weight.' She took a measured breath. 'And yes, maybe it was to spare you some of the comments floating around. I'm not a primary school teacher. I don't have time for all that shit.'

Taking in a long, slow breath, Sarah nodded. 'Alright, Sarge. I'll go.'

'And Sarah?'

'Yes?'

'Stop calling me Sarge. Only probationers do that. Call me Gabby. Or Ball Breaker behind my back. But Sarge is reserved for when the top brass is sniffing about.'

A soft smile touched Sarah's lips. 'Will do.'

As she slung her coat over the banister, Sarah reflected on the day she'd had. She liked Gabby more than she feared her now that she could see where she was coming from.

'Bad day?' her husband's voice rose from the living room.

'Are you still here?' she snapped. The conversation with Gabby had given her a clarity she hadn't had for months. Home was meant to be a place of comfort, not unease. 'I want you to leave,' she said, stalking into the living room. 'I know you have this twisted idea that you're looking out for me, but you're not welcome here anymore. Just go.' She turned and walked out of the room before he could say anything more. She knew he wouldn't follow her. He had no place here now.

As she soaked in the bath a while later, Sarah breathed in the silence of her cramped but comfortable home. Changes needed to be made, she knew that. In her diet, her lifestyle, and her job. But most of all she needed to learn to live on her own. Lavender steam relaxed her as she thought about her old friends. Elsie, Maggie, Lewis, David . . . they had all grown up here and all suffered in one way or another. What was it about Slayton that drew them all together, battle-scarred misfits of life?

Changed into a clean tracksuit, Sarah planned her attack. There was a late night of housework ahead of her. Not quite the excitement of CID tonight but it would keep her mind off things. And it was about time. Towel-drying her hair, she walked into the kitchen, exhaling a sigh of relief. Peace. David was gone, at least for now. These days, her husband seemed like the harbinger of doom, undermining her confidence and when it came to work, making her feel inadequate. She needed to make a clean break.

Her gaze fell on the shed at the end of her garden, his old domain. Clearing it of his things was another job for her to-do list, although she was nervous about what she might find. Outside, the fence rattled in a gust of wind. It was only gone eight and evening had closed in.

'Hey, puss,' she said, as Sherlock joined her in the kitchen. 'Would you like a cuddle?' His tail aloft, the ginger cat swerved Sarah's outstretched hands and made his exit through the cat flap. 'I guess that's a no, then,' Sarah said, her attention drawn to the mat beneath. There was an envelope sitting on it that hadn't been there before. Time stopped around her.

It wasn't the envelope which frightened her. It was the name written in blue fountain-pen ink. With trembling hands, she reached for it, blood pounding in her ears. It was a name she had not been addressed by in a very long time.

Sarah Middleton.

14

'Who's that?' Elsie called from the living room, as a lock rattled in the front door. Her body clock measured in mealtimes and she had run out of snacks.

'It's me,' Christian called cheerfully, letting himself into the hall.

'You're late,' she said. 'It's almost six o'clock.'

'I was at the library picking up your books.' He looked at her curiously as he let himself in. 'Who else would it be anyway?' His shirt tail was hanging out and his fringe was falling into his face.

'It might have been Sarah.' Elsie's eyes trailed over the books cradled in his arm.

'Who?'

'Sarah. She's a police officer. We used to go to school together. She called to see me today.'

'Right. The gate.' He released the books onto her bed.

'Yessir, the gate. She's done well for herself. She's going to visit again.' She frowned in disapproval at the books. 'I asked for Mary Cleveland.' It was the second time he'd let her down today; the latte he'd brought home at lunchtime had been lukewarm.

Christian was picking up the empty éclair box off the floor. 'They're all out on loan. You never mentioned any Sarah before.'

'We lost touch after school. I did have a life before you, you know.' She pointed at the book cover featuring a woman standing in front of a police car. 'Look at that. Her pants are so tight you can see her religion.'

'They're your usual reads, Mom. I did my best.' Muttering something about making sandwiches, he sloped off to the kitchen.

'I've run out of E45 cream!' she called after him. 'And I'm low on talcum powder. You'll have to pick up a batch from the pharmacy.' Her skin was a cracked landscape of red, her joints in constant pain. She had tried to clean and powder the weeping sores in the folds, but there was only so much she could do on her own. She rubbed the back of her neck as another dart of pain made itself known. When Christian was young, he would dutifully wash and powder every crack and crevice in her skin in exchange for a chocolate bar or a bag of crisps. But now he was eating healthily she had even less in common with him than before.

Tomorrow. She sighed. She would drag herself into the shower tomorrow, maybe even look at getting a wet room. 'What happened here?' Christian's voice echoed from the kitchen as he surveyed the cat litter trays lining the floor. 'Did your friend tidy up as well?'

'No, I did it,' Elsie said proudly. The ache in her lower back was a testament to that. It was burning like blazes, but she'd felt better about herself as a result. 'I changed my bed linen too.' Her old, stained sheets were sloshing around on a boil wash, along with her underwear. Christian did what he could, but it was a long time since either had been changed.

Christian was standing in the kitchen with his back turned to her, buttering a half loaf of bread into peanut butter and jelly sandwiches – a snack to keep her going until suppertime. The cats were eyeing him hopefully, protesting with hungry mews.

84

'That's good,' he said, kicking the fridge door shut. 'I've been busy too. I let the police into Blackhall Manor so they could have a look around. Some kids were messing around in there last night.'

Elsie thumbed through each of the books, already formulating the one-star reviews she was going to leave. *Lazy, gawdawful, porn-level writing. Double crapola, stinky ending, potty-mouthed filth.* A smile rose to her lips at the genius of her repertoire. She raised her face to her son as he returned, plate in hand. 'You'd think if kids were able to get into that creepy old place that law enforcement would too.'

'It doesn't work like that,' Christian called from the kitchen. He emptied a pint of milk into the plastic cat bowls. 'It all has to be above board. The gate is padlocked. We don't know how they got in.'

'That place is evil, pure and simple. The devil's playground.' Elsie pulled the wheeled table over as Christian walked in carrying a slab of sandwiches. She wanted to tell him that she was cutting down on calories, but she wasn't ready. Not yet. 'I'll have some of that nice apple pie and cream,' she said. 'And don't forget—'

'The chocolate milk. Coming right up.'

Elsie stared at the tower of sandwiches, dented by Christian's fingers where he had pressed into them while cutting them in half. She wished he would wash his hands before preparing food. She lifted each slice of limp bread, carefully checking its contents for cat hairs. Mention of Blackhall Manor was almost enough to steal her appetite away. She made a silent note to pray for the poor souls who lost their lives there. If ever there was a place devoid of the Lord's attention, it was there.

'Will you eat with me later?' she asked, as he rested the litre of chocolate milk on her table. Friday night was pizza night, and a takeaway would be ordered at eight.

'I ate at work,' he said, looking longingly at the door. Christian liked to go on his computer game and catch up with his online friends. But the evening stretched out so long in front of her, even five minutes in her son's company was better than nothing at all.

'What was the name of that officer you let into Blackhall?' Elsie countered. 'It wasn't Sarah, by any chance?'

'They were two male officers. Why?'

'You've got to keep this to yourself, mind.' Elsie smiled, tapping the side of her nose. She waited for Christian to pull up a stool. He lowered his hand to stroke Felix as the cat curled its tail around his legs.

'She seems a nice enough lady. She deserves to be able to get on with her life. I mean, it's bad enough, everything she's been through without people sticking their beaks in, wanting to talk to her.' With some satisfaction, she watched him drink in her words. It was nice to have his undivided attention for once.

'I'm not with you. Who are you talking about?'

'The girl in the Middleton family. The one who was shot last.'

Christian's face clouded in confusion. 'How would anyone speak to her? She's dead.'

'Rumour and conjecture. The whole thing was hushed up.'

Elsie bit into her sandwich. It tasted better than it looked. 'The wardrobe door was locked, so her dad shot right through it before turning the gun on himself.' She raised a hand to her head. 'The bullet skimmed her right here,' she said, pointing to her forehead. 'Left her with a scar. She covers it up with her fringe but it's still there, rightly enough. There's no denying who she is.'

'No denying who who is?' Christian scratched his cheek.

'Aren't you listening to me at all? Sarah, the police officer who came to see me earlier on. She's the sole survivor of the Blackhall Manor massacre.'

'The girl who was shot in the wardrobe lived?'

'Uh-huh,' Elsie nodded, taking another sandwich off the pile. 'She was in a coma for months. Then she was transferred to a private hospital and people forgot about her after that.'

'Huh,' Christian said, with a smile. 'Did she change her surname?' He looked at Elsie thoughtfully.

'Yeah, she goes by her mother's maiden name. Keeps her under the radar, I guess. She came back to Lower Slayton a while ago.' A smile rose to her face. Two proper conversations in one day. 'Anyhoo, I was thinking, if she can overcome all that and become a detective, then the least I can do is lose some weight.'

His expression thoughtful, Christian gave a slow nod in response. 'Sure, Mom, if it's what you want. But you may as well finish what's in the fridge first.' He glanced down at his watch. Elsie could see he was counting the seconds to leave.

'Go on then, go and play your game.'

As he rose from his stool, Elsie could see the subject of dieting didn't interest her son. Christian had heard it a million times before. The room fell gloomy and silent as he closed the door behind him. At least she had her books. Taking another bite of her sandwich, Elsie chewed methodically as she picked her next read. Above her, Christian's bedroom door slammed shut. She rubbed her chest as a slab of bread seemed to get stuck on the way down. 'Ow! What the—' She sucked in a wet breath as pain radiated outwards. White foam gathered in the corners of her mouth, her limbs jerking in sudden bouts.

'Christian!' she rasped in a spit-choked voice. Her teeth clenched as pain took her with force, watering her eyes and casting a sheen of sweat on her brow. In, out, she heaved for breath, her chest rising with exertion. The band around it was tightening. Her eyes rose to the picture of Jesus hanging on the wall. 'Sweet Lord,' she whispered through clenched teeth as she gripped the sides of the bed. 'Spare me . . . Godddd!' A spasm of pain distorted her words. Tears streaked from her eyes as she stared at the door. Nobody was coming. She was going to die alone.

15

'How are you feeling, little man?' Elliott's mother stroked his hair. It was daylight when he'd sat down in front of the television and he hadn't noticed it become dark. All the action was going on inside his head. It was dark all the time there.

His eyes swivelled towards the clock on the wall, gone six o'clock. 'Aren't you going to work?' His mum visited his dad in hospital when he was at school, and in the evenings she worked flexible hours as a cleaner in the Slayton Lakeside Hotel.

'Not today – no babysitters,' Maggie replied. 'Libby and Jahmelia aren't well, so I've called in sick. They can manage without me for one night.'

Elliott relaxed a little knowing his mum would be at home. Maybe tonight, he would be OK. He felt a little better after speaking to the policewoman too. But it couldn't take away the horrible feeling which started in his tummy and went all the way up to his chest. Last night, everything had spilled over. He'd been deep in his nightmare and hurt the person he loved most in the world. He had seen the scratches and bitemarks on Maggie's arm and they made him scared.

Almost before he could talk, Elliott felt the bad things around him, like the sickness in his tummy before he went to the dentist, or that time Mummy brought him to the doctor to get his injections. But the bad thoughts that came to him now played out like a movie that he could smell and feel too. Sometimes it showed him things that had happened, and sometimes he saw things that were going to come true. Every day it was getting harder to keep the bad thoughts out. He was seven and a quarter years old, but he didn't know what to do. Maggie settled on the sofa beside him, crossing her legs and bobbing her foot.

'Any tortoise facts for me today?'

Elliott searched his memory banks for something interesting. 'Tortoises have been around for over three hundred million years.'

'Wow. That's a long time.' Maggie's eyes widened in amazement, but Elliott wondered if she was pretending it was cool.

'Are you OK, Mummy?' He searched her face for an answer. 'Did I hurt you bad?'

Maggie's smile was as warm as the sun. She liked it when he called her Mummy, which was why he said it today. 'No, baby, you didn't. I'm fine. What happened last night?'

'I remember feeling scared,' he said in a small voice. 'You brought me back to bed.' Elliott wished that was all it was. He was so jealous of normal kids with normal lives and normal nightmares. Why did he have to be this way? He used to use up all his birthday and Christmas wishes asking for the dreams to be taken away, but he had given that up now.

His mother looked at him sorrowfully, her blonde lashes fluttering as she drew him close. 'How about I make us sausages, peas and mash? I'll do the gravy nice and thick.'

Elliott nodded enthusiastically, not because he was hungry, but because if Maggie hugged him for much longer he was scared he would cry. He rubbed a thumb over the medal. It had never been this bad in the day before. The Midnight Man was all around him, and in a few hours Elliott would have to go back to bed. Every night he tried to stay awake, but it never worked.

Maggie was in the kitchen, boiling the kettle and rattling saucepans when a sudden flash from last night's dreams invaded his mind. Frozen with fear, Elliott clutched his father's medal as the violence replayed on a horror carousel. The stinky smell of damp clothing, thick and heavy as it was pulled on. Voices in the dark. Flapping. Panting. Running through the trees. Elliott gripped the medal tightly, his breath coming fast as the darkness came alive. Cold. It was so cold: the breeze was watering his eyes and reddening his skin.

A deep, scary voice. An icy blade pressed against warm skin. The purple-blue vein in her neck. A low growl. Thick knuckles against an ivory handle. The angel's fear because she knew this was the end. Blonde hair splashed with red. A gargling, bubbling cry. *The angel is dead. But the Midnight Man still comes.*

His mother shook him awake, he didn't know how many minutes later. He swiped away the dribble from the corner of his mouth and picked up his daddy's medal from the floor. He had passed out. Maggie thought he was sleeping. It was better that way. His legs felt like jelly as he followed her to the kitchen. It was a small but warm space, with Maggie's paintings on the wall and some stuff she had bought from a charity shop after they moved in decorating the space. Some dying posies sat on the windowsill next to the big white sink. Stuck to the fridge were some of the drawings he'd made in school – the regular pictures, not the scary ones his teacher had made such a fuss about. After that, he'd learned to draw tortoises instead of what was in his head. He looked at the photo of his daddy, taken in happy times when he was well. They were at the zoo seeing the giant tortoises and Elliott was sitting on his father's shoulders. He'd felt like a giant that day too. But then they came home to Slayton, a place where the air was heavy somehow, and he always had a feeling of being watched. A lump rose in his throat and he swallowed it back down.

The smell of Bisto curled around him when he sat down to eat. Maggie's eyes were bright with worry as she asked for the hundredth time if he was OK. Nodding, he kept quiet. Quiet couldn't get him in trouble. Quiet was safe. In school, he tried extra hard to act like a regular kid, especially during the days he felt scared. But Miss Grogan watched him all the time. That's why she had called the children's so-shall-care. The women who came to their house didn't seem very caring to him. All they did was make Maggie worry, asking if anyone had hurt him. It wasn't Mummy's fault. It wasn't anyone's. After a few weeks the women from the so-shall-care stopped coming around. They said he had an 'overactive imagination' and was 'processing' what happened to his dad. But Elliott didn't want to be different. He wanted to be like everyone else.

He chewed his food mechanically as bits of the dream that wasn't a dream hung around. He couldn't find the right name for it. Nightmare, night stories . . . none of them fit. It was something from the other place. He imagined the other place being behind tracing paper, like the pages he'd got to trace and draw with in school: a thin sheet which kept that world from this. Most people couldn't see through it, but Elliott saw too much. He rested his hand over his eyelid as it began to twitch. It felt like an insect trapped beneath his skin. This was his punishment for seeing the world from behind someone else's eyes. Some *thing's* eyes. Blackhall Manor. The name gave him goosebumps all over. It was coming for him. It was sending the Midnight Man. His eyes flicked to his father's medal on the table next to his plate. He wasn't brave like his daddy. If he was brave he wouldn't have wet the bed.

'You OK, hun?' his mother said, resting her knife and fork. Elliott opened his mouth to speak. He wanted to tell her. For her to take him in her arms and hug the scary stuff away. But hugs could not stop them, and his mummy was sad enough. 'I'm fine.' Elliott gave her a watery smile before sticking his fork in his sausage and taking a bite.

16

Sitting at her kitchen table, Sarah stared at the letter which she'd found beneath the cat flap in the back door last night. Weary from lack of sleep, she sat hunched over the letter, her concentration broken by a long miaow. Sherlock's tail flapped from left to right as he demonstrated his disapproval of having to wait for his breakfast.

'Sorry, mate,' she said, fetching some cooked chicken breast from the fridge. 'We need to get you on a healthy diet, eh? No more pizzas, no more greasy chicken. Cat food for you, and Slimming World for me.' She caught sight of herself in the mirror; a study of loneliness as her words bounced around the walls of her kitchen. Another furtive glance at the letter. Her stomach clenched at the sight of it. *It's just hate mail,* she told herself. *As worthless as the paper it's written on.*

She plopped the chicken in Sherlock's bowl and topped up his water. At least the kitchen smelled clean. One cat was enough for anyone, God only knew how Elsie coped with six.

But she could only distract herself with cat thoughts for so long. The letter called her by her real name . . . her *childhood* name. She had only taken her mother's maiden name of Noble because of the anonymity it offered. Back then, when her mum's side of the family took her in, it seemed like the natural thing to do. She felt the familiar spiral of panic and shame spreading up her body. Just when the abuse about her husband had died down, it seemed that someone was intent on dragging up her own personal hell. What did the sender of this letter want with Sarah Middleton? It was the invasion that bothered her. Someone creeping around her overgrown garden. A hand darting through the cat flap. She had been so spooked last night that she'd done a full sweep of the house. The back door had been locked. There was no forced entry and she had thoroughly checked upstairs. So why was she still standing here, staring at the damned letter?

Letters were more personal than emails, more intimate somehow. Her senses heightened, she re-read the handwritten words.

Dear Sarah,

Congratulations are due. How you have managed to stay beneath the radar in a small town like Slayton is impressive. People underestimate you, don't they? But then, you have a forgettable face. Your clothes blend in . . . even your house feels like it's hiding. We're not that different, you know. I too am underestimated by the grand folks of Slayton. Not for much longer, I think.

You slouch when you walk, did you know that? You keep your hair long, so it shadows your face. You think people can't see who you really are. Don't worry. The residents of Slayton are too wrapped up in their own lives to notice little old you. Heaven forbid that the papers would get hold of your true identity. But then, Blackhall Manor has always stolen your limelight, hasn't it? You should pay the old place a visit. It would be happy to see you again.

I'm sure by now you're wondering who I am and why I'm writing to you. Maybe you think I'm a crackpot, or some kid with too much time on their hands. I imagine all sorts of thoughts are going through your head. I know a lot about you, Sarah, but I'm not here to suggest that we meet if that's what you're wondering. I don't think you're ready to play the Midnight Game yet, are you? Have you figured out who I am? No. Of course you haven't. You're not really cut out for policing, are you, Sarah? If incompetency was a sport, you'd come in first every time.

Let me help you a little, God knows you need it. I'm the one who wiped that privileged waste of space, Angelica Irving, out. And she had been so delighted by my invitation. She thought it made her special! Isn't that funny? All the reverence of their game playing . . . Don't feel bad for her. She invited me in. She drew her own blood because she was so desperate to spend the night with the Midnight Man. You could say she got what she asked for. Girls like Angelica usually do.

Have you figured it out yet, or are you ready to throw in the towel? But then, an incompetent loser like you wouldn't have the guts to enter the ring. I bet the cogs in that tiny brain of yours are turning now, aren't they? Save yourself the embarrassment of bringing this to your police bosses. You won't trace it back to me. It's circumstantial evidence. You'll have heard the term on one of those cop *shows that you watch. Does it make you sad, knowing you'll never make the grade? Even your cat hates you. But don't worry, your time is coming. You weren't meant to live, I'm just righting a wrong. Feel free to correct it any time you like. When you're gone, then I will be too. So do the world a favour and swallow those tablets in your bedside drawer.*

If that's not enough motivation for you to end your miserable life, then here's something else for free: there were four other players that night. Four other candles waiting to be snuffed out. For every day you're alive the game continues. You know what you need to do.

The Midnight Man

Sarah gripped the kitchen counter as the words hit her with force once again. Was Angelica Irving really dead? And was this her killer? Her eyes flicked to the window. Was he watching her now?

Snatching the letter, she ran to each window and drew the blinds before checking the door again. His mocking words rang in her mind, playing on her insecurities. Someone who would never make the grade. Someone who tugged at her fringe. She dropped her hand from her hair. It was as if he had seen into her soul. How did he know everything? Her life, her habits, where she lived. She knew she had to report this, but she could not bear the shame. She felt naked. Exposed. But her tormentor had mentioned four other players. Who were they? And who would write her a letter fuelled with so much hate? She started as the phone rang from the hall, the *dring dring* of the old-fashioned handset echoing in the empty space.

'Hello?' she said, hoping for a sales call, or her sergeant, or

BT broadband, anyone except . . . A heavy exhalation of breath. 'Hello, who's there?' she said, firmer this time. Nothing. Nothing but breath ruffling the phone line, and the low, ominous sense of hatred being conveyed without words. Slamming down the phone, she grabbed her boots from the floor and tugged them on. She was meant to have the weekend off, but she couldn't spend another second in her home. Fear quickened her movements as she grabbed her coat, scarf and car keys and marched out of the front door. She drove on autopilot to the police station. It was a prank. Nothing to be scared of. But the phone call, so soon after she picked up the letter. It gave a clear message – I am watching you. I will be back.

Sarah monitored her sergeant's expression as she read and re-read each word. She'd relayed details of the silent call, but it was the letter which intrigued her the most. As Sarah sat in front of Gabby's desk, she was in earshot of her colleagues who were immersed in their work. 'Where's the envelope?' Gabby said, her gaze falling on Sarah's empty hands.

'I . . . um, I left it at home. He delivered it by hand. No stamp. Through the cat flap in the back door.' The last thing Sarah wanted was her sergeant seeing her maiden name.

'The back door?' Gabby echoed Sarah's words.

'The front of my house is visible from the road. Maybe he was worried about being seen.'

'They . . . maybe *they* were worried about being seen,' Gabby corrected. 'Never assume. What's your home security like?'

'Crap,' Sarah replied. 'The fence needs replacing. Every time there's a storm it comes down.' Sarah's street led to the local playground and kids cycled past on their bikes all the time. But the back of Sarah's house led to a trail overgrown with brambles which was a cut-through into town. At night, it was dark and gloomy and only used by those in the know. She didn't tell her sergeant that some nights she went to bed and forgot to lock her back door. She didn't need anyone else calling her an incompetent loser today. She willed Gabby to keep talking, unable to escape the sound of the caller's breath. She imagined them, palms moist as they clung to the receiver, getting a kick out of her fear. Her sergeant's eyes flicked upwards, pinning her with a gaze.

'What's this rubbish about tablets?'

'Dunno,' Sarah lied. 'I keep some painkillers in my bedside drawer. Doesn't everyone?'

Satisfied, Gabby bowed her head as she re-read the words.

'I take it you've not heard from Angelica,' Sarah said, feeling a sudden urge to fill the silence.

'No, but we've requested a search party with sniffer dogs. We're going to start at the graveyard, then Slayton's old asylum and back to Blackhall Manor for a more detailed search.' Local officers had already searched Blackhall Manor but it made sense to request PolSA to investigate. Slayton's old asylum was another teenage hangout as it had been empty and abandoned for years. Situated beyond Lower Slayton, it was a mile outside of town. Gabby nodded towards the letter. 'This is probably related to David. You know what people are like around here.'

'Yes, that's probably what it is.' Sarah nodded. Her sergeant was most likely right, but it didn't explain how they knew her childhood name. Not that she'd bring it up now. She'd given away enough of herself today. Gabby looked thoughtful.

'What did they mean when they said Blackhall Manor would welcome you back?'

'I used to play there as a kid with my friends. Most kids in Slayton have dared each other to visit that place at some point.'

For a long time, it seemed Gabby wasn't going to say anything. Then she cleared her throat. 'They seem to know you very well. An old boyfriend, perhaps?'

'David was my *only* boyfriend.' A blush rose to Sarah's face. This always caused her embarrassment. But it was important in the context of this letter.

'Your only boyfriend?' Gabby repeated. 'Surely there must have been others . . .'

'I met him when I was twelve. He was seventeen.' The words made her feel dirty. It was something that had come back to haunt her with vicious regularity in the past year.

'And you . . . did you . . . ?' Gabby's tone dropped as she danced around the sensitive subject.

'Oh no, not until I was sixteen,' Sarah added hastily. But it was too late. She could see the judgement in her eyes. Her husband was a predator, even then. Except she had been too young to see it. By the time she was sixteen, she was head over heels in love. She rubbed her hands together, feeling like a suspect in an interview. 'Do you think he's telling the truth? I mean, about killing Angelica?'

'The best thing we can do with this is to keep it under our hats for now.' Gabby was non-committal. 'We don't want to worry her family, but we're trying to find out which other kids were playing the game too. I'll mark this up as sensitive on the system as it concerns you.' She returned her attention to the letter. 'Send it off for forensic analysis on the hurry-up. It's most likely some local crackpot, and I don't think it's related to the case. But they do seem to know a lot about you. Have you anywhere you could stay until things die down?'

Sarah thought about David's mother, and how she had a spare room. But there was no way she could darken her door. 'I'm fine,' she said. 'I've got Sherlock . . . my cat to keep me company.' Her smile faded as she remembered the words *even your cat hates you.* For someone to have such knowledge of her life . . . it was deeply unsettling. Gabby carefully placed the letter into a clear evidence bag. Sarah had penned details of the seizure on the outside, and a half-page MG11 statement would need to be written to cover it evidentially. The anonymous letter would be scanned and uploaded. It made her squirm to think that anyone with access to the investigation would be able to read the words online.

'I don't think your cat is going to defend you, Sherlock or not,' Gabby said. 'I've got a sofa, if you need somewhere to crash until you get your fence fixed.'

'No, honestly, I'm fine. I can stay with a friend if I need to.' But she was touched by the unexpected gesture. Gabby wasn't the ice queen she made herself out to be.

'I'll request a tag on your address then,' Gabby continued. 'Keep your phone on and charged. You know the drill.'

Sarah had safeguarded enough victims of stalking in the past to understand. Should she call 999, dispatch would be alerted to the flag on her address and allocate officers to attend. 'I do. Thanks.' Sarah picked up her bag, which was lying next to her feet. A small sense of relief washed over her. She had done the right thing. Hadn't she?

Gabby must have read the worry on her face. 'Don't stress

over this, Sarah. If I had a pound for every weird call or letter I've received when a case picks up attention, I could retire on the proceeds.' Gabby's desk phone began to ring. She picked it up, keeping her caller waiting as she issued Sarah with one final instruction. 'But for God's sake, get yourself some security cameras, and arrange to have your bloody fence fixed.'

'I will,' Sarah said, picking up a maternal tone. It made her heart wrench for her own mother, who was taken away so brutally. *Not my little girl.* The last words she heard her utter. She straightened her posture as she turned to leave. This time she was ready to meet her colleagues' eyes. She had faced far worse than this and survived.

17

'Plug in my fan, will you, son?' Elsie wafted a hand in front of her face. 'I'm hotter than a goat in a pepper patch.'

In fact, she hadn't felt this flustered since re-reading the Christian romance series by Caroline Brookes. The doctor who had left couldn't have been any more than thirty, and wouldn't have looked out of place on the cover of any one of those books. It was a long time since a man had touched her, even if it was to check her heart rate. And those eyes . . .

She leaned forward and gulped some flavoured water. No more chocolate milk for her. She closed her eyes, gratefully accepting the cool breeze as Christian flicked on the power switch of the fan. Yesterday's sudden attack of indigestion had been a warning. Doctor Costello's words were grave. This wasn't her first rodeo. She'd had heart problems in the past and she was several stones lighter back then. If she didn't lose weight soon, her ticker would give up the ghost and she would die.

'Why don't I take the router and put it in my room?' Christian said, his hand resting on the black plastic device. 'So if there's any problems with the signal, I can take care of it.'

'Really?' Elsie slammed down her empty glass. 'I'm lying here, near on dyin' and all you can think of is your darn Wi-Fi? I swear, Christian Abraham, if I upped and kicked the bucket here and now, you'd crawl over my body to get to that thing.'

'Sorry, Mom, I was only thinking of you.' Christian gave her an apologetic gaze before backing away from the bed. The only reason he didn't pay for his own broadband was because he spent every penny on online games. Christian didn't have any real-life friends. The only life he had was online. Some nights she would hear him, talking to people from halfway across the world. His conversations were engaging, and it was the only time she heard him laugh.

'Will you park your ass down here?' She pointed at the chair next to her bed as he fussed about, picking up empty sweet and crisp wrappers. He looked tired. She knew she worked him too hard. Holding down a full-time job as well as being her constant nursemaid . . . it was too much for him.

Clutching the empty wrappers, Christian did as he was told. Through gritted teeth, she had managed to call the doctor yesterday, as he sat upstairs oblivious, thanks to his headphones. He had lingered in the background, wringing his hands during the house call. She had refused the emergency services. She would not need to suffer the embarrassment of trying to squeeze herself into the ambulance. But something needed to be done.

'Son, listen to me. This is important.' She gave Christian an imploring look. 'This time I mean it. It's time I changed my life. I need your help.' She glanced at the shadows beneath Christian's eyes. 'This isn't good for either of us. You deserve a life of your own.' Not that he could cope without her. Christian was a star when it came to fulfilling his duties. But her father used to say that Christian only had 'one oar in the water'.

'You're not throwing me out, are you?' Christian's worried voice broke into her thoughts. 'I'll listen out next time. We could get baby monitors . . . so you can call me if you take a turn.'

Not a bad idea, Elsie thought. Baby monitors *would* save her shouting at the top of her lungs. An unwelcome image appeared, one of her wearing plus-sized adult diapers because she could no longer reach the restroom. She shook the thought away, taking in her son's weary face. 'Heavens to Betsy, I'm not throwing you out! Get that idea right out of your head. I'm just saying . . . I'm going to diet this time. It's now or never.' Having said that, the word 'diet' gave her an irrepressible urge to reach for the doughnuts.

Christian smiled nervously, shifting restlessly on the stool. 'Whatever you want. Write me a shopping list and I'll pick it up.'

Elsie gave him the beady eye. 'But you don't mean that, do you? It's easier to pick up a bucket of chicken from KFC than to make healthy home-cooked food.' Despite her son's smile, she picked up on his reservations. 'Spit it out,' she said. 'What's tugging your chain?'

Christian's cheeks reddened, as they always did when he was placed on the spot. 'You're so moody when you're dieting. It's hard enough now, but when I cut back your food, all you do is scream and shout.'

'No, I don't,' Elsie pouted, although come to think of it, the last time Christian confiscated her treats, she smashed one of her favourite vases against the wall.

'I'm doing the best I can,' Christian replied. 'But I'm tired, Mom. It's hard, doing everything on my own.'

'I get that,' Elsie said, guilt washing over her. 'I know you've given up your life to care for me. Which is why things need to change. If you just help me . . .' She heaved a sigh. She needed to make him understand. 'When I eat, everything else fades away. All my thoughts . . . they disappear. It's the only time I'm happy. But it's killing me too.' She looked around the room. She hadn't set foot outside these four walls in well over a year. 'I have two thrones. My bed and my toilet seat. That's as far as it goes. I move my ass from one to the other all day, and even that causes me pain.' Her hand fell to her constant companion, and she rhythmically stroked her cat. 'I haven't been outside since Lord knows when, and before you say it, yes, I know that's my fault.' She glanced to check for his understanding. 'My world is very small compared to yours, Christian, so please don't look at me like that, this is important. The doctor told me, plain and straight. I'll die if I don't sort myself out.' She swiped away her fringe, which was stuck to her forehead with sweat. She didn't want to feel this way anymore.

'I don't want you to die, Mom.' The look on Christian's face relayed sympathy. 'But I'm tired of getting my hopes up. We go through a few weeks of hell, then it's back to square one, only this time, you're bigger than before.' It was true. Each time Elsie lost weight, she found it impossible to keep it off.

'Well, don't hold back there, son . . .' Elsie said in a quiet voice, tears forming in her eyes. 'Have you ever stopped to wonder why I turned out this way?'

Doctor Costello had raised the question as he talked through her options. The young man had been so kind, he had just about melted her heart. But she could not discuss the real reasons for her compulsion. It was too horrific for anyone to comprehend, let alone her own son. To know he was the product of such darkness . . . it would be the end of him. She repressed the thought, scared he would see it on her face.

'Maybe I could shop online, order in the food myself . . . if you'll show me how.' Her parents had disapproved of computers – the devil's work, according to her father. Then again, according to Papa Abraham, there were few things in the modern world that weren't. These days, she used her laptop mainly for leaving Amazon and Goodreads book reviews.

'Don't worry about it.' Christian waved the suggestion away. 'I'll get you what you need.' Then he was gone, racing up the stairs, back to his online friends. Elsie wasn't the only one with a compulsion, but at least his wasn't damaging his health.

'Looks like it's just you and me, Felix.' Elsie spoke to her cat as he purred on her lap. Doctor Costello had spoken of counselling. Of getting to the root of Elsie's overeating. The truth was, she already knew the cause. She just wasn't strong enough to fight it.

18

Maggie stared at the marble sky as clouds rolled over the moon. She flicked the business card back and forth in her fingers, the cool night air clearing her thoughts. In her other hand was a cigarette – her guilty pleasure. She'd peeped in on Elliott before daring to light it, comforted to see him snoozing. The first hours were always the most peaceful and it was a relief to get him down early for once. But the hollows beneath his eyes relayed that sleep was not a safe place. He had battled to stay awake, finally slumbering in her arms as tiredness took hold. As much as she dreaded Elliott's nocturnal visions, her son felt it tenfold. They came and went in waves. After social services visited, they'd had a blessed respite and Maggie had dared to hope that Elliott could lead a normal life. Now it was starting all over again.

Sarah was the one person in the world who would understand. Was it too late to call her? She checked her watch. It was half past seven on Saturday night. She had such fond memories of their friendship. Of warm summers listening to Chesney Hawkes on their Walkmans and cycling to the BMX track. Meeting David and Lewis, who were a few years older, and spending forbidden time with them. Not that they'd got up to much back then. At twelve years of age their only interests were cycling around town, buying ice creams at the parlour, and splashing about in the lake. It was adjacent to the Slayton Lakeside Hotel which was equipped with a jetty and water sports centre. The lake was the first thing people saw when driving towards town, and the last thing they passed when they left. She'd spent many a happy summer's day in its waters. It was where she first met Lewis, with his dark wavy hair and tanned skin. She and Sarah had been swimming when he arrived with David in tow. She'd watched them splashing about with some old car tyre inner tubes, their goofy laughter filling the air. Maggie had seen them occasionally in town, but hadn't had the courage to approach them until that day. She smiled as she remembered how mortified Sarah had been when she'd gone up to them. Sarah had always been an introverted soul, but they'd had so much fun that day. The boys weren't like the other kids in school, they were more mature for a start. Lewis had quickly become the love of her life. But now he lay broken and silent, his eyes vacant when she sat next to his bed. Each week she relayed her news, her hollow words echoing around the room with no response. If ever she needed a friend, she needed one now.

Dialling Sarah's phone number she exhaled a stream of smoke before stubbing the cigarette into the ashtray at the back door. With Elliott's insights, it had been safer to keep her circle small. Sarah had kept a low profile too. They'd grown apart when they'd needed each other the most.

'Hello?' Sarah answered, after the fourth ring. There was hesitancy in her voice. She sounded spooked.

'It's me, Maggie,' she said, closing the kitchen door. She opened the glass cupboard above her head.

'Maggie,' Sarah said, with relief. 'Sorry . . . I thought it was a prank call.'

'Oh . . . sorry to bother you.' Maggie took a wine glass from the cupboard. 'Are you free for a chat?'

'God yes, I'd love that. I'll come straight over. Be with you by eight.' As the phone went dead, Maggie stared at the display. She'd meant a phone call, not a visit. She laughed at the situation. Sarah was even lonelier than her. At least her house was clean, she thought, resting a bottle of wine on the kitchen table. Wine and a catch-up with an old friend . . . not a bad way to spend a Saturday evening. She turned the dial on the wall up a couple of precious notches to draw in some extra heat.

Sarah was at her door in a flash, bottle of wine in hand. 'Snap,' Maggie said, gesturing at the Merlot as Sarah followed her into the kitchen.

'There's nothing better than a friend, unless it's a friend with wine. I stopped off for fish and chips on the way.' She raised the bag in her hand. 'The portions are massive. I hope you'll share.'

'Oh no, I've had supper, but I'll pick at a few chips.' It seemed rude to turn down Sarah's offer. They sat in the kitchen, the smell of salt and vinegar wafting from the plate before them as Sarah filled her friend in on her life to date.

'Listen to me, blabbering away. I hope I wasn't too forward, coming over like this.'

'Don't be silly. I rang you, remember?' It felt like old times, being in her friend's company. The years may have added a few extra wrinkles, but she was still the same warm-hearted Sarah that Maggie had come to love.

'So, your turn, Maggie. Fill me in.'

'There's not much to say.' She picked at the plate of chips. 'I've been holding the fort since Lewis ended up in hospital. We've got his army pension and his medical cover, so we're getting by. I work part-time in the Lakeside Hotel and I visit Lewis in hospital when I can. I'd bring Elliott but it upsets him, seeing his daddy so unwell.' Her heart heavy, Maggie paused to sip her wine. 'After all that time in Helmand Province and he almost gets blown up on a training exercise.' The story of how Lewis had saved his fellow soldiers had been all over the press. How the pilot of the army helicopter had suffered a heart attack. How Lewis had run towards the explosion as it hit the army base with force. He saved many lives, but at what cost? She glanced at her friend, who was looking equally sorrowful. 'Look at me, getting all maudlin. I have something that will cheer us both up.'

She reached for the old photo album she had taken down from the loft earlier that day. Laying it out before them, she flicked through each page. 'Oh my God, look at those dodgy perms!' Sarah laughed, pointing at a picture of her and Maggie as teens.

'I remember that batwing jumper,' Maggie smiled. 'I never took it off.'

'Ditto with me and my dungarees.' Sarah's eyes were alight as she turned each page. 'Is that . . .' Sarah squinted at an old photograph. 'Simon Irving?'

'So it is,' Maggie replied. The photo had been taken on the first night Slayton held an outdoor cinema screening. *Jurassic Park* had pulled crowds far and wide. Unlike Sarah and her friends, Irving attended a private school in Benrith, but he sometimes hung out with local teens. 'Did he ever try it on with you?' Maggie said, thoughtfully.

'Once,' Sarah replied. 'But I think it was for a bet. You?'

'Same.' Maggie recalled the time he'd tried to get her into his car.

'Knob,' they said in unison, before laughing aloud. Shaking her head, Maggie turned the page.

'Look, there's Elsie. Remember her? Her father found her at the screening and marched her home. Poor thing. I was so embarrassed for her.'

'I'd forgotten about that . . .' Sarah stared at the photo of Elsie, her hair tied up in ringlets and ribbons. 'I saw her, you know, after I left you yesterday. She's really struggling with her weight.'

'We all have our demons,' Maggie said, quietly.

'True,' Sarah agreed. 'But don't you think we have more than most? If I didn't know any better, I'd say Slayton is cursed.'

Maggie sipped her wine, comforted by its plummy notes. 'And yet we're all still here. I thought you weren't coming back.'

'It was David's idea,' Sarah said. 'I was quite happy working in police HQ. But then he was offered the sergeant's job and said he could get me on his team. I couldn't turn down the offer of a position in CID.'

The room fell silent as Maggie turned another page. Sarah looked so young next to David in the faded old photographs. She was a shy and nerdy girl, immature for her age. She met Maggie's eyes.

'I didn't know . . . I'm supposed to be a detective, Maggie, and I had no idea he had a thing for young girls. I would never have married him.'

Sarah's face was drawn. Her voice dropped as she continued. 'I thought we had a good life. As good as I could hope for after what happened . . .'

'Hey, it's all in the past now.' Maggie squeezed her friend's hand. 'You weren't to know. None of us were.' They sat in silence as the dishwasher swished in the background. It was an old model which barely worked, but the sound of the water was almost hypnotic. Maggie took another large sip of wine.

'How's Elliott coping?' Sarah asked, her composure back.

Maggie blinked to bring herself back to ground. It was an obvious change of subject but Maggie was happy to go along with it. She had seen Sarah gaze at her scratched arm when she'd last called around.

'He has night terrors, bad ones,' Maggie said flatly. 'That's where the bites and scratches came from. Social services got involved for a while then out of the blue, it all stopped. That was months ago. Seems the night terrors are back again, worse than before.'

Sarah looked deep in thought. 'The last time I was here, Elliott said something to me. I haven't been able to get it out of my head.'

'What's that?' Maggie rested her glass on the table. Talk of Elliott reminded her that she could not afford to get drunk.

Sarah tilted her glass as she accepted a top-up. 'He said the Midnight Man is coming, and something about the angel being dead. Does that mean anything to you?'

'No.' Maggie looked at her in genuine puzzlement. 'Should it?'

'Well . . .' Sarah paused to take another sip of wine. 'I probably shouldn't say anything. Can I trust you to keep a secret?'

'Of course,' Maggie nodded vehemently. As friends, Sarah and Maggie had kept each other's secrets all the time.

'Simon Irving's daughter Angelica went missing on Halloween night. Her brother said she'd arranged to play some midnight game with friends. It looks like they went to Blackhall Manor. She's not been seen since.'

Mention of the Manor made Maggie straighten in her chair. 'Oh. I see. How do you feel about that?'

'I'm scared for her, if I'm honest. That place is falling apart.'

Maggie sensed more behind her friend's words. What she had been through as a child put her own problems in the shade.

'I was wondering,' Sarah said. 'Could Elliott have picked it up from the babysitters?'

'It's possible . . .' Maggie paused for thought. 'Come to think of it, Libby and Jahmelia couldn't come over tonight. I thought it was weird, them crying off sick at the same time.'

'Interesting.' Sarah made a mental note to do some digging on their whereabouts when she got back to work. Her expression grew serious as she prepared to confide in her friend. 'I got a letter addressed to my old name of Sarah Middleton. It was really nasty. It said I was supposed to *die* that night. They signed off as the Midnight Man.'

'Bloody hell.'

'I know. And Maggie, they said they'd killed Angelica, and that they were watching me.' She plucked nervously at her hair.

Maggie looked into her eyes, searching. 'When did you get this?'

'Yesterday. Someone shoved it through my cat flap. I got a heavy breather phone call too. I reported it to work. They're fully aware.'

Maggie suppressed a shudder. 'What did they make of it?'

'My sarge says it's just a crackpot. They all come out of the woodwork when kids go missing. But I don't know, Maggie, the things this person knew about me . . .'

'And you went home on your own?' Maggie exclaimed. 'No wonder you were happy to hear from me.'

'You've no idea!' Sarah laughed, but her face was haunted by recent events.

'You don't think Angelica's dead, do you?'

114

'I hope not. But Elliott has picked the Midnight Man up from somewhere.'

'Kids in Slayton play that game every year.' Maggie rubbed her arms. Her words were hollow. Her son's insights were more powerful than she was letting on. The back door rattled on its hinges as the wind gusted outside.

'Yeah, that's probably it.' Sarah cast an eye at the clock on the wall as it ticked away the seconds. 'Anyway, I should be off.'

'You're not going anywhere.' Maggie rose from the table and picked up the empty wine bottle for recycling. 'I've got a spare room. I'll put some fresh sheets on the bed.'

'I couldn't . . .' Sarah said, but her expression was one of relief.

'I won't hear otherwise.' Truth be told, Maggie was grateful for another body in the house in case Elliott woke up. He was not the only one dreading going to bed. 'Now sit. I'll make us some coffees.'

Their peace was shattered when Elliott's cries filled the air. Maggie raced down the corridor, joined by her friend. A familiar sense of fear twisted her gut.

'Night terror?' Sarah said, her eyes wide.

'Sounds like it,' Maggie whispered, as Sarah followed her into the room. 'Be careful. He doesn't know what he's doing.'

Elliott kicked and thrashed in his bed, his sheet tangled around his legs as his screams filled the air. The room was graveyard cold.

Tentatively, Maggie approached, but it was Sarah that Elliott called to.

'Help!' he screamed, reaching out for her. Maggie could barely stand to see her little boy so upset.

115

'It's OK. Go to him,' she said, as Sarah looked to her for approval.

Sarah's reaction seemed instinctive as Elliott buried himself in her arms. 'Make it stop,' he cried, his chest juddering as he sobbed. 'Please. Take it away.'

'Hey, it's OK,' Sarah said. 'I've got you. Take a breath. They won't get past me.'

Maggie watched Sarah soothe her child as she sat on the bed, gently rocking him.

'What was it?' Sarah said, softly. 'What did you see?'

'The woods,' Elliott sobbed. Giant hiccups claimed his breathing, and he muttered beneath his breath as Sarah soothed him back to sleep.

'Shh. It's gone now. I've got it . . . let it go.'

Fighting back tears, Maggie smoothed her son's hair. Sarah looked at her apologetically, before resting him back on the pillow where he fell straight into a fitful sleep. Maggie checked beneath the covers. He hadn't wet the bed. His father's medal was beneath the pillow as usual. She tucked in his Teenage Mutant Ninja Turtles duvet and pushed his soft toy under his arm. He was just a child – far too young for such trauma. They stood together in silence, watching over him. His face was pale but peaceful now, no longer ravaged by fear.

Maggie glanced at Sarah's arms. She had come out of it unscathed. 'He'll be alright now,' Sarah said softly, as they crept from his room.

'How did you . . . how did you do that?' Maggie felt as if the air had been stolen from her lungs.

'To be honest, I don't know,' Sarah said. 'I didn't mean to intrude.'

'You didn't,' Maggie said. All she felt was relief. They both wandered into the living room, dazed.

'I need to make a phone call.' Sarah pulled her phone from her bag. 'Don't worry, I'll keep Elliott out of it. But I think I know where Angelica Irving is.'

Maggie didn't disagree. Her son hadn't been wrong yet.

19

What's normal for the spider is chaos for the fly. *The words danced across my mind as I walked between strobes of flashlights on the path towards Blackhall Woods. My face was ruddy from the cold, and the moon was high in the sky. I managed to fix my face into the same look of dismay mixed with determination as those around me. I was good at blending into the background. A chameleon of sorts.*

Several locals had turned out for the search as well as members of the police force. Word had spread quickly on Angelica's Facebook page. But unlike everyone else who joined, I knew exactly where she was. The hems of my trousers were damp as I trod through the boggy ground.

Angelica was buried in these woodlands in a shallow grave camouflaged by broken branches. I could have walked the short distance from the grounds of Blackhall Manor to the encompassing woods, but I could not risk being seen. So I had laid her in the boot of the car, knees against her chest, grey mottled lips pressed against plastic sheeting until the time was right. Then I drove her deep into the woods. Beneath the cover of darkness, I unwrapped her from her plastic cocoon. I recalled the slice of my shovel and how easily it had parted the dark, moist soil. Then I set to work, methodically cutting and ripping, my gloves soaked with congealed blood as I

completed the next steps of the game. I took no pleasure from it.
Bodily fluids revolted me. They were even more unpleasant to deal
with when they were cold.

By the time I shovelled dirt over her corpse, my thoughts had
already moved forward. Now here I was amongst the search team,
pretending to look for her. My hood up and my head down, I mixed
with the locals who were blind to what was before their eyes. I was
surprised to see the police still about. Detailed searches were usually
carried out in daylight. Had they received a tip-off? There was purpose
in their movements and they were using sniffer dogs.

The wind whipped around me as I reached the centre of the woods,
the rain pitter-pattering on my coat. People were still calling Angelica's
name. I thrust my hands into my pockets and waited for her to be
found. I was imagining the state of her when I saw Sarah Middleton's
pale face suddenly appear in the thick of the crowd. My heart beat
a little faster. Down but not out . . . at least, not yet. I felt a thrill at
what was to come.

She was shoulder to shoulder with a black police officer, deep
in conversation as the pair negotiated the leaf-slick path. She was
only a female sergeant, nobody of any great importance. The pair of
them appeared to be having strong words. I tried to get closer, but I
didn't want to draw attention to myself. She was bound to be on her
guard, given she had received my letter. I wish I could have seen her
face when she read it. I knew she wouldn't swallow those tablets. I
didn't want her to. There was only one way for her to die when the
time came. My nostrils flared as a rush of anger enveloped me. She
would regret ever coming back here. She should have stayed playing
dead. I pulled my scarf up over my chin as another bluster of wind
skinned my cheeks. Stumbling on a tree root, I regained my footing

as I negotiated the dank earth. Bare branches creaked above me in the rising November winds.

A sudden rush of urgency. Sarah picked up speed before me, updating her police airwaves while other officers gestured at us to stay back. A signal went up, deep in the woodlands, exactly where I had buried her. Angelica had been found . . . but she was not the only player. I was not finished yet.

20

A cool breeze swept down the school corridor, chilling the flesh on Libby's legs as she sat on her chair. It had been the school's idea, bringing in a counsellor to help Angelica's class with their grief, and now she was sitting in the hall, waiting her turn to go in. She only hoped Isobel and Bethany would hold their tongues.

'Remember the pact,' she'd whispered, as they were pulled from class to attend. *If you tell, you'll go to hell.* The words on the invite had been more of a threat than a pact, but she had claimed it just the same. 'We will if you will,' Isobel had rasped in return. Now she was sitting with Jahmelia in the corridor waiting for them to come out. Piped whale music played from the tannoys; some weird new incentive to help the students keep calm. Even with all this, Libby couldn't believe that Angelica was dead. It did not compute. Because if it fully sank in, Libby was the one to blame. She hadn't sent out the invites, but she knew better than to visit Blackhall Manor in the dead of night. The others had looked to her for reason, yet instead of tracking Angelica down, she'd insisted they stay and play.

Had Angelica's murderer been hiding in the shadows, watching them wander around the building with only a candle to guide their way? The killer could have chosen any one of them. She could not reconcile what she had done. Her eyes were red-rimmed and puffy, the skin on her nose raw. She was meant to be the sensible one; now they would never see Angelica again. She replayed events in her mind as she tried to understand what had possessed her.

Everything about Slayton was boring. Just hanging out with Angelica had boosted her street cred no end. But she only went to Blackhall Manor because she thought Angelica had orchestrated it. Also, if she was brutally honest with herself, a little piece of her wanted to get one over on the girl who thought she was better than everyone else. She had read about houses in America where people paid to be scared out of their wits. The places weren't really haunted, they were set up to look that way. But deep down she'd known Blackhall Manor wasn't like that. People steered clear for a reason. She picked the bits of tissue which had fallen onto her skirt.

'I've been having nightmares,' Jahmelia whispered. 'They're so bad that I'm scared to go to sleep.' She was rocking ever so slightly, her hands bunched into fists on her lap. Her eyes were as wide as saucers, and she looked even younger than she did before.

'Me too.' Libby checked up and down the corridor as she replied. 'I keep dreaming we're back there. I can't get it out of my head.'

Jahmelia cast a sideways glance at her friend. 'Mum and Dad have been grilling me . . . even Grandma's been ringing me night and day!' A pause. 'He comes to me in my sleep, Libby – the Midnight Man. He's going to get me. I'm next.'

'You don't believe that, do you, Jay?' But her friend's fearful expression relayed that she did. 'Here.' Libby reached into her schoolbag and pulled out a Mars bar from the front pocket. 'Mum

122

packed two in my lunchbox by mistake.' She hadn't, but Libby didn't have the appetite for chocolate today.

'Thanks,' Jahmelia said, gratefully taking the snack. All Libby wanted to do was to curl up in bed. She tried to imagine what her parents would say, that there were no such things as supernatural beings, much less some 'Midnight Man' out to get her because she had played some stupid game. But *someone*, or *something*, had murdered Angelica, and while her school friend may have been a pain, she couldn't think of one person in Slayton who would set out to hurt her like that. Their invites were personalised. He knew each of them.

'What do you think he did to her?' Jahmelia said in a small voice, a fleck of chocolate on the side of her mouth. 'Mum and Dad won't tell me anything.'

Libby shrugged. She didn't want to think about Angelica's last moments, or how scared she must have been. If her parents found out what she'd been up to that night, they'd never trust her again. But it was nothing compared to what Angelica's parents must be feeling. Slayton was a small town. The thought of bumping into them was too much to bear. She sniffled.

'You can't say anything. Remember the pact.'

'If you tell, you'll go to hell.' Jahmelia swallowed hard, her eyes shiny with tears. 'I looked it up online, Libs. If the Midnight Man catches you, he kills you and pulls out your insides, *piece by piece*.'

'That's crazy, stop panicking.' Libby placed a hand on Jahmelia's arm to quieten her friend as a group of sixth formers walked past. They delivered sympathetic looks before continuing towards the canteen. Each year group were identified by the colour stripe on their school uniform ties. Libby had been getting a lot of sympathy smiles today. But that would all change if they found out that she had carried on playing after Angelica disappeared. The thought brought fresh tears to Libby's eyes. What happened to sisterhood? Her parents would be so ashamed if they knew. As for Angelica's mum and dad . . .

Angelica's family were powerful. The Irvings owned the company which employed her father, for a start. They would need someone to blame, and what if they blamed her entire family? Mr Irving could drive them out of town. She'd heard of it happening to other families. One wrong step and you lost everything you owned. Thoughts swirled like leaves in a whirlwind. There was no going back. They had stained their blood next to their names and invited the Midnight Man in. All she could hope for was that the prophecy was fulfilled. The game was over. It had to be. She would never play again.

21

Sarah brushed the crumbs from her lunchtime tuna sandwich off her trousers. She was sitting in the job car, parked up in Slayton police station car park, staring at the tall, grey building ahead. She'd once been so excited to work from this building, being a detective on her husband's team. It seemed a much more interesting prospect than walking the streets in uniform or helping with scene guard. She'd passed her CID exams with flying colours. She knew she'd get flak for being married to her sergeant but it helped that she hadn't taken his surname. If only that was all she'd had to contend with. She had no idea how bad things would get.

Today, she felt on the outside of things, but she only had herself to blame. At least she'd been called in for a few hours of overtime yesterday. But while her colleagues were attending briefings and arranging media appeals, Sarah was on the ground with uniformed officers taking statements and conducting door-to-door enquiries. It wasn't the return to CID she had imagined, but it *had* borne fruit. She had not been prepared for the brutality of it. The sight of Angelica with her internal organs exposed, lying naked in a shallow grave – it had stolen the breath from her lungs. Who could have done such a horrific thing? And why?

Her thoughts were interrupted by the sound of rotary blades chopping the air. Shrinking back in her seat, she cast her eyes upwards, relieved it was a police helicopter. At least the KCOM News budget didn't stretch to choppers. They'd picked up the story as soon as they heard Simon Irving's daughter was missing and their van had been seen driving around Slayton ever since. Had the Irvings been a regular family, they wouldn't have cared. Now details of the crime were splashed all over the news, sending the town into panic. She could see it in the worried faces of everyone she spoke to, and had heard that locks and Ring cameras were selling out in the local shops.

Sarah could see where townsfolk were coming from. If Simon Irving's daughter could be murdered in a safe part of town, what hope was there for them? They didn't yet know about Blackhall Manor, or the game Angelica had played. Her thoughts returned to the letter. If Angelica had played the game with four other teenagers, who were they? Her social media gave nothing away, and her online search history was being checked. But despite efforts to find her mobile phone, police had been unable to triangulate a signal and it was either powered down or destroyed.

As the helicopter disappeared from view, Sarah locked the car and headed towards the station, her expression fixed as her mind worked over the details of the case. How had Elliott known exactly where Angelica was buried? Someone must know something, and Elliott was picking up on it . . . Only the night before Angelica went missing, Jahmelia and Libby had babysat Elliott. She imagined the girls patiently listening as he talked about tortoises to them. Had he overheard them discussing the Midnight Game when he was meant to be asleep? Angelica was in their year in school. But Sarah had spoken to Libby and Jahmelia at length, along with the rest of Angelica's friends. Not one had admitted to seeing Angelica the night she disappeared. That poor girl, who was on the cusp of adult life, to be left in the woods in such a state . . . Sarah pressed her fob against the security panel and the heavy door clicked open.

Maggie had treated her as if she was some kind of messiah, sent from above to help her child. 'You understand him,' she'd said on Saturday evening, breathy with relief. Sarah loved her old friend dearly, but when you thought about it logically, Elliott was just desperate for someone to confide in. It must have been tough for the little boy, seeing a man as strong as his father become incapacitated overnight; it wasn't surprising that it had triggered something. And Sarah was a police officer, a symbol of all that was good to a child like Elliott. No wonder he'd been ready to offload. But how did he know Angelica was buried in the woods? Sarah couldn't fathom it as she strode down the gloomy corridor with her tangle of thoughts.

The station was buzzing with activity. She passed her DI's office, having a sneaky peek through the glass in his door. Head down, he was deep in conversation as he spoke on the phone. Various newspapers were spread out on his desk. She had already seen the headlines as she popped into her local newsagents on the way to work. The story of the murdered teen was front page on all the papers from the nationals to the *Slayton Gazette*. Sarah carried on walking. At least they'd found her body. She'd told her sergeant the tip-off had been anonymous but it was time to be up front about Elliott. She entered the CID office; disappointed to see that Gabby wasn't at her desk.

'You OK there?' Yvonne said, holding several dog-eared files in her hand. Yvonne was one of the longstanding members of CID and was only a few years younger than Sarah. Her dark hair was perfectly straightened, her arched brows pencilled in.

'Oh hi, Yvonne, just waiting to speak to Gabby. Do you know where she is?'

'She's in a meeting with Angelica's parents, due back any minute now.' She regarded Sarah with a smile. 'Well done on the lead, how did you manage that? You're putting the rest of us to shame.' Yvonne shifted her folders to the other arm, obviously in no hurry to leave. Sarah could imagine the snide comments Yvonne had said about her behind her back. She didn't trust her, but Gabby wanted everyone working as a team. There was no room for lone wolves in CID. She was more of a lame dog than a lone wolf, but still . . .

'I have my contacts.' A protective feeling rose in Sarah. She knew how the others would react to Elliott's involvement.

Yvonne tilted her head to one side. 'Anything that's related to the case needs to be brought up, Sarah.' She paused for thought. 'You're not holding out on us, are you? Because—'

'No, God no, of course not,' Sarah jumped in, emitting a stilted laugh. She panicked as Yvonne stared her down. 'It's just . . . there's this young boy. I spoke to his mum, Maggie Carter, about a prowler on Halloween night.' Sarah wasn't ready to confide in Yvonne about their friendship. It had nothing to do with the case.

'Are you talking about Elliott Carter?' Yvonne said evenly.

'Yes, you know him?'

'Slayton is a small place. He's an interesting boy.'

'Yes. He's very . . . insightful.' Sarah shoved her hands into her trouser pockets and tilted on the balls of her feet.

'He's helped police with enquiries in the past.'

'Really?' Sarah frowned. 'His mum never said.'

'That he's psychic? It's not something you blurt out in conversation, I suppose, but yeah, I've spoken to him before.'

128

'*You* have? In a police capacity?'

Yvonne nodded. 'Oh yeah, yeah, thanks to Gabby. She's very open-minded.' She lowered her voice as she leaned in to Sarah. 'She tends to keep her beliefs under wraps. Not everyone appreciates her point of view.'

'What point of view is that?' From the corner of the room, Sarah saw one of her male colleagues give them a curious glance. She returned her attention to Yvonne, who was getting friendlier by the minute. Sarah couldn't deny that it felt good to break the ice.

'She's very spiritual,' Yvonne whispered. 'You'd never think it, would you?'

Sarah was having a hard time equating her sergeant with the woman Yvonne was portraying. 'No, she doesn't strike me as the type.'

'Yeah, don't call her a type either, she hates that. I mean, she hates most things; they don't call her the Ball Breaker for nothing . . .' Yvonne broke into a short laugh. 'But you'll gain her respect if you show some consideration for her beliefs. You poor thing, you could do with it. You've not had the best of starts.' She delivered a pitying look before glancing over her shoulder. 'But don't talk about it here because the others will only take the piss. Speak to her in private, she'll like that.' Their conversation was interrupted by the shrill ring of Yvonne's desk phone. She glanced over Sarah's shoulder before giving her a wink. 'She's coming. Good luck!'

Sarah nodded in acknowledgement, feeling uncertain about what had just happened. From what she could tell about Yvonne, she was a spiky character who took her time accepting people into the fold. Right now, Sarah didn't know her well enough to

129

trust her, but she *had* left them short-staffed and she had to start somewhere. She switched her focus to Gabby, who didn't look all that happy to see her. Sarah inhaled a deep breath. *Carpe diem, seize the day.*

'Sarge, can I speak to you for a minute?'

'As long as it's worth my while.' Gabby sighed. 'Walk with me. You have as long as it takes to get to the vending machine.' She fished her purse out of her bag from behind her desk and took out some coins. 'Why aren't you at Blackhall Manor?' she asked, the second the office door closed behind them. Sarah was grateful that she had reserved the tongue-lashing for in private. 'I tasked you to meet with the officers conducting today's search.' Given the discovery of Angelica's body in the nearby woodlands, officers had returned to the property for a more thorough search.

Sarah's smile faltered. 'I am . . . I mean, I got someone else to cover it.' The thought of going back there again made her feel sick to her stomach.

'And the source of your unwillingness is . . .'

Sarah opened her mouth to respond, but nothing came out.

'So, you think you know better than me, because I'm the one who gave the order after all and I've been in the job twenty-five years . . . how long have you served again?' Gabby knew full well that Sarah had not been long out of probation before joining CID.

'Well,' Sarah said, 'I have some information about the case, and I wanted to run it by you first.'

'In that case I'm all ears.' Gabby came to a halt outside the vending machine full of chocolate, energy drinks and crisps.

'You asked me last night who my informant was. It's Elliott Carter.'

'Uh-huh,' Gabby said, non-committally. 'I know of the boy.'

Sarah felt encouraged by this news. Was there a grain of truth in Yvonne's words? 'The first time Elliott spoke to me, he said something about the Midnight Man, and that an angel was dead.'

'Right,' Gabby said shortly, sorting through her change. She deposited some coins into the machine and pressed the code for a Mars bar. Sarah watched as the bar of chocolate dropped with a clunk.

'On Saturday night, I went to see him and he mentioned the chestnut tree that borders the fence in Blackhall Woods. That's how I knew where she was.' The sting of a memory made itself known: her father, telling Robin not to be scared of Blackhall Woods because it was really the Hundred Acre Wood. Her little brother's eyes alight as their father relayed that chestnut trees were rare in such a crowded forest, so it *had to* belong to Mr Owl. She pushed the memory back to the deepest chambers of her mind. It was one of many too painful to touch upon.

'In here,' Gabby directed her into a side office used by the neighbourhood policing team. It was mercifully empty, and a place that offered more privacy than the corridor which echoed their words.

'You've been questioning a vulnerable young boy about a murder investigation without any instruction from me?' Gabby looked at her curiously as she leaned against a desk.

'Well . . . I wouldn't quite put it like that,' Sarah replied.

'Was he your informant or not?'

Sarah nodded, unable to meet her gaze.

'So, you had me beg the senior investigating officer to divert the PolSA team on the basis of the dreams of a seven-year-old boy?'

'Um . . . I guess that's correct.' Sarah couldn't see her sergeant's face as she turned to close the door, but she wasn't encouraged by her tone.

'And according to Elliott, the Midnight Man took Angelica? A supernatural entity is our number one suspect.'

'Well . . .' Sarah paused, failing to sense the enthusiasm that Yvonne had spoken about. 'It's how Elliott interpreted him.'

Gabby levelled her with a hard stare. 'We are in the middle of an investigation into the murder of the daughter of Slayton's most prominent businessman.' She paused only to draw breath. 'You took it upon yourself to involve a vulnerable young child who has a history with social services in the investigation. While you're at it, Detective Constable Noble, why don't you ring the papers and get them involved too?' Gabby smiled, but it was a cold smile. There was a fire of fury behind her eyes.

'So, you don't believe in psychics?' Sarah said quietly, her cheeks burning as she inwardly cursed Yvonne for putting the idea in her head.

'No, Sarah, I don't. What would give you that idea?'

Sarah felt the cold realisation that she had been played. She could have told Gabby that Yvonne had tried to set her up, but that wouldn't improve her plight. She wished the ground would swallow her up. Her day could not get any worse.

'Now tell me the real reason why you ignored my instructions to go to Blackhall Manor?'

'I can't,' she said. 'I'll do anything you want, but please don't send me there.'

'You're in CID! I don't sugar-coat shit. I'm not Willy Wonka.' Gabby looked at her gravely. 'But maybe you were right. Maybe you're not up to the job.'

'What?' Sarah said, her eyes moist with tears. 'No . . . I . . .'

'It's not your fault.' Gabby took a soothing breath. 'I overestimated you. Maybe you *should* give your notice in, Sarah. Let the job go to someone who's more capable.'

'You don't understand,' Sarah said, her voice low.

'No, I don't understand.' Gabby matched her tone. 'I thought I saw something in you, Sarah. Saw potential way beyond your present situation. I respected you for climbing out of that hole your husband pushed you into. I really thought you'd make a go of this. But this . . . Elliott . . . what is going through your mind? Was it seeing Angelica's body? Do you need more time off? Because if you do . . .'

Sarah knew she was on the verge of losing her position in the team. 'There's something you need to know,' she mumbled. 'I can't go back to Blackhall Manor because part of me died there.'

Gabby's eyes creased in confusion.

'I'm Sarah Middleton. Daughter of Nigel Middleton, the man who shot his family in cold blood.'

'No, there were no survivors.'

'That's what my family wanted people to believe.' Sarah inhaled. 'He killed my little brother first. Mum locked me in the wardrobe while he was shooting my gran and grandad, and she kept the key.' Sadness coursed through her as she returned to Blackhall Manor. To the smell of gunpowder. The sound of her mother's guttural screams. 'She was shot trying to defend me. I remember hearing my father's footsteps . . . then the police sirens. He blasted through the wardrobe, but I was hiding under some coats and the bullet skimmed my head.' She pushed back her fringe, displaying the jagged scar on her forehead. 'They found Dad dead. Everyone was dead . . . except for me. In the wardrobe. Bleeding.'

Her eyes met Gabby's and she saw her own pain reflected back at her. 'They saved my life, but I was in a coma for months. My other grandparents moved me to a private hospital in the next county and the media lost interest. The locals presumed I'd died and that was the way we wanted it to stay.' She sighed at the memory of everyone fussing around her. How she had sat in the bedroom of her grandparents' house for months, feeling numb. Taking her mother's maiden name, she'd tried to reinvent herself but like Elliott, her nightmares dragged her into a world of terror time and time again. The death of her family was something she had been unable to process for years. Her mother's parents had been too paralysed by grief to be able to help her.

'It's not difficult to get a rumour going in Slayton if you have the right people on your side,' Sarah continued. 'And I had friends back then, friends who thought I deserved some peace after everything I went through.' Maggie. What a star she had been, even at that young age. 'Besides,' Sarah said. 'They were right. Part of me died with my family that day. Fourteen-year-old Sarah Middleton is back in the house still sitting in that wardrobe and I cannot bear to step inside there. So please don't make me go back.'

Gabby turned her head, swiping a tear from her eye. She coughed, clearing her throat. Sarah was flooded with relief. 'Who owns the house?' Gabby's face was devoid of the anger it had radiated just moments before.

'I do. I pay a management company to take care of security and a local estate agency has a key. I know the locals have been campaigning to have it knocked down for years. But I can't. I still feel like I'm there.' She paused for breath. 'He called my name. My father called my name so he could find me and shoot me before the police arrived. And I wanted to answer him. Because a part of me still believed that my daddy would keep me safe.' Closing her eyes, she swallowed back her grief. She would not cry any more tears over this. Not today.

'You should have told us,' Gabby said. 'You should've declared it when you joined the police.'

'DI Lee knows everything on a confidential basis. I didn't want people treating me differently. *Please* don't make me go back.'

'Of course I won't. God.'

'Sarge, with all respect, a few minutes ago you were asking me if I was crazy and suggesting I quit CID. I am more than capable of taking statements and I can be relied upon. I only mentioned the supernatural because one of our glorious team said it would impress you because you are such a great believer in alternative explanations.'

'Who?' Gabby's brows knotted in a frown.

Sarah shook her head. 'It doesn't matter. I won't be taken in again. Please don't tell anyone about this. I don't want people to look at me with pity – the way you're looking at me now. I just want a chance to live a normal life, move on.' The air between them was heavy with her grief.

'Do you need me to organise help? Counselling?'

Sarah offered a watery smile. 'I've been counselled up to my eyeballs. All I want is to get on with my job.'

Gabby nodded. 'For what it's worth, you got me at a bad time. I've just had to explain to Angelica's parents that their daughter's internal organs were removed from her body before *that monster*

135

buried her in a shallow grave.' Sarah winced as something flickered in her memory. Such horrific details were usually held back unless the victim's family insisted on knowing every painful truth.

'We'll catch him,' Sarah uttered, nodding to herself.

'I know. And Sarah . . .' Gabby touched her lightly on the arm. 'I wasn't wrong. You are as strong as I first thought you were, and more.' Her gaze went to the door as a tannoy called her name from the hall. 'Best we get back to work, eh? We have a murder to investigate.'

22

Sarah thought she was alone in the office for once, as her colleagues attended the 5 p.m. police press release. She wriggled her toes in her boots. Her hair was frizzy from the rain, her legs stiff from conducting door-to-door enquiries all afternoon. The residents of Lower Slayton were a strange and vulnerable breed. One middle-aged man had answered the door wearing nothing but a string vest and socks. Another old dear, her eyes cloudy with cataracts, let her all the way into her kitchen before asking where her Tesco grocery delivery was. Some residents were lonely and needed reassurance, but not one could shed light on Angelica Irving's movements that night.

Sarah clicked on her emails, methodically deleting the ones she didn't need. She didn't see Richie looming over her, and she jumped as he cleared his throat. If he was going to take the piss, she wasn't in the mood. His sleeves were rolled up to his elbows, his skin tanned. Richie had a charming, easy-going way about him. Today, charisma would be lost on her. After what happened with Yvonne, she didn't trust her colleagues an inch.

'Yes?' she said, stony-faced as she swivelled her chair to face him. Most likely he was used to Yvonne hanging on his every word. He rubbed his chin, taken aback.

'I just wanted to say . . . It was out of order, what Yvonne did.'

He folded his arms, his brown eyes holding no malice. 'That's not how we do things here.'

'Really?' Sarah said. 'Because it seems very much how you lot act. I'm not deaf, you know. I hear the snide comments. It hasn't exactly been easy, coming back here after . . .' She sighed. She'd had enough of raking over the embers of her past today.

Richie looked at her thoughtfully. 'Gabby's a decent sergeant but she's not perfect. She's good at handling caseloads, schedules . . . but she's deficient when it comes to the emotional stuff.'

'I gathered that.' Sarah recalled how she had turned away to wipe a tear from her eye.

'She should have welcomed you back, at the least. Reintroduced you to the team. It feels like unfinished business, you know. All that stuff with David . . .'

'I had nothing to do with that.' Her husband's misdemeanours might not be a pleasant topic of conversation, but it felt good to clear the air. She returned her attention to her emails, but Richie was still standing there, with a stupid grin on his face. 'You don't remember me, do you?'

Sarah's hands twitched with the urge to tug on her fringe. 'Remember you? Why, should I?'

Her desk creaked as Richie leaned against it; his legs crossed at the ankles. 'We went to school together. One year, you invited me to a party at Blackhall Manor. God, that was a spooky old place. I never went back again . . .' He took in the look on her face. 'Oh. Shit, sorry. I've put my size nines in it, haven't I?'

There's no escaping it, Sarah thought, feeling a twist in her gut. Soon everyone would know who she was. 'No . . . no, it's OK.' She snapped on the smile reserved for strangers. 'I've met a few old school friends this week. Does anyone else know?'

Richie shook his head. 'They won't hear it from me. Not unless you want them to.'

'So that's why you're talking to me . . . out of sympathy, is that it? Because at least I knew where I was when people were being mean.'

'I just wanted to let you know that you had an ally.'

'An ally. You don't know me. Why would you say that?' The phone on the desk rang and Richie reached across and muted it.

'That might be important,' Sarah said.

'It can wait,' Richie replied, never taking his eyes off her. 'Listen, I don't mean to cause offence.'

'You haven't,' Sarah replied. 'I just want to know the real reason you're standing here, blocking my light.'

A smile touched Richie's face as he moved the desk light positioned over her desk. 'Alright then. It's Blackhall Manor.'

The moment lingered longer than was comfortable before Sarah rolled her eyes. Of course. 'I get it. You're one of those local protesters, aren't you? You want me to knock the thing down.'

'No. The opposite, in fact.' He ran a hand through his hair. 'What happened to your family. It's always stayed with me. It doesn't seem right.'

Sarah snorted. 'And here was me thinking it was perfectly normal for a loving father to massacre his family. Your police training has served you well.'

'Jeez, you're defensive,' Richie countered. 'I mean, I looked at the investigation. It was shoddy, at best and wholly negligent, at worst.' His silver thumb ring glinted as he gesticulated. A Help

139

for Heroes bracelet sat between leather bands on his wrist. Sarah realised she was staring and looked away.

'What was there to investigate?' she said at last. 'My father was suffering from depression, most likely PTSD.' But she remembered something her grandparents had told her. How her family had made it all go away.

'But did he, though?' Richie looked contemplative. 'Or was that how they filed the report? Are you one hundred per cent sure your father was holding the gun that night?'

Sarah stared at him, disbelieving. 'Why are you interested in this now? Why can't I be left in peace?'

'I didn't mean to upset you. Look.' He grabbed a pen from the table and scribbled on the notepad on her desk. 'It's the name of a small private conspiracy site on Facebook. We just want to help.'

'We?' Sarah said, aghast. Voices rose from the hall as her colleagues returned. Richie raised a hand. 'No pressure. Just . . . just think about joining. It's a safe space.'

As Yvonne walked in, Sarah turned to her computer, but not before she caught a flash of annoyance on her face.

'Shouldn't you be going home, Ms Part-Timer? The grown-ups have work to do.'

The friend act hadn't lasted very long. Sarah quietly shut off her computer before rising from her chair. Her thoughts crowding in, she grabbed her bag from the floor and walked out the door.

23

'Guess I seized the wrong blooming day,' Sarah muttered, her car seat upholstery giving a little wheeze. She was shaking from frustration, thinking of a million comebacks she would never have the courage to say. In just one line, Yvonne had humiliated her yet again. So much for rule three: Don't take any crap. Maybe she deserved it, after leaving them short-staffed for so long. Maybe they needed an outlet, given David wasn't there to face up to what he had done. Perhaps it was a case of keeping her head down and riding the storm.

She looked up through the windscreen. The sky was heavy with impending darkness and she had the town hall meeting to attend tonight. Her thoughts returned to Richie and his bizarre request for her to join the Facebook group. She'd known him for a few weeks before she left CID for a year. Why hadn't he asked her then? Perhaps he'd been gearing up to it before she went off sick. Decades had passed since Blackhall. It was reasonable to think she could handle it, given she was an adult now. But more to the point, there were people in the world who were looking at the bigger picture. For years, her father's actions had haunted her. She never thought he was capable of such cold-blooded acts, but during her many counselling sessions, she was told to accept it and move on. She thought of her little brother, so innocent and sweet . . . a ball of grief lodged in her chest. 'Don't cry, you silly sausage,' she whispered to herself as she swallowed back her tears. It would be good if she could get through one day of adhering to her self-imposed rules. Even if it was only rule five: Act normal. But how could she when the past wouldn't let her go?

Should she be fighting for her father's reputation or was that disrespectful to the family she had lost? It was odd that her father had been buried next to her mother and brother, given what he had done. Unless . . . A cool breeze curled in through the crack in her car window, raising goosebumps on her skin. She had always avoided the media coverage of what happened for fear of reports about her father. But what if they weren't labelling him a monster? What if they were defending him? She slipped her phone from her pocket and typed in the details of the Facebook group. Chewing her bottom lip she requested to join. Her Facebook page was marked as private, and she was there under her mother's maiden name, Sarah Noble. Nobody but Richie should know who she was. Her heart gave a little flutter as her request was immediately accepted. This was either going to make her day better, or a whole lot worse.

She scrolled through the numerous posts, with pictures, maps and more. No wonder she'd had to hire security to keep people away from Blackhall. The group was rife with speculation about Angelica's murder. She swept past all the fresh comments, on to the older ones. There were so many theories, interspersed with warnings that anything negative about the family would be removed and the user banned. She glanced through the admins, seeing the name Damien Richardson. So that's why he said the group was a 'safe space'. But how was her father not to blame? She had been there. She'd heard her mother cry out, '*Not my little girl,*' after calling Sarah's father's name. The hairs stood sentry on her arms. Not *my* little girl. Why not *our* little girl? Thinking back, her mother always used the term in the collective. It was always *our* children, even when they argued. Her mum always said that raising children was a family effort, you never did it alone.

Sarah automatically tugged at her hair. She had never stopped to consider that. Her memories of that night had been pushed into the darkest chambers of her mind, where they rusted, degraded . . . *But I saw him,* she thought. *Didn't I?*

Her eyes lit on a comment from Sharon Young in New York. 'Sarah was in the wardrobe when the shooter walked in. It was dark. She was in shock. What if it wasn't her dad?'

'But he called my name . . .' Sarah said, chilled by the theory. Her bones rigid, she had peered through the tiny keyhole. Clutching herself, her teeth had chattered, caught in the frozen grip of fear.

No wonder Richie had wanted to talk to her. Was it weird that he was interested in the case? After all, he grew up here. He had the inquisitive mind of a detective. *I know you intimately.* The words from the hate mail she had received returned to haunt her. What was that Richie said about her husband? *Unfinished business.* Could Richie have had a hand in it? He had been to Blackhall Manor. He also had a reason to hate her, given her husband's behaviour . . . David had been his sergeant, after all. No. It couldn't be . . . She shifted uncomfortably as niggles crept in. Snorting, Sarah turned the ignition of her car. Her imagination was galloping away with her.

She manoeuvred the car from the car park, her thoughts only half on the busy road. There had been a moment between her and her father before she had gone to bed that night. The look he gave her as she said goodnight held nothing but love. She closed her mind to the thought. It was too much to bear.

She turned off towards Pine Heights. This gated community was not quite as grand as Slayton Crest, but still a development of exclusive properties with price tags of half a million pounds upwards. She drove freely through the tall black metal gates. There were no barriers at the entrance of Pine Heights, no CCTV to capture her presence as she passed through.

The girl who answered the door was wearing a pink onesie with a unicorn horn attached to the hood. Her afro hair was tied in cute, pink-ribboned bunches and at about five feet tall, she looked far too innocent to be getting involved with deadly Halloween games. But in a predominantly white community, there was a likelihood that Jahmelia would have done anything to fit in. 'Hi, Jahmelia, remember me? Is it OK if we talk one more time?' Sarah said, as she displayed her warrant card. The girl nodded slowly, her gaze returning to the hall as she called for her mum.

'It's nothing to worry about,' Sarah said after Jahmelia's mother let her inside. She reminded her of someone. Perhaps someone she'd seen in town . . . 'Would it be OK if I had another quick word with your daughter?'

'You're welcome to, but she's already spoken to the police several times now.' Pointing to the left, she led Sarah into the living room. The house was tastefully decorated with cream-coloured furniture and a family portrait on the main wall. Jahmelia was the middle child, with an older and younger brother. According to police files, her father was an architect. Like many people in Slayton, he was employed by Irving Industries.

'It's nothing to worry about,' she said to Jahmelia's mother, Bryony, as she left her ankle boots outside the living-room door. 'It's just a quick visit to see if anything has jogged Jahmelia's memory, or if she's heard anything in school.'

'Jahmelia wasn't friends with Angelica,' Bryony instantly replied. But the look on Jahmelia's face said otherwise. It was a look Sarah knew well. Her shoulders hunched, the young girl was brooding, burdened by a secret she was too scared to share.

'Your husband works for Irving Industries, is that right?' Sarah said.

'For now,' Bryony nodded. 'But we didn't encourage any kind of friendship. From the moment we met Angelica we knew she was a bad influence.' She looked to her daughter then back to Sarah. 'Sometimes I wish we'd never come to Slayton, but it's convenient for work.'

Sarah returned her attention to Jahmelia. 'Is there anything you'd like to share with me, Jahmelia, anything at all? You're not in any trouble.' Jahmelia shook her head.

'Has anyone asked you to keep a secret? Threatened you?'

'No,' she uttered quietly.

'And you didn't know *anything* about the Midnight Game?'

'She's already been through all this,' Bryony butted in. 'She was in the tent at the bottom of the garden with Libby. They didn't leave it all night.' She appeared annoyed as Sarah pushed the subject. This was obviously sore ground. 'Besides . . .' Bryony continued. 'If Jahmelia did know anything, her grandmother would have got it out of her by now. *That woman* is like the Spanish Inquisition.' The words were not spoken fondly, and Sarah sensed tension there.

She was interrupted by the delicate chime of a doorbell. 'Excuse me,' she said, pointedly checking her watch. 'That's her.'

At least it bought Sarah a few seconds alone with the child. 'You're Elliott's babysitter, aren't you?' she continued. 'He's a nice boy, isn't he?'

Jahmelia brightened. 'He's the best. I like babysitting him.'

Sarah's smile faded. 'He's been having nightmares about the Midnight Man. It's making him really upset. Could he have overheard you talking about it with Libby? Did you mention the game at all?'

Voices rose from the hall as Jahmelia's mother welcomed her visitor inside. Jahmelia stared, unblinking, at the door.

'Because if you're scared, you can talk to me. Elliott did. He feels much better now.'

Jahmelia's eyes glistened with tears as Sarah spoke of keeping her safe. 'It's not your fault. None of this is. You don't need to be afraid.'

The young girl took a breath to speak before her gaze returned to the door. She knew something, Sarah could feel it. She was on the cusp of confiding in her. The door swung open, putting paid to any disclosure. Jumping from the sofa, Jahmelia ran from the room.

'What the hell are you doing with my granddaughter?'

Sarah jumped from the chair as if she had received an electric shock. It was Gabby, and she was not best pleased.

'Sarge . . . Gabby . . . I mean . . .' Sarah stuttered, as the woman approached.

Gabby turned and shooed Bryony away. 'Check on Jahmelia. See if she's OK.'

'Of course she's alright, we were only chatting,' Sarah said, before being silenced with a glare.

'Who authorised you to come here and harass my granddaughter? Because if anyone's going to be doing the harassing, it's me.'

'I didn't know,' Sarah said. 'I just thought that . . . . well, Jahmelia is Elliott's babysitter. He could have overheard her talking with Libby about the game. I just wanted to speak to her one more time.'

'That's a conversation you should be having with me, not Jahmelia,' Gabby countered.

'I didn't know she was your granddaughter. You never said.'

'Unlike most of the people in my office, I separate my personal and work life. You're done here, Sarah. Chop chop.' She clapped her hands together, ushering her along. 'Get yourself home. We have a busy day ahead of us tomorrow.'

Sarah knew better than to reason. 'I'll see you at the town hall meeting.'

Gabby raised an eyebrow as she showed her the door. 'You're going then?'

'Of course I'm going,' Sarah asserted herself. 'I live here, don't I?'

An amused smile touched Gabby's lips. 'Right. In that case, I'll see you in an hour.'

Sarah wasn't attending the meeting as a concerned neighbour. Angelica's killer was local, she was sure of it. There was a good chance they would appear. Despite her sergeant's reservations, Sarah wasn't giving up the fight.

24

The steady beat of Taylor Swift's 'Love Story' pulsed in Libby's ears. She was grateful for the break from her parents, who had been hounding her since Angelica's death. Her lie about spending Halloween night in Jahmelia's tent had grown so big, there was no going back now. She lay on her bed facing her window, the string of fairy lights on the headboard bathing the room in a soft, comforting glow. The scent of lemon, rosemary and chamomile felt like a warm comfort blanket. It was lovely of Maggie and Elliott to buy her the Calm candle. Closing her eyes, she inhaled its scent as it flickered on her bedside table.

Her eyes snapped open as she sensed movement, and in that split second her world froze. Numb with fear, she caught sight of a reflection on the pane of her bedroom window. Someone was standing over her. A solid mass of black. She opened her mouth to scream and was silenced by a leather-gloved hand over her mouth. Her teeth crashed against her gum as she tried to bite down. White starbursts flashed in her vision as she received a sudden blow to the head. Fighting for breath, she swallowed the trickle of blood running from her gums. She kicked and thrashed in the bed, her eyes wild with fear as she tried to gain sight of her attacker. She screamed into the pillow as her head was pushed down, but it was a muffled cry. Her left earbud was ripped out in the struggle, and instead of Taylor Swift, all she could hear was a wet, rasping breath. And the smell . . . damp blankets, sweat and something else . . . Her eyes grew wide as she emitted another muffled scream. Fire. The candle had shifted on her bedside and had caught onto her curtains. She wriggled and squirmed as a muffled gargle left her throat. Her attacker was on top of her now, forcing her face down further into her pillow. Panic filled her being as her lungs burned for breath. Grunting, she felt them fumble . . . *oh God no. Please no.*

Then a zipping sound, hard plastic ties against her wrists as they were tightly bound. *Zip ties,* she thought. *They're zip ties.* The weight of the body pinning her down shifted as they swivelled, fastening ties on her ankles. Levering her face to one side she inhaled a wet, rasping breath. In the window, she watched the black figure, head down, intent on immobilising her. Before she could scream, her face was pushed back down into the pillow, one of her earbuds squashed up against her nose. On Taylor Swift sang, '*oh, oh, oh, oh,*' while Libby was bone cold with fear.

Was this how Angelica ended up before she was found in the woods? *If the Midnight Man catches you, he kills you and pulls out your insides, piece by piece.* Jahmelia's words returned to haunt her. She wanted to scream that she had won the game. She didn't deserve to die! Tears streamed down the side of her face as the attacker worked in silence to immobilise her. She shook her head furiously as a rag was wrapped around her mouth. Gagging, she recognised the rotting, sour smell. Blackhall Manor.

Her heart felt like it was going to beat its way out of her chest. Suddenly, her vision was lost as black material was pulled over her head. The pull of a cord tightened it around her neck. She was a fish flopping out of water, at the mercy of the person holding the line. A pair of strong arms grappled with her body as they launched her over their shoulder. Struggling to see, she made out shifting shadows of light and dark as she hung, partially upside down. Then the bounce, bounce, as he carried her down each stair before reaching their open back door. Cool fresh air curled around her skin. Where was her brother? She screamed beneath the gag. Was he dead or alive? Would she ever see her family again? Libby had never longed for her mother so badly. Spittle dampened the cloth around her mouth as she was taken into the night. The creak of a car boot followed. Then the searing pain of banging her head as she was thrown inside. The terrifying feel of a plastic liner beneath her body, and the stench of something decaying. She pushed back the thought that Angelica had been here before as the darkness swallowed her whole.

25

Nervous energy flowed through me like electricity. I was still sweating from the rush. It took all of my restraint to sit still behind the wheel of my car. My limbs were still shaking from the flood of adrenalin minutes before. I did it. I actually did it. Walked into Libby's house like I owned the place. She had stained her blood on a card, signing her life over to the Midnight Man. Now, she was unconscious in the boot of my car. The plastic lining was one of many precautions I'd taken. There was no rush the second time around.

I was taking a chance, coming back into town this evening but I hadn't been able to resist driving down the side road on a slow crawl. I shrank back into my seat, confident I wouldn't be spotted. People were too focused on the town meeting in the school hall to worry about me. A yellow ribbon fluttered from a lamp-post – a pathetic tribute to the blonde teenager I had rid the town of. Soon there would be more ribbons . . . more posters . . . maybe even more town hall get-togethers while they pointed the finger of blame.

Off you go little sheep, into your pen. With a keen eye, I watched the townspeople crowd into the high school. All families who had left their children at home. Of course, they'd be in the hands of older siblings, but most of them spent their evenings glued to a screen of some kind, as my current catch would testify.

I watched Mr Palmer shout at a skateboarder, swinging his crutch around like a fucking bayonet. Palmer was the Neighbourhood Watch coordinator, ergo self-appointed town sheriff. As always, his face was set in its usual grimace. I had done him a favour, bringing purpose to his pathetic life. My gaze switched to old Mrs Peterson as she strode purposefully up the path. Another pent-up pensioner with a bee in her bonnet. Then there were the families employed by Irving Industries, in their plush new homes and top-of-the-range cars. Jahmelia's parents crossed the road, a papoose wrapped around the woman's body. I knew them all and I had shaken the foundations of their privileged worlds. Fifteen-year-old Angelica was lying in a morgue freezer, as disposable as the empty Coke can in the footwell of my car. I could have waited to take Libby if I hadn't been ready. In time, they would forget what had happened. The grip on their children's hands would ease, they would stop glaring at each other with suspicion in their eyes.

My hands tightened around the steering wheel as I watched the locals file in, two by two. The crooked businessmen and councillors who were trying to turn Slayton into something it was not. It would always be the home of Blackhall Manor, a cursed place on cursed land. A place where even the dead could resurrect. Sarah 'loser' Middleton. She was the real reason I had driven here. A vein throbbed in my forehead as I waited for a sighting. She should have died that day. How was she still alive? The woman was a fucking rubber ball. Enjoy it while you can, bitch, I muttered beneath my breath. The buzz from taking Libby was being replaced by rage as thoughts of Sarah tormented my mind. Who did she think she was, coming back after all these years? She didn't care about other people. All she thought about was herself. It wouldn't surprise me if she was the first to hide when her father got his gun. She could have tried to save her family, *but she was only ever interested in looking after number one. Every day since she returned it was all I could think about.* Finish what was started. Finish her. *I stared out at the streets, feeling the dull throb of a headache. Slipping my hand into my pocket, I pulled out a strip of tablets and popped two from the foil. I swallowed them dry, my thoughts stalled by movement in the boot of the car.*

I caught the smell of something stringent. Vomit? Had Freckle Face puked into her gag? Or maybe it was the cleaning fluid I used to clean up after the blonde's corpse. I turned over the engine. I had stayed far too long. Libby needed dealing with. The game would not play itself.

26

As Sarah pulled into home she could not escape the image of Angelica – her open eyes crusted with dirt as she stared into the abyss. She recalled her own encounter with death. Remembered the police finding her cowering in the back of the shattered wardrobe. As much as she had tried to escape it, the memory had clung like a leech, through her adolescence and into adulthood. But there were no second chances for Angelica. No momentary brushes she could escape. Angelica's last moments were too monstrous to contemplate. Every resident of Slayton was in danger for as long as her killer was free.

Never had Sarah felt so reluctant to shove her key into her own front door. It was why she'd stopped off at a coffee shop, spending an hour on a crossword as she nursed her latte. It seemed bizarre, how she could focus on word puzzles when a killer was roaming free, but playing with words was the only thing that could calm her down. Help her to think. She remembered after the shooting, when she'd rocked in her hospital bed reciting the alphabet backwards again and again. Her lips silently moving Z, Y, X, W, V, U . . . It was her brain's way of keeping her functional. To stop speaking completely meant she would lose herself to the trauma. Then Grandad Noble, his eyes red with grief as he brought her crossword puzzles and word searches to keep her occupied. That was when Sarah discovered the real power in words.

Now she was late for the town hall meeting but couldn't leave until she'd fed her cat. Softly, she opened the door, pausing to listen for any unusual sounds before stepping lightly into her hall. She approached the kitchen, half-expecting to find another taunting letter on her floor. A clatter rose from within. There was someone in there. Her fingers curled into a fist. What she'd give for her telescopic baton right now. It was secured in a police locker, along with her CS gas. If she was found in possession of either off duty, she would be in hot water. Right now, it would have been worth the risk. She quickly swung open the door before taking a step back.

'Sherlock!' Sarah's hand fell to her chest, as her cat jumped down from the sink. On the floor was the plastic cereal bowl he'd sent crashing down. 'You nearly gave me a heart attack.' Her gaze fell to the floor beneath the cat flap and she exhaled a relieved breath. There was nothing there.

For now, the phone was silent, and there was no sign of her husband. Muttering to herself, she gave Sherlock extra helpings before heading into town.

At least she wasn't on stage, the first in line to face the residents' anger. The local secondary school was packed and things were well underway. Given the town hall was undergoing renovations, the school theatre was deemed the best place to hold the meeting. Whispering apologies, Sarah shuffled through the crowds to find an empty chair. Schools had their own unique smell and Slayton Academy was no exception as it emitted a mixture of old books and gym kit bags. As Sarah took a seat, she felt a pang of sadness as her gaze fell on the stage. She hadn't attended this school for very long, but this was where her parents should have sat as they watched her, and Robin after her, perform in the school play. But her little brother remained forever four years old, the boy who never got to grow up. The thought came from nowhere, and she blinked it away. She needed to keep her wits about her. A lot was riding on tonight.

Gabby spoke with confidence, dressed smartly in a charcoal suit, black heels and a white shirt, flanked by a cast of middle-aged white men. She was the only woman on the stage, and the only person there that Sarah trusted. Simon Irving wasn't on stage. After his loss, it was hardly surprising. Nobody expected him to attend. After going through the preliminaries, Gabby updated the crowd before her. By now, the chairs had been filled, and people were standing at the back. The mood was sombre, their faces grim. Sarah glanced around the room for Maggie before realising that she wouldn't have been able to get a babysitter to watch Elliott. But what about every other child whose parents were here? Who was minding them?

Bryony and her husband were sitting with their baby in the front row, their eldest son no doubt babysitting Jahmelia. Libby's parents were there, but no Libby. Then again, she had a big brother too. Due to the nature of the meeting, Sarah understood why children weren't allowed, but they could have made some provisions in one of the classrooms. She continued to scan the room. Father Aloysius, Slayton's only Catholic priest sat stiffly, his face gaunt. Next to him was Doctor Hamilton, a no-nonsense woman who Sarah admired because of her straight-talking approach. Jimmy Morrissey was there too, the owner of Morrissey's newsagents, and Slayton's high school teachers took up the whole of the front row. It felt like they were fighting a war, and the assembled townsfolk had gathered as a show of strength.

'We've identified several sets of fingerprints at a location close to the crime scene,' Gabby's voice echoed around the open space. She was talking about Blackhall Manor. Anyone familiar with the area would have known that. 'There's one person in particular we're keen to speak to. Further investigations are underway to facilitate that.' Gabby glanced around the hall. 'Before you ask for more details, we can't disclose anything further at this stage. But I can assure you that every member of my team is working around the clock.'

A pang of jealousy burned in Sarah's chest. *Everyone except me.*

'Never mind that, we want to know how this happened in the first place!' A gruff voice rang out from the crowd. It was Mr Palmer, a resident of Upper Slayton. Sarah remembered her husband saying what a pain in the arse he was due to his overzealous involvement in the local Neighbourhood Watch. Mr Palmer stood with his arms tightly folded, awaiting a response. He was a pock-faced man, and a keen runner. Sarah had grown used to seeing him on the roads. Not that he got very far, the number of times he stopped to talk to neighbours along the way. Today, he leaned on a crutch, and Sarah wondered if he'd had an injury of some sort. Her attention switched to Gabby, a reed in a storm as the locals voiced their annoyance in turn. DI Lee had been called away and left Gabby to hold the fort on her own. It wasn't like Bernard to let people down. As the cameras closed in on a shot of Gabby's face, it was disconcerting to see so many reporters here. But one camera belonged to the Slayton Police media department and she watched it pan the room. The crowd didn't know it, but they were being filmed. Sometimes perpetrators of crimes attended meetings like these to keep one step ahead.

Not every murder made such big news, but Slayton's history gave the case an edge. People wanted to hear about the residents of the town with the dark past. It brought an extra twist that the daughter of the man who had promised a secure neighbourhood had been murdered. A suited man stood at the front of the room, jabbing the air with his finger. 'We bought these houses in good faith. The developer made a promise. Upper Slayton is meant to be safe.'

Sarah noticed the name 'Upper' Slayton had been used, not Slayton as a whole. She rolled her eyes. They'd be talking about building a wall to separate them next.

'Slayton is a safe community,' Gabby spoke. 'This was a one-off, a tragic, unfortunate event.'

Mr Palmer stood for a second time to voice his discontent. 'But it wasn't a one-off, was it? What about Blackhall Manor? I said it before and I'll say it again, that place should be knocked to the ground.'

Gabby gave him a withering look. 'Mr Palmer, what happened in Blackhall Manor was twenty-five years ago.'

'What about that pervy police officer? That was last year!'

Sarah's face burned as a few heads turned to peer at her. She tugged her fringe, realised what she was doing, then sat on her hands. She would forever be known as the wife of the 'pervy' police officer.

'Nothing was proved,' Gabby responded firmly, and Sarah shrank in her chair a little more. The hall was growing uncomfortably warm, and her armpits were damp with sweat.

'Only because you lot covered it up!' Mr Palmer bellowed, encouraged by several nodding heads. 'I don't know why I came to live here. If the police can't protect us from perverts and murderers, then who can?'

'Councillor Dean, I've got a deposit on a new property.' A bearded middle-aged man remained seated as he spoke. 'Is it safe to live here?' With evident relief, Gabby took a seat and allowed Councillor Dean to take the microphone. Red-faced and sweating, his neck bulged over the tight collar of his shirt.

'I can assure you,' Councillor Dean said. 'Slayton is perfectly safe.'

'Slayton is safe? Tell that to Angelica Irving's family!' a woman from the crowd shouted. She didn't stand. Most likely didn't want her face seen. A steady click of footsteps rose from the curtain on the left. A low mumble spread as Simon Irving walked onto the stage. Had he been watching from the wings all this time, or had he just got here?

As always, he was smartly dressed, from his expensive leather shoes to the silver tiepin and cufflinks catching the stage light. Scanning the crowd, he took the mic.

'Most of you here know me. Angelica was my daughter. We are devastated by her loss.' Slowly exhaling, he pulled a tissue from his suit pocket, but no tears came. The room fell into a hush as Irving cleared his throat.

'I'm here tonight to reassure you. I've spoken at length to the police. I'm confident this will not happen again. No other family will suffer our agony.' He brought the tissue to his face before continuing. 'This was a game. One with a tragic ending. My daughter has paid the price.' He looked from left to right, taking in the crowd. 'House prices are booming. Any property purchased in Upper Slayton is as good an investment now as it ever has been.'

What the hell? Sarah thought. *His daughter has just died and he's talking about investments?*

'Thank you for your support,' he continued, pocketing the tissue that seemed little more than a prop. 'But my family and I would like to be left alone to grieve.' Stepping back from the microphone, he turned and left the stage.

The crowd fell into eerie silence. Sarah was stunned. This wasn't natural. Any parent in his situation would be baying for blood, not worrying about house sales. She caught the surprised expression on Gabby's face as Mr Irving left. She seemed taken aback too. After a short pause, Superintendent Marsh took the microphone, giving advice on general safety and taking questions from the floor.

Sarah had heard enough. Pushing past the crowd she walked through the internal double doors to use the bathroom. She knew her way around the school, which had been refurbished in recent years. As well as attending briefly as a pupil, she'd given talks to various classes while working in uniform. Her footsteps echoed down the corridor, the walls adorned with student posters, trophy cases and lists of upcoming events. She stilled at the sounds of harsh whispers rising from a classroom.

'I didn't expect to see you here.' Sarah leaned against the wall to listen. It sounded like Councillor Dean.

'I didn't do it for you,' a second man replied, an edge to his tone. 'I've got too much money wrapped up in these developments for things to go pear-shaped now.'

Sarah listened intently. It was Simon Irving.

'As for Blackhall . . . the less said about that, the better. We don't want that rearing its ugly head again.'

'I'm doing everything I can to keep it out of the press.'

A sudden thump of fist against wood. 'Your best isn't good enough! Do I need to remind you what's at stake here?'

'I . . . I . . . of course you don't,' Dean stuttered in response. Silence. 'Once again, I'm sorry for your loss,' Dean continued. 'Do they have a suspect yet?'

'Yes they do, and when they bring him in I'm going to string him up by the balls. My wife's at home now, in bits. I can barely get a coherent sentence out of her. I only hope me coming here tonight pays off.'

Sarah shook her head in disgust. He had come to protect his investment. The councillor was in his pocket, that much was evident. But what had he meant about Blackhall? Was it the bad publicity of the murders he was trying to avoid, or was there something more? *Do I need to remind you what's at stake?* Had his visit been motivated by greed? What about Angelica? Her funeral hadn't even taken place yet. A pair of squeaky shoes echoed as a caretaker walked purposefully down the hall. Darting into the girls' toilets, Sarah's thoughts went into overdrive. She knew better than anyone that people reacted differently to grief. But something about this set-up felt all wrong.

27

Libby's breath was quick and panicked as she came to. She didn't remember the journey which brought her here, and the bag was still over her head – but she recognised the location by the smell clawing at the back of her throat. She was back in Blackhall Manor, in the bowels of the building where the stench was magnified tenfold. She groped in the darkness, feeling a mass of tiny beads on the floor. A whine rose up her throat as she recalled the rat droppings littering the rooms. She was barefoot, bound and in fear for her life. Around her, rotting timbers creaked steadily, as if the house was breathing. She thought of the Sunday school lesson about Jonah, trapped in the belly of a whale. Libby blinked in an attempt to clear her vision. There were no shadows, no dots of light. The room was devoured by darkness. Her throat was scratchy from screaming for help, her face wet with tears and snot. A visceral shudder drove deep into her bones.

She shifted into a sitting position, her back against a wall. She was alive, and she was still in one piece. But for how long? Her heart was galloping in her chest, every instinct screaming at her to escape. A wisp of a sound caught her attention. The echo of a child crying. A reverberation from the past? Blackhall Manor was a place of last breaths – but it was not having hers if she could help it. The back of her head throbbed. She must be concussed.

Was he here, playing games with her? She whimpered, biting down on the gag which tasted of spit and dirt. As she stretched out her legs, her toes touched what felt like another wall. This was too narrow to be a basement. It felt as claustrophobic as a coffin but she couldn't just sit here trembling in the dark. Edging her chin to her knees, she pushed the gag from her mouth, heaving a deep breath. 'Is anyone here?' she said softly, waiting for her attacker to pounce. Nothing. A yelp escaped her lips as a slick, fat body of fur ran over her bare feet. She was blind to the horrors in the darkness. 'Is there anyone here?' Silence. She coughed and inhaled dust. The clicking of tiny legs scurried past her on the wall. She felt surrounded by insects.

If only her mum were here. She would know what to do. 'I can't,' she cried. 'Please. Mum . . . I want my mum!' Slouching onto her knees, she sobbed. She knew she should fight. The Midnight Man would not be far away. She felt a subtle shift in temperature. Goosebumps rose on her skin as a soft voice whispered in her ear. *'You can and you will. You're my special girl.'*

'Who's there?' Libby started. Torn cobwebs tickled her body as she leaned against the wall. The presence was everywhere. It was the same presence she had felt the first time she got here. *'Not my little girl.'* Not her mother, no. But someone's. A strange comfort washed over her. She wasn't Angelica. She hadn't run away from the Midnight Game. She was Libby and she could do this. She wriggled her wrists against the zip ties, and she moved along the back wall until she came to a hard, rigid post. Her limbs tense, she sawed against the wood, the bindings rubbing against her skin.

Urgency grew with the sense of dread. Time was running out. Sweat trickled down the curve of her back. Her muscles taut, she continued to saw. The smell of the space was becoming unbearable. It felt like the walls were closing in. No. She was *in* the walls. The thought drove another shard of panic through her chest. The bindings hurt as she exerted force on her torn wrists, but it was nothing compared to what would happen when the Midnight Man returned.

She jerked at the sudden sound of a door slamming in the distance. He was coming for her. She buried her head between her knees in an attempt to remove the hood. She could not do this blind. It jerked against her windpipe as she tugged. There was some kind of tie at the end. Another thought struck. She *could* get the hood off, but did she want to be bound when she did? The thought of what was in here with her was terrifying. She ground the zip ties harder against the pillar of wood, grunting as they finally broke. Her wrists felt like they were on fire, but she didn't have time to worry about them. She fumbled with the tie at the end of the makeshift hood, which turned out to be her brother's black gym sack. Pushing her hair from her face, she threw panicked glances left and right. Her gaze moved around the narrow space as her eyes adjusted. She could hardly see a thing. She shrank from the feel of cobwebs as she touched the walls. *Think,* she told herself, *you got in here, you'll find a way out.* But she couldn't see. She squirmed against the ties biting into her ankles, too scared to call for help. What if it was him? Groping in the dark, she tried to find a door. But the dusty cobwebbed tunnel seemed to go on forever. Out of nowhere, the flutter of a moth caught her eye. Its white wings glowed in the darkness. Entranced, she followed it, her breath catching in her throat as it led her to a chink of light. She pressed her hand against it. Then knocked . . . it was wood.

The wall was made of wood. The timbers creaked and splintered as she pressed both hands against them. Drawing back, she put her weight behind it as she threw her body against the wall. Hope flared as bigger chinks of light bled through the cracked timbers. Bracing herself, she forced her weight against the wall for the second time.

A sudden crack of rotting timber was followed by a blast of light as she came out the other side. She thumped onto the floor, her ankles still bound. She was free of her prison, but still in Blackhall Manor. She breathed through the pain, her stomach lurching as she heard heavy, rushed footsteps on stairs. The Midnight Man was coming. Her hand fell to her stomach, to a gush of blood. It trickled through her fingers as shock pervaded her body. A shard of timber was embedded in the soft flesh. She lay, keening on the floor, too weak to try and escape as the footsteps approached. Through a haze of pain, she cried out. A damning sense of finality told her it was too late.

28

Sarah pushed her hands deep into her Barbour coat. It had been a steal from the local charity shop and given the inclement weather, it was certainly proving its worth. She was already sick of the cold and had months of it ahead of her. Storm clouds blotted out the moon, draining Slayton of colour, and the tinny sound of an empty beer can kept company with her as it gusted down the street. She strode past a burnt-out car with a 'Police Aware' sticker flapping on its shell. Maggie's bungalow was on Stellar Avenue, one of the more deprived areas of town. It was a quarter of a mile from the police station, and a mile from where Sarah lived. It was tragic to see the once-thriving community falling into decline. When residents of Lower Slayton first objected to Irving's mass housing development plans, he had promised them the world. Newly tarmacked roads, a youth club and doctors' surgery to accommodate the extra families living in the area. But once his plans were passed, his promises fell away and the land set aside for extra services was used to accommodate more homes. He'd invested in Slayton police station, and donated money to the hospital but the residents of Lower Slayton had been forgotten. Now the roads were potholed from all the extra traffic and the schools were filled to capacity.

A street lamp overhead blinked three times before giving up

and petering out. Sarah chose her steps wisely. Broken pavements were another thing to look out for. Despite it all, she had been happy to respond when Maggie texted half an hour before. Libby and Jahmelia were grounded until Angelica's killer was found and the hotel where Maggie worked was short-staffed. Slayton had its fair share of tourists throughout the year and now the number of journalists taking up residence was growing by the day.

'Sorry to call you over at such short notice.' Maggie rubbed her hands together as she let Sarah inside. Her hair was tied up with a paisley headscarf and she was wearing a blue tabard beneath her coat.

'No problem.' Sarah smiled. 'I may as well watch *Blue Bloods* here as at home.'

'That's a cop programme, isn't it? Aren't you ever off duty?'

'Two words. Tom Selleck.' Sarah still had a crush on him from watching old *Magnum P.I.* re-runs as a teen.

'Well, there's wine in the fridge,' Maggie replied, smiling. 'Help yourself.'

'I don't drink while babysitting but thank you.' Sarah waved her friend away. 'Now off you go, you don't want to be late.'

'I'm only working a few hours. My shift ends at midnight. You've got my mobile number if you need anything.' Maggie gazed at the darkening streets. She looked older in the faltering light, and every worry line was evident on her face. 'Ring me if you have any problems and I'll come straight home.'

Sarah locked the door as soon as Maggie was safely in her car. She glanced at the instructions Maggie had left in the event of a night terror. *Turn on the light, give him a drink, don't shake him awake, tell him it's OK, speak in soothing tones.* A cough arose from the hall.

Elliott stood in his bedroom doorway, wearing turtle-patterned pyjamas and Gruffalo slippers that had seen better days. Sarah looked at the oversized woollen gloves and his big worried eyes before giving him a reassuring smile. Tonight, his father's medal was pinned to the pocket of his pyjamas. Medals like these were valuable. Sarah found it endearing that Maggie let her son wear it around their home.

'Hello, you. Aren't you meant to be in bed?'

'I can't sleep.' Elliott approached shyly. 'Please can I watch TV with you?'

Sarah checked her watch. It was almost nine. 'Go on then. You can stay up for half an hour . . . as long as you watch something child friendly.'

He sat on the navy sofa, enveloped in cushions of various shapes and sizes. The living room was small but functional, tastefully decorated in dark colours with splashes of yellow and pink. On the wall were some of Maggie's scenic paintings, and on the floor, an old deep-pile navy rug. 'It might be easier if you took off the gloves,' Sarah smiled, as he fiddled with the remote control. 'Are you cold?' The room was comfortably warm, heated by a small electric fire with flickering fake flames.

Elliott shook his head. His brooding expression told her there was more at play.

He opened his mouth to speak and closed it again. He looked so sad that it almost broke Sarah's heart. 'Elliott . . . are you OK? You can talk to me. You know that, don't you?' She paused to let the words sink in. 'When I joined the police, I made a vow to keep people safe. Your mummy is my friend, which makes you my friend too.'

He nodded, turning his doe eyes towards her, but the words did not come. It seemed he didn't trust Sarah as much awake as when he was asleep. She didn't blame him. Trust took time. Trust had to be earned. 'Tell you what,' Sarah said, softly. 'How about we play a game? Do you like games?'

He responded with a nod. Sarah recalled a game her mother used to play with her when she was little and feeling down. It was a way of getting stuff off her mind without betraying confidences. Not that she'd had too much to unburden at that age. 'It's called "if I ask",' Sarah continued, recalling the name. 'I ask you the same question from three different people. In this round I'll be your mum, Libby and me. You reply in three different ways, but only *one* answer is the truth. I have to guess who you're telling the truth to.' She laughed as his forehead wrinkled. 'It's not as complicated as it sounds, I promise.'

Elliott brightened, the remote control discarded. *Blue Bloods* would have to wait for now. Sarah crossed her legs, making herself comfortable. 'So, here's the question. Are you ready?'

'Yes,' he said, his expression turning solemn. This seemed more than a game to him.

'We'll start with a warm-up question, so take your time.' She gave him a look which conveyed that this was a safe place. 'Why are you wearing gloves? First answer goes to your mum.'

'Because I'm cold.' He stared at his hands. Sarah knew this wasn't the truthful answer. He wouldn't have wanted his mum to feel sad.

'OK. And how about if Libby asked?'

'They're Daddy's gloves,' he replied instantly. By the size of them, this seemed true. But there was another reason why Elliott had chosen to wear them to bed.

169

'And now me.'

Elliott finally met her gaze. 'I don't want to scratch Maggie again.'

'I see. Well, I'm here tonight so you don't have to worry about that.' Sarah held out her hand. 'Also, I've brought some microwave popcorn. Want to take off those gloves and give me a hand? Then we can play the rest of the game.' She didn't need to ask twice. The gloves disposed of, Elliott enjoyed the novelty of making popcorn at home.

A few minutes later they were back on the sofa, snacks in hand. 'You can ask me another question now,' Elliott said, watching her intently with a fistful of popcorn. It was as if he had read her mind. Sarah had been wondering if she was doing the right thing by continuing with the game.

'OK, but this is a big question, Elliott. You don't have to answer if you don't want to.'

Elliott munched on his popcorn, with a determined expression. 'It's OK,' he said.

Sarah nodded in response. 'Right. Here goes then. Who do you think the Midnight Man is? First answer goes to Maggie.'

'The Midnight Man is a bad dream,' Elliott said instantly. He blinked, his long dark lashes full of innocence.

'OK,' Sarah said, pleased he had the swing of it. 'The next answer is to Libby. What would you tell her?'

'I've never heard of the Midnight Man.' Elliott's chin dipped onto his chest.

'Interesting,' Sarah replied with a smile. 'Third and final answer is to me.'

She followed Elliott's gaze to the window, but the curtains were closed. Was he worrying about the Midnight Man? In Slayton, monsters were no longer confined to under the bed.

'Remember,' Sarah said, regaining his attention. 'You can trust me.' She felt a sharp pang of guilt as she spoke. Should she be doing this? But this wasn't police questioning. Sarah was asking as a friend. Elliott was a troubled little boy who needed to get something off his chest.

'I don't know.' His chewing came to a halt. Sarah was about to tell him it didn't matter, when he continued. 'He's wearing a hood. It's dark inside and he's cross, very cross.' His voice dropped low. 'Maggie doesn't like me saying this word, but it's like he *hates* everything. In here.' His hand rested on his heart. He looked at Sarah, awaiting her response. The look was so innocent, so trusting, that for a moment, Sarah was lost for words. How did this odd little boy cope with the rest of the world? She imagined him in school, and the years that lay ahead. No wonder Maggie was protective.

'I think you gave me the truthful answer, am I right?'

Elliott nodded.

'You can ask me a question now if you want.'

Elliott seemed to like the sound of this. He smiled a little before cocking his head to one side.

'Where's Libby?'

Shifting on the sofa, Sarah met his gaze. 'Your mummy said she was on curfew, didn't she?'

'Yes,' Elliott said. 'I had a bad feeling, because Libby played the game.'

'Wait, what?' Sarah interrupted. 'She played the game? When? With who?'

'On Halloween night.' His long lashes blinked as he looked at

171

her with sincerity. 'But she's OK. Maggie brought me to see her. We bought her a candle . . .' His words faded as he stared into the artificial flames. 'Fire. There's fire.'

'Elliott,' Sarah said, as he stared, open-mouthed. 'Are you OK?' No response came. 'Elliott?' she said again, touching his arm. 'Do you know who else she played with? What about Jahmelia?' But the little boy offered no response. Eventually, he shrugged, his gaze becoming vacant. 'It was just a dream.' He followed up with a yawn, stretching his arms wide.

Sarah checked her watch. 'We should get you to bed.' She thought she was helping him, but maybe she was wrong bombarding him with questions. Was she doing him more harm than good? Elliott needed a child psychiatrist. She was out of her depth. 'Sweetie,' she said, as the television played a game show on mute. 'Would you like me to read you a story?'

'I want to sleep in Maggie's bed.' Elliott blinked his huge eyes, finally meeting her gaze. He yawned, his expression lighter. Just like before, the burden of his secret had been lifted.

'I don't see why not. What story would you like?'

'*Harry Potter*,' he replied instantly.

As she followed him to the bedroom, his words and worries returned to haunt her. Fire? She would have to look into it. She couldn't call Gabby; the woman would never believe her. For now, all she could do was wait.

29

Tuesday, 5th November 2019

The warm light of dawn had long since crept in, but Elsie felt out of sync with the day. The smooth sounds of 'Fly Me to the Moon' played on the classic radio channel, but even that couldn't improve her mood. She curled her hand around her ginger tabby, Toni, and pulled her to her chest. Felix, Officer Dibble and T.C. were here too. It was unusual for so many of her cats to visit her at the same time. Like her, they must have felt something was wrong. A knock at the front door broke into her thoughts.

'Christiaaaan!' she called at the top of her lungs, shifting upright in her bed. 'There's somebody at the door!' She waited. Nothing. 'The darn thing won't open itself!'

'Alright, Mom, give me a minute.' Christian darted down the stairs, still buttoning up his shirt. He poked his head into the living room. 'Everything OK?' he said, as Boo Boo jumped up to join the others. Only one of her brood of six was missing. It wasn't unusual for them to go AWOL for days on end. 'Why are the cats on your bed?'

'Don't worry about the darn cats. Answer the door.' She hadn't meant to be so sharp but the presence of almost all her cats at once felt like a bad omen. The last time this happened, she had her first heart attack. She'd been lucky, it had been mild. But she didn't weigh as much then as she did now. 'Alright, precious,' she said to Felix as he gave Toni the evil eye. 'There's room for everyone.'

She eyed the empty family-sized bag of crisps that Christian had left by the side of her bed. Her mouth instantly watered. The stress of it all was playing havoc with her diet. She listened keenly as Christian opened the door, straining to hear the identity of their caller. Most likely, it was the police. A second girl going missing was big news. But the television in the corner of the room was layered in dust so she hadn't seen any of the media reports. She didn't watch mainstream TV. Far too much fornication going on there. She scratched at her smock. The material must have shrunk in the wash. Grunting, she shifted her legs a little further apart and pulled the light blanket up to her waist. Today, she was itchier than a flea on a hotplate. At least *she* didn't have to worry about being kidnapped.

Christian's voice rose from the hall as he allowed their guest inside. It was Sarah. She was calling early. It wasn't yet seven thirty. She was dressed in black trousers, wearing a crisp white shirt beneath a wax jacket of some sort.

'I was hoping to catch you before I went to work. Not too early, am I?' she said, with an apologetic smile.

'Are you on duty?'

'No, not yet.'

Elsie's eyes fell to the bag of shopping in Sarah's hand. 'Then come in. That for me?'

'Yes,' Sarah smiled. 'It's a care package. I thought you could do with some cheering up.'

'That sure is sweet of you.' Elsie beckoned her over and shooed the cats off the bed. She couldn't wait to see what goodies she had brought. Christian had already gone back upstairs. His day began at six, when he would feed the cats, clean out the litter trays then help her wash before preparing her breakfast and tidying up the house. Only then would she allow him to play a quick game on his computer before getting ready for work.

She watched as Sarah rested the tote bag on the table and wheeled it towards Elsie's bed. Elsie cast an eye over the bag. It was from Turn the Page, a small independent bookshop in town. 'I got a jumbo pack of Frontline, for the cats,' Sarah said. 'You squirt it on the back of their neck, and it lasts for six weeks. Then you won't have to use the flea powder. That stuff can't be good for your lungs.'

'That's sure thoughtful,' Elsie replied, wondering if there was anything in the bag for her. She'd heard a new bakery opened in town, and she was dying to try their cakes.

Sarah reached into the bag. 'Now don't take offence, but I got you a book.' Elsie eyed the title *The Obesity Code*, and sighed. Something told her there wouldn't be any cakes.

'You said you wanted to lose weight and well . . . I thought this would help. There's some pamphlets too.' She glanced uncertainly at Elsie as she rested them on the table. 'I got them from the doctors'. I got some smellies too. Candles, body butter, hair products . . . just some things to make you feel nice.'

And smell nicer than I do now too, Elsie thought, as she cast an eye over the products. Her thoughts darkened. This was a lot of expense. 'Why are you doing this? Because I ain't no charity case. Christian looks after me. We're doing OK.' In Elsie's experience, people didn't give stuff away for free – not unless they wanted something in return.

Sarah pursed her lips. 'I feel like I owe you. Maggie and I . . . well, we should have made more of an effort in school. It must have been a lonely time for you.'

'Water under the bridge.' Elsie twisted the lid from a container of body butter and gave it a sniff. It smelled as coconutty as a Bounty bar. In truth, the scars of the past would never leave her. Things could have been different if she'd had someone to confide in. Not just for her, but for Christian too.

'Well, I'm here for you now, even if I wasn't back then. Anything you need to help you on your journey.' She patted Elsie's hand. 'You can do this.' Elsie warmed at the sentiment. It was a long time since anyone believed in her. She gave Sarah a furtive smile.

'Maybe some evening you could come over. I'm not very good with the internet and I could do with some help ordering . . .' She lowered her voice as she leaned in. 'Ladies' underwear.'

'Of course!' Sarah said cheerfully. 'I'll bring my laptop.' She checked her watch. 'God, is that the time? I'd best get to work.'

Elsie gave her a knowing nod. 'You must be busy with everything that's happened. I'm surprised you found time to come here.' Felix jumped back onto the bed, giving Sarah the evil eye. His tail thumped against the blanket rhythmically, a puff of white powder rising with each signal of discontent.

'Yes, it's tragic, what happened to Angelica,' Sarah said.

'I didn't mean Angelica,' Elsie continued, her cat arching as she stroked his fur. 'I'm talking about last night. Honestly, if my Christian hadn't found her when he did . . . I dread to think what could have happened to that poor girl.'

Sarah stared at her as if she was speaking a foreign language. 'I'm not with you.'

Elsie looked at her curiously. 'Didn't you know? I figured with you being in law enforcement an' all . . . My Christian. He's a hero. He saved that missing girl.'

'What missing girl?' Sarah's brows knitted together. 'Saved her from what?'

Elsie appeared tickled by Sarah's lack of knowledge on the matter. 'I thought you were a detective?' Her gaze fell on Christian as he returned downstairs. He was holding a black leather briefcase, a dab of bloodstained tissue stuck to his chin. Pride swelled in her bosom. She didn't know he had it in him. 'Tell her,' she instructed. 'Tell her what a hero you've been.'

'Mom . . .' His cheeks burned as he was put on the spot. 'I was just in the right place at the right time.' He opened a dresser drawer and pulled out a lint roller.

'He's being modest,' Elsie said, happy to share his glory. 'Last night, he was in Blackhall Manor checking security after the police finished with the place. Then he heard this banging coming from the walls!' She raised her hands theatrically. 'Most people would have upped and ran from that creepy old place. But not my Christian. He went to investigate. Next thing you know, that Libby girl crashed right through the wall! She was bleeding and bound. Would you believe it?'

'Is this true?' Sarah turned to Christian. Her mouth was parted in disbelief as she waited for him to answer. 'Christian?' she repeated as he shifted from one foot to the other.

'Yes,' Christian eventually said, barely able to meet her gaze. 'She was trapped in a gap in the walls. Police are crawling all over the place.'

Elsie watched as Sarah stood, stunned.

'Who knows what would have happened if Christian hadn't been there to save her,' Elsie piped up, when it was apparent Christian wasn't going to elaborate. He had always been shy around women, but today he looked like he wanted the ground to swallow him whole. But that was OK. She could talk on his behalf. 'That poor gal would have been killed.'

'All I did was call the ambulance, Mom,' Christian said, pressing the roller against the cat hairs which clung to his trouser legs.

Sarah looked aghast. 'I'd better go, sounds like I have a busy day ahead. I'll let myself out.' She mumbled her goodbyes before marching out the front door.

'She's strange,' Christian said, throwing the roller back in the drawer.

'So is the world we live in.' Elsie looked him over with a concerned eye. He had paled in Sarah's presence and there was a tremble in his hands. 'Honey, are you sure you're OK, going back to work today? You could have been killed last night.' Her son was a sensitive soul. He would feel the effects for a long time to come. Christian delivered a weak smile.

'I'm fine. Just glad I could help.' He checked his watch. 'I have to go.'

Elsie straightened in her bed. Just a few more minutes of company would make her day. 'It must have been scary, her jumping out on you like that.' She was dying to hear the all the gory details, but Christian couldn't get away quickly enough.

'I'm gonna be late. I'll be back at lunchtime to check on you.'

As the door slammed behind him, Elsie was left alone. Her eyes trailed over the care package and she heaved a mournful sigh. She would have preferred cake.

30

When Sarah scurried into the office just after 8 a.m., the edge in the atmosphere was enough to silence the jibes of previous days. She was old news now. Once, she would have been grateful, but not like this. Officers were working every available hour as they scrutinised the case. Sarah rooted in her desk drawer for a spare phone charger. Pens rolled around the space, along with half-used boxes of staples and a curled-up block of Post-it notes. *Typical,* she thought, finding the tail of the charger lead and pulling it from the drawer. *The one night I stay at Maggie's and all hell breaks loose.*

The information she had gleaned about Libby had come too late. While they were at the town meeting, Libby had been abducted, her brother barricaded into his room. It was only thanks to their indoor sprinkler system that the whole house didn't go up in flames. Now Libby was in hospital recovering from her injuries. At least she'd managed to get away.

Bernard, their DI had attended the hospital with Richie to obtain her account but the information she'd imparted was vague. As with any serious investigation, persons of interest had been flagged but that did not make them suspects. Angelica's father, Simon Irving, and her brother, Ryan, had been marked on the board for further intelligence checks. Christian Abraham was also there. Given he had access to so many places, that was no surprise. As

Sarah approached her desk, she noticed Gabby looked stressed. With the Midnight Man still on the prowl, she had good reason to be. She spoke in low tones as she updated Sarah on Libby's abduction and recovery.

'We've got intel to say she's one of four other girls who played this Midnight Game.'

Sarah's eyebrows rose. 'Just like the letter said. Who's the informant?'

'A source from Angelica's school. They've got an online system where students can report things to the school anonymously.'

'Can the school narrow their source down?'

'It came from a school library computer. I've been told the only kids in there at the time were twins – Bethany and Isobel Clarke.' A chill swept through the office. Open windows meant clear minds. Given the hours officers must have been working, they needed all the help they could get.

'Do you want me to speak to them?'

'Not yet. The school wants to talk to their parents first.'

Gabby appeared to scan the room. Their colleagues were head down at their desks, laser-focused on their tasks. Yvonne rose to close the window. Gabby's voice lowered to a whisper. 'If the DI finds out Jahmelia is my granddaughter, I'll be taken off the case. So, keep it zipped for now. I need you with me on this.'

'Absolutely,' Sarah nodded. 'Whatever you say.' She plugged in her charger and attached her phone. But Gabby wasn't finished with her yet.

'You knew Libby was involved, didn't you? That's why you went to see Jahmelia. You know they're as thick as thieves.'

The last thing Sarah wanted was Gabby charging head first in such a delicate situation. 'I pieced it together when Elliott mentioned the Midnight Man. He probably overheard them talking about it when they were babysitting. How else would he have known?' Sarah spoke softly, conscious that Yvonne was eyeing them both. 'I babysat for Maggie last night. I asked Elliott if he knew anything more.'

'And?' Gabby searched Sarah's face for answers. 'What did he say?'

Sarah felt like she was walking a tightrope. A balancing act between loyalty towards Maggie and allegiance to her job. What good would come from telling Gabby that Elliott had seen a spooky Midnight Man in his dreams? That was back in the realms of the supernatural, and she knew how Gabby felt about that.

'He was worried about Libby, he seems to think she played the game.' Sarah recalled Elliott staring into the artificial flames. *There's fire.*

'And what did he say about Jahmelia?' Gabby looked sick.

'Nothing. He didn't say anything. But given they were together that night . . .' Sarah's words trailed away.

This obviously wasn't what Gabby wanted to hear. 'You know as well as I do, Sarah, this killer is not going to stop. Jahmelia could be next.' She glanced over Sarah's shoulder for the second time. 'Go back to Maggie's. Find out what they know . . .' Her words came to an abrupt halt as Yvonne approached.

'I've got the fire inspector's report. They're blaming a candle which caught the curtains in Libby's bedroom.'

'That's fine,' Gabby said, waving Yvonne away. 'Upload it to the system. I'll view it online.' Turning on her heels, Yvonne returned to her desk.

Sarah shuffled uncomfortably as she waited for instruction.

'Um . . . Sarge, what is it you want me to do? I'm pretty sure Elliott's told me everything he knows. I could try speaking to Jahmelia again . . .'

'No chance. She's on curfew. My delightful daughter won't even let *me* near her.' Gabby's fingers bit into her forearm as she pulled Sarah closer. 'Visit Libby in hospital. Take Elliott with you. See if you can get either of them to talk. And think about that letter you showed me. There was nothing useful from forensics, but I might have been too quick to dismiss it.' She released her grip. 'Please. For Jahmelia. She's not street smart like Libby. We need to get this bastard off the streets before he hurts anyone else.' A look of understanding passed between them. 'I've assigned you to making local enquiries for the next few hours. Whatever it takes, you have my blessing. Do what you can.'

Sarah knew better than to argue with her sergeant, but this felt off-grid. Her job was to commit words to paper and create a legible account. Having said that, it was satisfying, earning Gabby's trust. If her sergeant needed her to pull out all the stops then she would. The thought of anything happening to Jahmelia was enough to spur anyone on. Libby had been lucky, but the Midnight Man would not make a second mistake.

31

Elsie relaxed as the front door clicked shut. Another visit from a police officer, albeit not a very nice one. Elsie saw the way she'd looked at her, with a mixture of pity and disgust. The police seemed very interested in her family of late. They said they had to take a statement to eliminate Christian from their enquiries because he was connected with Blackhall Manor. But Christian had been at work. Elsie wasn't stupid. She knew when someone was digging. Still, she didn't think she had anything to worry about. She relaxed back into her bed as her mind turned things over. She'd given them a full family history to steer the focus away from Christian. That had made the officer's mascara-laden eyes pop. It had actually felt good to get things off her chest. She was adept at blocking out bad feelings. From a very young age, she implemented the coping mechanism to deal with those who forced their will upon her. Food was her anaesthetic and as her body expanded it had earned her the benefit of her father's disgust.

Her eyes fell on the picture of her parents which taunted her from the yellowed wall. Why did she do this to herself, this form of self-flagellation? What sort of a masochist was she? Even now, after her parents were gone, their soulless eyes tortured her. *A cleft in your chin instead of your foot, but no less a devil for that* . . . The words of Sylvia Plath had imprinted themselves on her heart. Plath's poem was imbued with such a sense of hatred for her father, it made Elsie feel a little less alone. Like Plath, she was killing herself too.

She glanced at the cats gathering around her bed and the trinkets crowding each dusty shelf. At the dog-eared books featuring muscle-bound heroes and the litter trays which carried an odour she had grown accustomed to. At the sweet wrappers, the crisp packets and litres of chocolate milk. This was her life. She was only as happy as she had a right to be.

Silence, close your eyes, kneel.

The bones of a memory returned as the words echoed from the corridors of her mind: the red velvet cushion introduced to their weekly sessions after her teacher noticed her knees were grazed. Then afterwards, her mother entering the room and tidying the cushion away. Out of sight, out of mind – at least, for another week. The most hurtful betrayal was her mother's blind eye to her father's weekly 'blessings' which carried on long after Elsie was old enough to understand they were wrong. There was no peace when Elsie closed her eyes. In her darkest hours she could still hear the rasping sound of her father's zip being undone. His heavy breath as his hand guided hers, shouting both prayers and obscenities as he demanded she follow his instruction to 'cleanse her soul by releasing the power of his righteous seed'.

With a creeping sense of horror she wondered about her son. *What if he remembered what he saw?* The question made her grip her blankets and draw them up to her chest. Her bed was her safe place. Nobody could see her here. She was invisible to the world. But what if Christian *had* remembered? He was just four years old the night he hid in her room, a silent witness to her father's evil. Nobody knew he was there until it was too late. It was over twenty years ago. What if the sight had planted a compulsion which grew into something black and evil – a sickness he could not control? Was that the real reason why the police were snooping around? Did they think Christian was involved in that awful Midnight Game the poor girls had played? The question was insistent, tugging on the skirts of her consciousness for an answer. She had bigged up her son, gushing about how heroic he'd been. But who was she trying to convince? What if Christian wasn't Libby's saviour after all?

She thought back to Halloween night, to when he'd changed the batteries in her novelty clock. She had given her son an alibi, saying he'd been home at midnight. But was it midnight when Christian noticed their damaged garden gate? And why had he encouraged her to report such a minor thing to the police? She hadn't heard any kids messing about, much less seen them take her gate off its hinges. Christian had been awfully quiet in his room that night. It was almost as if he wasn't there.

On the surface, he was a good boy, always willing to lend a hand. But like her, he had an addictive personality. Christian's compulsion wasn't food, it was computer games. One in particular. *Beyond the Darkness*. It was about a bunch of teenagers trapped in a creepy hotel. One by one, a ghostly figure picked them off.

It wasn't just the game that made Elsie uneasy, it was Christian's growing resemblance to his father. What if he'd taken on his personality? He was an evil man. Christian couldn't help what he was. But at least he knew the truth. Elsie sighed. It had not been easy, explaining his parentage last year, but he had seemed to take it OK.

She paused to drink from the bottle on her table. It was a small but positive step, replacing chocolate milk with water. With help from Sarah, there was hope on the horizon. She was starting to imagine a way out of the prison she had created for herself. But not before she put her mind at rest about her son. She could have a little peek in his room. Her imagination was probably running away with her, and he wouldn't like it if he knew, but one look couldn't do any harm. *Still* . . . she thought, as she lumbered out of bed. *It's like climbing Mount Kilimanjaro.*

It had been years since she'd ventured upstairs, so Christian had no need to lock his bedroom door. Her eyes flicked to the clock on the wall. She had at least an hour before he returned home for lunch. She forced one foot before the other as she shuffled towards the stairs. Already, sweat was beading her brow. *One step at a time,* she told herself. She was in no rush. With each stair, she paused for breath, heaving herself up. 'C'mon Elsie,' she encouraged herself as she gasped for air. 'You got this.' She was almost there.

At the top stair, she bent over, feeling like someone had lit a bonfire between her chafed thighs. She rubbed a clammy hand over her chest. Her heart felt like it was going to near on pop out. 'Almost there,' she gasped, pressing her hand against the wall for support. The carpet was thick with dirt and cat hairs, and there was a stink wafting from the bathroom. Why had she turned such a blind eye to housekeeping? Her parents would roll over in their graves. She only noticed the bulb on the landing had been removed when she tried to turn it on. Squinting, she adjusted her eyes to the dim light. Every door on the landing was closed.

Standing outside Christian's room, she asked herself if she really wanted to enter uninvited. Judging from the rest of upstairs, it would not be in a good state. But this was about more than housekeeping. What was he doing up here? The door swung open against her weight, and she gripped the frame for support. Slack-jawed, her eyes danced around the mess. The space was dark and stuffy, the blinds shut tight. She stared at the map of Slayton pinned to the wall. At the pictures of Blackhall Manor and the accompanying woodlands. What did he want with those? Her nose wrinkled at the smell of leftover food piled on plates next to his bed. He hadn't been eating healthy at all. This was worse than downstairs . . . The stale air made her want to open the window. Her eyes fell on the weights in the corner of the room. To the barbell next to them on the floor. So that was how he'd grown so strong. She flicked on the light and fear bloomed, large and ugly, as she caught sight of a hooded figure standing in front of the wardrobe. Elsie wheezed, her chest tight. She needed to get out. Blinking a second time, she realised that it was just a cloak hung on the door of the wardrobe. 'Gosh darn it,' she said, her hand falling to her chest in relief. But why was it there? What was it for? She'd heard of gameplay but . . . Shuffling over, fuelled by curiosity, she lifted the worn sleeve, yelping in horror as an earwig slid onto her hand. Something about this room was all wrong. She needed to get out. To call Christian this instant and demand he tell her what was going on. She reluctantly turned her gaze back to the hood. He couldn't be mixed up in any of this Midnight Man silliness, could he?

Sweat prickled her brow. She was feeling none too good. The climb upstairs had taken it out of her. She needed to get back to her bed. Turning off the light she headed towards the stairs, vowing to make Christian clean his room up. Her mind swirling with thoughts, she did not see her cat Toni at her feet until it was too late. As she lifted her foot to avoid her, she missed the first, second and third step. Grasping for the banister, she cried out in pain as she bumped and crashed her way down the stairs. 'Oww!' she screamed, before the breath was forced from her lungs. Stars exploded in her vision as she was thrown to the ground. A low moan escaped her lips as she lay on her back, staring at the cobwebs in the corners of the ceiling that she had never got around to cleaning. As her cats gathered near her, Elsie closed her eyes, surrendering to the darkness as it dragged her in.

32

Maggie was humming the theme tune to *Coronation Street* today. Elliott's grip on her hand tightened. Hospitals made his skin itch. In his other hand was the card he made for Libby. He'd glued pasta and pink glitter around the 'Get Well Soon' he'd drawn in yellow pen. But the deeper they got into hospital, the worse he felt. He wrinkled his nose at the smell of cleaning fluid, staring straight ahead. He didn't know what to say to Libby because he hadn't spoken up. Now he felt like that time he ate mud in the playground and found something wriggling in the back of his mouth. He smacked his mouth at the memory of the dare. His teacher said that if you saw something bad or scary you should always speak up. But Maggie said that sometimes keeping secrets was a good thing.

This morning, Maggie told him about Libby and he was so happy she was OK that he'd cried. Last night, he'd sensed her lost in darkness so thick that he could barely make her out. Until his mother spoke to him, he couldn't put his worries into words. Now, he understood. Libby was hidden in a place with no windows or doors. The feeling of insects on his skin . . . a bad smell. She was trapped in the walls. Not like Angelica though, she was in the *other* place. The Midnight Game was still being played and it would not stop until it was done. How could Libby

189

have been so silly? Even Elliott knew that you shouldn't play dangerous games.

'Are you OK, sweetie?' Maggie looked at him with the same scared face that all the mummies and daddies in Slayton were wearing now. Most kids were on curfew. The Scouts and Brownies were cancelled, and every pole was decorated with a yellow ribbon. People peeked through their blinds, and whispered in corners. The killer was one of them. Elliott couldn't explain this aloud because he could barely understand it himself. He nodded in response to his mummy's question. It was an automatic thing now.

Maggie said that Libby was barely speaking, and that they had to do what they could to help. They had some magazines from a bargain shop near home which Elliott had helped to choose, and grapes. Elliott stood next to Maggie at the elevator, silently watching. It was not good to get in the way of the game. The Midnight Man saw everything. Elliott listened as a trolley rattled past. Heard the squeak of rubber shoes against tiled floors. He had a sudden thought and tugged on his mother's hand.

'Can we go and see Daddy?'

'Daddy's in Benrith hospital, sweetheart.' Maggie smoothed over his hair. 'He's not up to visitors yet.' Elliott sighed. The last time he saw his daddy, he looked like something from the robot programmes on TV, with tubes coming out of him that came from machines with blinking lights, and bandages on his face. But that had been so long ago, when Elliott was six years old. He was seven now, almost grown up.

His mother bent down to his level. 'As soon as he's well enough, I promise I'll take you to see him. But today we need to think about

Libby. She's had a horrible time and she needs some cheering up. Do you think we can do that?'

Elliott nodded, putting on his special smile. As the lift doors opened, he spied Sarah waiting in the corridor, chewing on her thumbnail. The sad cloud that followed her was back today, but she still looked brave. If Sarah was at his school she would climb right to the top of the bars without even looking down, he could tell.

'Hello, Elliott,' she said brightly. 'I think you're growing taller every day.' Elliott responded with a shrug. His jeans had inched up near his ankles, and his toes were squished in his shoes, but he hadn't said anything because his mummy would have to work even harder to buy him new things. He liked it better when she was at home.

'Thanks for bringing Elliott,' Sarah said to Maggie, as the three of them approached Libby's room. 'It's important that we let Libby lead the way. If she tells us to go, we go. Whatever she wants. She's in control.'

Maggie agreed and turned to Elliott. 'She's not long out of surgery,' she added. 'She's probably sore, so best not to jump onto the bed.' Elliott nodded. He wasn't in a jumping around kind of mood anyway.

Libby's room was small but bright, with flowers in glasses adding splashes of yellow and green like in Maggie's paintings at home. Libby had her own room. She didn't share with anyone else. There was a bandage on the back of her head, and another on her side where the chunk of wood had jabbed her skin. Elliott had felt that. Blackhall Manor didn't like letting people go.

Libby was awake, staring at the ceiling. She pulled the blankets up to her chest as Maggie walked in ahead of them. 'It's OK, sweetheart,'

Maggie said, softly. 'Elliott's here to visit. Is it OK if he comes in?' Libby smiled as she caught sight of him trailing in. Slowly, she held out her hand. Without hesitation, Elliott joined her, taking her hand in his own. A gentle stillness passed between them. 'And this is Sarah,' Maggie said, pulling over a chair. 'She's my friend. We went to school together.'

'She's my friend too,' Elliott said, looking at Libby in earnest as he sat in the chair next to her bed. Her eyes looked empty, but her shoulders dropped half an inch.

'Is it OK if she joins us?' Maggie continued, placing the grapes and magazines on the table over her bed. Libby responded with a nod. Elliott felt swallowed up by her sadness. Something inside Libby was broken. But she had been able to get away. She had beaten the Midnight Man, and Elliott knew that would make him cross.

Her hands in her trouser pockets, Sarah joined Elliott's side. 'I used to live in Blackhall Manor,' she said. 'And now I work for the police. The thing is . . .' She took a deep breath. 'The man who took you. He's not going to stop.' She rocked slightly on the balls of her feet. 'I know you're tired, and probably very scared, but I need you to tell me everything you know. Anything at all. There isn't a lot of time . . .'

Libby's eyes were already swimming with tears. 'I don't know who it was,' she said. 'I already told the police . . . I only saw his reflection in my window before he pulled the hood over my head. He was strong . . . dressed in black.' A sob hitched in her throat. 'I banged my head when he put me into the boot, and then I woke up inside the walls.'

'That's OK, sweetie, I don't want to upset you.' Silence fell as Maggie passed Libby some tissues. 'Do you want us to go?' Sarah eventually asked, and Libby responded with a small nod. As Elliott went to leave, Libby's grip on his hand tightened.

'I'll be right outside,' Sarah said, following Maggie out. 'Get better soon, Libby. You're safe here.'

Libby turned to Elliott as soon as the door clicked shut. 'Don't go near Blackhall Manor. Promise me.'

'I won't,' Elliott replied. After a beat he remembered something. 'Did you know that tortoises like being scratched? They can feel it when you touch their shell.'

'That's lovely.' Libby gave him a teary smile. 'I hope your mum lets you get one someday. You'd be the best tortoise owner in the world.'

Elliott hoped so too. But Maggie said tortoises lived too long. They sat in a happy silence until Libby began to doze.

'If you tell, you'll go to hell.' Libby was talking in her sleep, her eyes closed.

Elliott's chest tightened. He had heard those words in his dreams. They were the words of the Midnight Man. He sat quietly at Libby's bedside, trying to be brave. The image of a hooded figure rose in his mind. It was as if he was feeding off Libby's connection with the Midnight Man. His pulse quickened as the image sharpened. *Two faces,* he thought, hugging himself in the chair. *The Midnight Man has two faces.* One good, one bad.

33

'Poor taste, isn't it?' Maggie pointed to her newspaper. 'Taking a photo of the funeral.'

Sarah squinted at the black and white image. She had been looking over Maggie's shoulder at the crossword competition, not the story next to it. Anything to kill the time as they sat, waiting for Elliott to emerge from Libby's room.

'Is that Angelica's funeral?' she said, taking in the image of a family standing at a graveside, hands clasped, heads bowed. She may not like Simon Irving, but even he deserved time to mourn.

'Yeah . . . it is.' Maggie looked down her reading glasses which were perched on the end of her nose. 'That's Elsie's son, isn't it? I thought it was family only. What's he doing there?' Much had been made of the Irving family's request for complete privacy, with promises of a memorial mass for the public to attend later on.

'You know him?' Sarah looked at her friend curiously. She'd never mentioned keeping in touch with Elsie.

'I should do, he works for Moving & Rentals in Upper Slayton. I rent my house through them.'

'Strange. As you say, I wonder what he was doing there?' Sarah scanned the picture of Christian, standing a foot away from everyone else. With his thick black hair and ill-fitting suit, he looked out of place next to the family, who seemed perfect in every way even in their tailored mourning black.

'He must have slipped through, like the photographer,' Maggie snorted, folding the newspaper in half. 'Bloody rag.'

'I'll have that,' Sarah said, as Maggie stretched to throw it in the bin. She slipped the paper into her bag and raised her head at the sound of Elliott's squeaky trainers as he plodded down the hall. He looked a pitiful sight, his head down as he avoided eye contact with the nurses who passed him. Maggie was too proud to accept charity, but the kid really needed some new clothes. Anyone could see his jeans were too short, and his sweatshirt was clean but worn. She'd considered offering to take him shopping, but it was too early in their renewed friendship for that.

'How did it go?' Maggie asked as he drew up beside them both, his hand interlocking with hers. Her face looked hopeful. 'Did Libby say anything?'

Elliott screwed up his forehead. 'No. Sorry.'

'Never mind.' Sarah squeezed his shoulder. 'You made her day better. Now if it's OK with your mummy, I think I owe you a chocolate bar.' His face brightened as they headed back down to the hospital shop. If Libby had said anything to him, he wasn't ready to share it with her, and she wasn't going to push. She saw a little of herself in Elliott. She knew how hard it was, standing beneath the shadow of authority as question after question was fired at you. But Elliott was a good kid – thoughtful, caring and kind. She needed to handle him with care.

She glanced down at the newspaper nestled in her bag. Could the same be said for Christian Abraham? At first she thought his odd behaviour was down to living with his mother for longer than seemed good for him. He seemed awkward in her company, even furtive as he failed to meet her eye. Being his mother's carer from an early age must have affected him. But being introverted was not a crime. He had a job; he may not be the most charismatic member of the community, but it didn't make him a killer.

It wasn't just the newspaper photo which linked Christian to Angelica though, his fingerprints had turned up at Blackhall Manor too. Her DI had been quick to rule him out, given his occupation. He managed the building, after all. But was it more than a coincidence that Christian was at Blackhall when Libby was found? What if he hadn't been saving her? What if he had returned to silence her for good, but changed his plan when she tried to escape? If it was designed to get the police off his scent it had worked. Now he would be deemed a hero rather than a suspect.

Sarah thought again about the sombre photograph at the graveside, and the lone figure with bowed head. Had Christian been the one to bury Angelica the first time around?

34

Sarah stared out her car windscreen at the stray dog ambling past, his black fur slick with rain. There were lots of them in Lower Slayton. They usually came out in the early hours, when the roads were quiet, but tonight the streets outside Elsie's mid-terraced home were devoid of people, apart from some police community support officers on patrol. People's perceptions had altered, and there was a collective anger brewing as they placed their children on curfew. It was almost a week since Angelica disappeared. A lot was going on behind the scenes, and teams of officers were working hard to track down the killer dubbed the Midnight Man. But locals' tempers were fraying. It wasn't helped by the media, who splashed headlines such as **Midnight Man Terrorises Slayton** across their front pages. The story started in the *Slayton Gazette* as details of the game were leaked to the press. Word spread on social media under #TheMidnightMan before being picked up by the nationals. It had been met with a macabre fascination, featuring on YouTube true crime channels to KCOM News. Most adults in Slayton hadn't heard of the game until now, much less understood it. Tales of the pagan ritual were interspersed with segments about Blackhall Manor's dark past. The daily reminders of Sarah's history made her scar itch. Heaven forbid they find out who she was – they would have a field day. Not to mention the fact she was assigned to the crime.

If only she'd been able to interview Isobel and Bethany, she could have uncovered more. But by the time she'd got to their house, the twins had been whisked away to Ireland to stay with relatives. 'It's the safest place for them,' their father had insisted, while stating they had nothing to do with Angelica's murder. *Talk about contradicting himself,* Sarah thought. If they had nothing to do with the Midnight Game, why had they been taken to Ireland? It was obvious the family were scared half to death. She was glad the twins were safe, but it was a frustrating end to a fruitless shift.

Sarah couldn't help thinking about the letter. *For every day you're alive the game continues. He's goading me,* she thought. *But into what? My suicide would not make an impact on the world. He must want something more. Press attention? Revenge? Or is this all part of some sick game?* Her gut instinct nagged that Christian Abraham needed more consideration than police were giving him. She tapped the top of her steering wheel as she worked out an excuse for rocking up at Elsie's door again. She *had* promised to help her buy some underwear online. Her car keys jangling in her hand, she approached Elsie's home with a newfound stride. A puff of black smoke bloomed from over the rooftops as darkness closed in. Someone must be having a bonfire. This year's Bonfire Night celebrations were muted, apart from a couple of organised firework displays in town.

The front door opened before Sarah got to it. Christian's hands were full of black plastic bin bags and she watched him stack them outside. 'Having a tidy?' she said cheerfully, visiting under the guise of a social call.

'I . . .' Christian said, seemingly at a loss for words. His shirt sleeves were rolled up to his elbows, and there was a dusting of what looked like soot on the leg of his jeans. Sarah walked through the open door before he could stop her.

'I just want a quick word with your mum, I won't be long.' She wiped her feet on the grate before carrying on through to the living room. Unlike the houses in Upper Slayton, this was not a place you needed to take your shoes off. 'Oh,' she said to herself, staring at Elsie's bed which was stripped of its sheets. 'You *have* been busy. Elsie? Are you about?' Perhaps her previous visit had inspired Elsie in more ways than one. The house looked much bigger and brighter, now it had been cleared of all its clutter.

Christian's shadow grew large in the doorway. 'She's not here.'

'Oh right, has she gone to the doctor's?' Sarah said, hopefully. The look on Christian's face relayed that it was something far more serious than that. She followed his gaze to the empty bed, almost tripping on the cat winding its tail around the back of her legs.

Christian picked up a pile of books from the ground and threw them in a bin bag. Sarah caught sight of *The Obesity Code* at the top of the pile and sighed. This wasn't good.

'Mom's at the hospital,' he eventually said. 'She fell down the stairs.' Turning his back on her, he carried another two bags outside. Sarah stared, open-mouthed as she digested his words.

No. Surely not. But then Elsie wasn't steady on her feet. Just getting up the stairs would have caused her enormous effort. 'How is she? Is she going to be OK?'

'They're running tests. That's all they'll say.' He plucked the

Kit-Cat clock off the wall, gave it a rub with a duster and put it back.

'Christian. What are you doing?' Sarah pinched the top of her nose as she contained a sneeze.

'Cleaning up,' he replied quietly. 'I want to make the place nice for when she comes home.' Every word he spoke seemed an effort and he could not meet her eye.

'But this sounds serious.' Sarah watched him intently as he continued to dust and clean. The air was thick with the smell of smoke and Mr Sheen. Two of Elsie's cats followed him around the room, miaowing pitifully. 'Shouldn't you be at the hospital?'

'I've just come back from there. The doctors sent me home to get some sleep.'

'Then can I make you a cup of tea?' She knew the trauma of a sudden shock, but Christian's behaviour was bizarre. 'You must be upset.'

'No time for tea,' Christian said, picking up two more bags. 'I need to get rid of these old clothes.' She followed him out to the back garden which consisted of a scrub lawn and some sorrowful-looking shrubs. A barrel was blazing in the middle of the patio. So that was where the smoke had come from. It hissed and crackled beneath the evening sky as he threw in a handful of baggy clothes. Mesmerised, he watched the flames take hold of the stained material and turn it into ash. 'They had to get a special ambulance. One that could take her weight. They stretchered her out through the back double doors.' His words were flat as he looked straight ahead. It was like he was talking to himself.

Sarah stood, her hands in her trouser pockets, bristling from the cold. She'd have to invest in a decent scarf and gloves if she was intending on spending so much time outdoors. She raised her hands to the heat as Elsie's old clothes burned. It felt as if he was giving his mum a funeral. Except she wasn't dead.

Why was she even still standing here? If Christian wanted to clean up the house, he was well within his rights. But then she remembered how unfit Elsie had been, and how answering the front door had been an effort in itself.

'What was she doing upstairs?'

The answer came instantly in the same flat tone. 'Probably looking for chocolate. She's meant to be cutting down.' He stood, motionless, watching the smoke rise.

'Is there anyone I can call?' Sarah drove a hand through her hair. Already, she could smell the stink of smoke on her clothes.

'For what?' Christian looked at her blankly before going back inside.

She watched his gaze flit around the room, landing on a picture of Elsie's parents. In one swift movement, he pulled it off the wall and threw it in the bin.

'Won't she want to keep that?' Sarah said.

'No. She won't.' Christian looked at her, an edge of bitterness in his tone. 'Because Mom doesn't have any family – only me.' His cheeks inflamed, he finally looked Sarah in the eye. 'She doesn't have any friends either, so don't pretend that you care.' His gaze fell on the cheap ornaments lining the shelves next to her bed. 'I'd like you to go now. I've got a lot to do.' He turned his back on her, his head bowed as he retreated from the conversation.

'Sorry,' she said. 'I'll . . . I'll leave you to it then.' A wave of guilt washed over her. He was right. It *was* a bit late to show concern, but she did genuinely care. 'I'll visit her as soon as I can.'

In the absence of a reply, she let herself out the front door. Black bags were piled up next to the green recycling bin, their contents spilling onto the path. Bending, she picked up some worn-looking romance books. Elsie had always been a bookworm. A sad smile graced her face as she flicked through the stained pages . . . tea, ketchup, cake crumbs between the folds. Carefully, she placed them back into the bag, picking up an A5 journal from the ground. 'The Country Girl Romance Series by Caroline Brookes,' she said softly, tracing a finger over the words. She opened the pages, all handwritten. It seemed Caroline Brookes was a pen name. Had Elsie written this? Giving one quick glance towards the door, she slipped the journal beneath her coat.

She had only driven half a mile up the road before she pulled the car over. Switching off the engine, she heaved a heavy sigh. Elsie had seemed so hopeful the last time they spoke, and now she could be about to die.

Her glance fell on the journal resting on the passenger seat. Why had she taken it? More to the point, why was Christian dumping Elsie's things? Was it really in an effort to clean the place up? Clearing her throat, she began to flick through the pages.

'Elsie, you dark horse,' she said with a sniffle. It seemed that Elsie, for all her prudish ways, was a romance writer. And quite a raunchy one at that. She'd been writing a chapter a day. Each one was interspersed with notes, doodles and updates. Elsie was living vicariously through her books. Sarah flicked through the journal, stopping on a heavily dog-eared page. The words that were scrawled across it were tear-stained.

'*Silence, close your eyes, kneel. Silence, close your eyes, kneel. Silence, close your eyes, kneel.*' Written again and again, until the words blurred into one. She stared in disbelief at the scribbles. This was a freehand outpouring of emotion – but what did it mean?

35

My mind raced as I sat in my car. I checked my watch. Almost 10 p.m. The time teenagers were in bed but not yet asleep. I was parked beneath a broken street lamp, grateful for the darkness. Seeing so much of Sarah was messing with my head. It took all of my strength not to jump her as she marched to her car, and drag her to Blackhall there and then. But I had a formula. One where the end result was me not getting caught. I couldn't see myself in prison. Where was the justice in that? Not when she was the one so blatantly in the wrong. Things were moving too quickly, though. I needed to accelerate my plans.

Why was Sarah pretending to show concern for Elsie now? It wasn't as if she'd had any time for her in school. It was probably Sarah's fault that Elsie had been snooping around. She'd been putting ideas in her head. Something had made Elsie go upstairs. But there was little that could implicate me – apart from the cloak, and given Halloween had just passed, that could be explained away. Just the same, there were too many threads hanging loose for my liking. Closing my eyes, I inhaled a deep breath. It was easy to get overwhelmed. I reminded myself that it came down to just one thing: finish the Midnight Game. Player one was dead. Player two was in hospital. Player three would soon be in the morgue. Next time I would be more careful. The dead couldn't tell tales, after all.

The mobile on my passenger seat beeped with a text and I glanced down. It was player three, Jahmelia, replying to the text I'd sent from a burner phone, pretending to be Libby. I had asked for a meetup – in secret, of course, while explaining my old phone had been lost.

Cool! I didn't know you were out of hospital. Mum and Dad won't tell me anything.

Am OK . . . *I texted*. But the police have been here. Need 2CU. I'm scared x

Jahmelia's response was instant.

Glad UR OK but I'm freaking out 2. Sorry. I can't keep the Midnight Game a secret anymore.

A gasp of surprise left my parted lips. Well now, that was quicker than expected. I knew she was nervous, but I didn't think she'd cave just yet.

I checked my surroundings before crafting a reply.

OK, but we should get our stories straight. We cd B in big trouble for holding back so long. Meet in the playground. Don't get caught. Xox

I stared at the text, wondering if I could convince its recipient that it was Libby talking.

Now? x

The one-word response gave me the reassurance I needed. How dumb is this kid?

I replied with a thumbs up and added.

Am here. Don't let me down, Jay. Xox

I waited for her response. Jahmelia wasn't the rebellious type, but I was counting on the use of her nickname, gleaned from their old messages, being enough to seal the deal. The playground was only five minutes' walk from where Jahmelia lived. It would be deserted at this hour, and Jahmelia would take the shortcut where I would be waiting. I tapped my fingers against the steering wheel, awaiting her response.

OK. Mikey's playing his VR, and Mum and Dad think I'm in bed. CU soon x

I pulled out of the junction and headed towards the park. A breath of relief escaped my lips. Everything was back on track. The next stage of the game was underway.

36

Wednesday, 6th November 2019

Sarah was deep in thought as she entered the police station corridor before eight on Wednesday morning. She'd had a terrible night's sleep as she tried to work out the right thing to do. She had read and re-read Elsie's journal until she was word blind. She had a viable lead, but could she convince Gabby it was worth pursuing?

A voice rose ahead of her, snapping her from her thoughts. It was Yvonne, talking to the DI outside of the CID briefing room. Judging by the number of officers coming out, Sarah had missed an impromptu briefing. Had something new come in? Her footsteps slowed as she listened to the conversation. 'I'm sure it's just an oversight on Gabby's behalf.' Yvonne's head was tilted to one side as she spoke with her usual fake sincerity. 'But I don't think it's acceptable for her to be working the case now her granddaughter is involved.'

'Thanks for bringing it to my attention,' Bernard said, too involved in the conversation to notice Sarah approaching. 'I wasn't aware Jahmelia was related.'

'Yes, well, as I said. It's an oversight. But I know this case better than anyone. I'm the best person to fill her shoes.'

Fill her shoes? Sarah slowed her pace. Yvonne must have

overheard them talking about Jahmelia and now she was trying to get Gabby kicked off the case.

'Consider the ball well and truly in your court.' Bernard clasped his hands together. 'If you're up for it, then I'm happy to give you the responsibility. It's all hands on deck right now.'

'Thanks, boss,' Yvonne called after him. 'I won't let you down!' But the smile dissolved from her face as Sarah came into view.

'Morning.' Sarah fell into step with Yvonne as they entered the CID office. The weather was dull and gloomy and the weak early morning sun filtered through the vertical blinds. Sarah smiled at the cleaners as they left. The floors had been freshly hoovered and the computer stations were gleaming. Soon they would be covered with paperwork and coffee cups.

A whiteboard took up space at the end of the room, littered with details of the investigation and crime scene photographs. There were more whiteboards in the briefing room, featuring locations, dates and theories. One solely held details of the Midnight Game. Her colleagues had picked the game apart, trying to work out a connection between the killer and his need to play. Sarah visited the room when she could, tapping her chin and staring at the boards as she waited for answers to materialise. But not today.

Her colleagues took their seats as they filtered in from the briefing. It seemed everyone had been called in except for her. Sarah glanced around the room as Yvonne failed to reply. 'Where's Gabby?'

'She's taken time off to be with her family. I'm acting sergeant now,' Yvonne said briskly.

Sarah's spirits plummeted as the news sank in. She had hoped for some divine intervention to stop such an atrocity taking place. She glanced over at Richie who was in conversation with uniformed officers as he spread out a map on his desk. The office was bustling with activity. They had obviously been called in early. Something new must have come in.

'Have we had a new lead?' Sarah followed Yvonne to Gabby's desk. Yvonne raised an eyebrow as she checked the clock on the wall.

'I suppose you haven't heard, given you've just rocked up.'

Sarah frowned. That was hardly fair. Her shift started at eight and it was just gone quarter to.

'The early bird gets the worm,' Yvonne continued, 'as Saint Bernard would say.'

She'd be after his job soon too, Sarah thought, inwardly rolling her eyes.

She slipped off her Barbour jacket and rested it on the back of her chair. 'If I'd been called, I would have come straight in.'

But Yvonne was unmoved. 'Jahmelia's missing. Her parents called it in an hour ago when she didn't get up for breakfast.' She shifted on her heels. 'I'll set you some tasks on the system.'

Sarah's stomach lurched. Jahmelia was gone? But her parents must have been watching her every move. How could this have happened? Aware of Yvonne's presence, she regained her composure as she remembered the journal in her bag. 'I have a lead. It's a journal from Elsie's house.'

As she handed over the book, Yvonne sat at Gabby's desk and settled back into her swivel chair. Most acting sergeants continued to work from their own desks, but Yvonne seemed to be enjoying the power trip. She thumbed through the pages of Elsie's old journal. 'What am I looking at, apart from badly written soft porn?'

'It belongs to Elsie Abraham. Christian Abraham is her son. It was in a bag of stuff he'd put out for the bin.'

Sarah's stomach rumbled as she stood. For the first time in years, she had left her house without breakfast. Food was no longer part of her every waking thought. She licked the dryness from her lips as she prepared to state her case.

'Given the content, I can't say I blame him.' She threw the journal back onto the desk. 'What's your point?'

'He could be the Midnight Man.'

'And how did you come to that conclusion?'

Sarah pointed at the journal. 'I went to school with Elsie. Whoever sent me the letter that's on the system seemed to know me quite well.'

'Next reason,' Yvonne said impatiently. 'There *is* more, isn't there? You're accusing a young man of murder. You must have more than that.'

'I do,' Sarah said, but her reasoning was falling away, and she scratched around in her mind to retrieve all the facts which had been so glaringly obvious after she left Elsie's house last night. 'He's an estate agent. He works for his uncle's firm. He's the keyholder for Blackhall Manor, as well as other properties around here. He could have a spare to my house for all I know. It feels like he's been there.' Sarah didn't mention the tablets in her bedside table that she had stockpiled in case things got too much.

'OK,' Yvonne said. 'Is that it?'

'His fingerprints were found at Blackhall Manor and . . .'

'But that relates to your previous point,' Yvonne interrupted. 'Given he's a keyholder tasked with keeping an eye on the place, it would be strange if his fingerprints *didn't* show up. It's in his

210

statement. He goes in, checks the rooms for vagrants, sets the mousetraps. Please tell me you've more on him than that.'

I will if you stop interrupting me, Sarah thought. 'His mum gave him an alibi, but he could have messed with the clock on the wall. She sleeps in the front room. Well, she did, until yesterday.' Sarah glanced over her shoulder. Her colleagues had their heads down. Some were making notes, others were staring at their computers. But they had to be listening just the same. It seemed a day couldn't pass without her being berated before her team.

'So you were there?' Yvonne continued.

'I popped in for a personal visit. Elsie's not been well.'

'I'm not surprised, given the size of her. That woman has one foot on a banana skin and the other one in the grave. If you ask me . . .'

'She's in hospital,' Sarah interrupted. 'Fell down the stairs, according to Christian.'

'Oh. I see. She's only young. That *is* a shame.' She pulled back her shirt sleeve and looked at her watch. 'Anything else?'

Dammit, Sarah thought. If she was granted more access to the investigation rather than being sent out to take statements she might be more au fait with the case. 'I think Elsie was abused by her father and it really messed her up. Christian could be the result of incest.' She reached for the journal and opened the tear-stained page. '*Silence, close your eyes, kneel,*' scratched into the page with a heavy pen over and over again. 'I think this is referring to abuse. Nobody helped her when she was young. It's why she turned to food.' Sarah sighed. The theory sounded much more sensible in her head. 'She's always spoken about her ex, but she's never been married. Christian's birth certificate doesn't name the father. There's no record of another man in her life.'

'So Christian is a child of incest *and* a murderer because we don't know his father's identity?'

'I . . .' Sarah frowned as her reasoning deserted her. She hated being placed on the spot. 'He fits the profile. He's a loner, he's never had proper socialisation. He's cared for his mother all his life. I remember her from school, her parents were odd . . .' A blush stained her cheeks as her argument fell away. 'And it's the way he looks at me, you know? Like he has a dark secret or something.'

'So, he's creepy – as is half the population of Lower Slayton. Is that it?'

'He was at Angelica's funeral. It was meant to be for family only, which raises the question – why was he there?'

Yvonne raised a manicured hand. 'OK, Sarah, let me stop you before you embarrass yourself any further. Do you think we aren't aware of everything you've told me and more?' She did not wait for a response. 'We're way ahead of you.'

Yvonne wore a half smile as she spoke down to her. 'It's not public knowledge yet but Christian Abraham is Simon Irving's son. Angelica was his half-sister. Hence why we've not rushed in to make an arrest.'

Sarah's mouth dropped open. 'I . . . I didn't know.'

'How would you? You're a statement taker. You're not investigating this case. You've got to be careful, throwing accusations around. Simon Irving is a powerful man.'

'I wasn't throwing anything,' Sarah said, in an effort to defend herself.

'So you didn't just march in here with a bent-up journal and say you knew who the Midnight Man was?'

'I . . . I was just trying to help.'

'But we don't need your help,' Yvonne said. 'We're all over this.'

'Fine,' Sarah replied. 'But as the DI said, all hands on deck. I need time to catch up with the case.'

'Not necessary, but you can have an hour. Start by reading the statement I took from Elsie. While you were on a fool's errand to the hospital, I popped out to see her. She gave me a full background of her family situation. Now, some would argue that it wasn't needed, but in a small town like Slayton, everyone knows everyone.' Yvonne cast an eye over the uniformed officers leaving the room. 'Given Christian's presence in so many aspects of the case, I pre-empted the SIO's request for more information.'

'I still don't think we should rule him out,' Sarah said.

'Yeah, yeah. I gather that. But thankfully you're not leading the investigation,' Yvonne replied. '"Softly softly, catchy monkey," as the DI says.'

But Sarah wasn't ready to concede just yet. 'Christian is gutting the house. He's lit a fire in his garden. There could be evidence there.'

'That house is a health hazard. Good luck to him, I say.'

'But why is he spring cleaning when his mother's unconscious in hospital . . .' Sarah said. 'He's involved somehow. I can feel it.'

'Are you acting sergeant?' Richie's voice rose from behind. He had a habit of making Sarah jump and this time was no exception.

Yvonne responded with a nod.

'Excuse me, I was here first.' Sarah looked from Richie to Yvonne, her nerves frayed. 'What about the letter? It's obviously someone who knows me.'

'You think so?' Yvonne's eyebrows rose a notch. 'Given your track record, I wouldn't be surprised if you wrote it yourself.'

'That's harsh,' Sarah said, heat rising to her face. She shoved Elsie's journal back into her bag. She was wasting her time here.

'I'm only saying what everyone's thinking.' Yvonne's stiff laughter filled the air. 'It's not that long since you were talking to your husband's ghost!' The office fell quiet. She had gone there. Laid Sarah's most embarrassing moment bare. Yvonne's manner was unprofessional and not the way a sergeant should behave.

'Excuse me.' Sarah brushed past Richie. She'd had enough humiliation for today.

'That was out of order,' she heard him say to Yvonne as she marched out the door.

The ladies' toilets were mercifully empty. There were just four cubicles in the windowless space, available only to police station staff. A roof fan whirred limply as it sucked out stale air. It smelt permanently of sweet 'seasonal berries' which squirted from its automatic dispenser every thirty minutes without fail. Sitting on the lid of the toilet, Sarah grabbed some tissue from the dispenser and blotted away her tears. She hated that she cried when she was embarrassed. You'd think that she'd be used to it by now. She tried to recount the rules she'd set herself but found she couldn't remember them. *Oh yeah,* she recalled, *act normal.* It seemed that ship had sailed. Thanks to Yvonne shooting her mouth off, everyone knew why she'd been placed on restricted duties to begin with.

She heard the main door creak open and sighed. Three knocks on the cubicle followed. 'Occupied,' she said. The tips of a man's leather shoes came into view.

'It's me.' Richie's voice echoed from the other side of the door.

Silence.

'Are you OK?'

'What are you doing in here?'

'Asking if you're OK.'

Quietly, Sarah wiped her nose.

'She went too far. She shouldn't have brought that stuff up.'

Sarah sniffed. 'Maybe she's right. I keep getting it wrong. I'm not cut out for this.'

'Don't play into her hands. It's exactly what she wants.'

'I still talk to him, you know,' Sarah said. 'Despite everything that's happened . . . I know he's dead. But it was so hard, the way he went. I needed to have it out with him, so I found myself shouting at thin air.'

'No judgement here,' Richie said. 'We all do what we can to get by.'

'Then after a while, I'd hear him in my head, imagining what he would say.' She shook her head. 'You must think I'm crazy.'

'Not me,' Richie replied. 'I talk to toilet cubicle doors.'

Sarah gave him a watery smile as she unlocked the door and came out. The truth was, she hadn't heard David's imaginary voice since she told him to go. She hated herself for missing it. How messed-up was that?

'Why are you being so nice to me?'

'Because if anyone deserves a little bit of TLC, it's you.' He looked at her earnestly. 'I saw you joined the Facebook group. What do you think?'

'Everyone seems nice . . .' Sarah brushed past him to the sink. 'If a little obsessed.' She washed her hands robotically, even though she hadn't used the loo.

'You know there are officers in Blackhall Manor now, searching?' He looked at her curiously. 'The crawlspace . . . there's more than one.'

215

'They're not on the plans.' Sarah pulled down two paper towels to dry her hands. 'Grandad used to talk about them when I was little. He forbade me and Robin from looking. Apparently our ancestors were not very nice people. I think Grandad was scared of what we might find there.'

'And you've never been tempted to check them out?'

Sarah threw the scrunched-up paper towels in the bin. 'Would you be tempted to revisit the place where your family was blown to bits?'

'Sorry. Stupid question,' Richie replied.

'Seems like it's the day for them. I've got to get back to work.'

Richie touched her forearm. 'If you have a hunch then don't ignore it. Just come to me, not Yvonne. She'll step on anything you have to say.'

'Thanks.' Sarah opened the door. 'After you.' At least she had one friend to talk to. But was he a friend she could trust?

37

Sarah sat, head down, at her desk. Her world was closing in and she needed a second to catch her breath. Search teams were out hunting for Jahmelia and local appeals were underway. Statements had been taken from the family by the night shift who'd been covering when the call came in. *Think of a word,* she told herself, something to distract her from this mess. Yvonne had left the office for a meeting with DI Lee, and she prayed her name would not be raised. *Advokate*, she thought, from her police training days. Mnemonics had featured heavily during her college days in Police HQ.

The letter A stood for amount – to question the amount of time the suspect was under observation by the witness. D was for distance between witness and suspect. V was for visibility conditions . . . With each recall, Sarah gathered herself together. It would be OK. Yvonne was just being Yvonne. The senior investigating officer would see sense. She brought up Elsie's statement on the system. Statements were written in five parts and she went straight to the meat of the interview. Yvonne was known for writing MG11 statements in the witnesses' voices, which was rare in the general scheme of things. It was a nice touch, and she had certainly captured Elsie, which made it all the more poignant. With a rising sense of gloom, she read.

At this point I would like to talk about Christian's father. I have signed a gagging order but I am willing to break this to provide some background to the police. I have provided Detective Constable Yvonne Townsend with a copy of this order to show that I am telling the truth. I met Christian's father in July 1994. I was fourteen years old. My parents were very strict. I wasn't allowed out on my own. But that night I was allowed to attend the screening of *Jurassic Park* in Slayton's outdoor cinema. I told my mother I was going with my friends, Maggie and Sarah, but in truth they hadn't invited me. I wasn't part of their gang.

'No,' Sarah said quietly as she took in Elsie's words. She was right. Sarah's gang of four had been watertight. Her heart melted for Elsie, the awkward young girl desperate to fit in. Sighing, she scanned the rest of the page.

I didn't realise then that my date had only met me as part of a dare. He said he liked me. He drove me somewhere we could be alone. I cried myself stupid when he later told me why he'd taken my virginity. Slayton is a small town, and every summer the privileged kids would make up a dare. This wasn't a twenty-four-hour thing – they took it real serious. They played the long game. The summer Christian was conceived, the dare was to see how many cherries they could pop over the course of six weeks. I was a prime candidate as the pretty girls were wary of their games. Out of all the girls he'd slept with, I was the only one to get pregnant.

Sarah's jaw stiffened. It was all slotting into place. Simon Irving. She recalled both Irving and Elsie in the photographs at Slayton's outdoor cinema event.

'Arrogant bastard,' she muttered beneath her breath. Always in the background, always lurking. Slayton's so-called saviour was nothing but a predator. He thought he was untouchable. She remembered how he had flirted with her, how she'd pulled away as he tried to drag her into his car. Anger rising, she forced herself to read on.

I told the father before I told my parents. It was too late to have an abortion by then. There was a meeting between the parents. An illegitimate child had not been factored into their son's life plans. A pay-out was offered, and a monthly amount for the rest of Christian's life. All I'd wanted was for someone to rescue me, but I hadn't the sense that God gave a goose. As Mom once said, 'If you can't play with the big dogs, stay under the porch,' and that's just what I did.

So my baby was born, and my parents used the hush money from the baby's grandparents to buy what would become my home. But my father was an abuser. DC Townsend has asked me if I would like to go into detail and I have declined. Just to say that what he called his 'blessings' ended when my son was four. Unknown to us, Christian became a witness to what my papa forced me to do. That's when I gained the courage to stand up and say *no more*.

Christian's father is Simon Irving. What a life he has made for himself. He has never missed a payment. I cannot fault him for that. But he's the same mean son of a bitch that

he always was. Christian is a good boy. I will always stand
by that. He had nothing to do with these murders, or this
Midnight Game business. He has cared for me as soon as
he was old enough to run and fetch. He is a quiet, loving
boy. All he's ever done is try to help. I would also like to
add that DC Townsend has offered to refer me to victim
support which I have declined.

'Oh Elsie,' Sarah said beneath her breath. If only she had known.
But she was barely fourteen years of age – how could she have
understood? Sitting at her desk, Sarah knocked back the last of the
coffee that Richie had kindly made her. No wonder Christian was
at Angelica's funeral – he was Simon Irving's son. She recalled him
throwing the picture of Elsie's father into the rubbish bin and the
haunted expression that seemed to be part of him. But didn't Elliott
carry a similar expression, and perhaps at times, even herself?

Christian wasn't the result of incest and Angelica was his
half-sister. Had she been suspecting the wrong person all this
time? But if Christian wasn't the Midnight Man – then who was?

38

Elliott sat in the middle of the school bus. The back was where all the noisy kids sat, and the front was too busy. He liked sitting in the middle on his own. The other kids teased him for not listening when they were talking, and when he did join in, he never said the right thing. His hands felt empty without his daddy's medal but he wasn't allowed to bring it to school. Not since Tommy Young tried to take it and Elliott screamed the classroom down. He got into trouble and Miss Grogan said his daddy was a hero, but the medal was too special and Elliott wasn't to bring it to school again.

As the bus chugged along, Elliott looked out the window. Lucy Mayweather slipped into the seat behind him. Elliott didn't like Lucy. Sometimes when Miss Grogan wasn't looking, Lucy stuck out her tongue. Lucy Mayweather and Tommy Young were best friends. Elliott hunched in his seat, feeling the thump, thump, thump of Lucy Mayweather's shoes as she kicked from behind. Tommy Young was laughing, but Elliott just sat forward in his seat, pretending she wasn't there. As the bus trundled along, his heart lifted at the sight of the small red car parked up outside his house. He wondered if Jahmelia had been found. Everybody was talking about her. They said a prayer in assembly and later they made new yellow ribbons to be tied around town. He wasn't sure how the ribbons were supposed to help but Miss Grogan said they would 'keep her in people's minds'.

Jahmelia was in Elliott's mind every hour of the day. Sarah had already phoned to ask if Elliott knew anything, but Elliott didn't like speaking on the phone. He wasn't sure if other people could listen in. He rose from his seat, taking care not to forget his schoolbag. Lucy Mayweather took the gum from her mouth and stuck it to the side of his bag. But all Elliott could think about was Jahmelia, as he felt her in the air. She was somewhere as black as night in a place that smelled like the school toilets the time they broke and wouldn't flush. He reached into his bag and took a sip of water from his refillable bottle. But the thirst he felt was Jahmelia's thirst, and not easily quenched.

He walked down his short driveway, his stomach clenched as he remembered Libby's words. '*If you tell, you'll go to hell.*'

Maggie opened the door to let him in, taking his schoolbag as he kicked off his shoes. 'There's chewing gum on your bag,' she said, tutting as she raised it in the air. 'How did that get there?' Elliott shrugged as Maggie pulled some tissue from beneath her sleeve and took it off.

'Did you learn anything new in school today?' She asked him that every day.

'No,' he replied, because he didn't want to think about school. Last week they studied the Galapagos Islands. He'd talked about that lots, telling Maggie that the group of islands had once been named 'islands of the tortoises.' When he was grown up he would go there, when things were better at home. He followed his mum through to the kitchen where Sarah was standing, holding a mug in the palm of her hand. She placed it on the table, next to his daddy's medal.

She said she wanted to talk to him about Jahmelia again, but Elliott didn't know what to say. All sorts of fears were shaking loose inside him, like rotten apples bouncing off a tree. '*If you tell, you'll go to hell.*' He was next. He slipped the medal into his trouser pocket.

'Chicken nuggets and chips OK?' Maggie said, even though there was a police officer in their kitchen wanting to know where his babysitter was.

'Yes please, Mummy.' He caught his mother's smile, small but real.

Last night Elliott had dreamed about the Midnight Man again. He decided to tell Sarah what he knew. Maybe he could be brave too, like his daddy.

'I saw him,' Elliott whispered, as Sarah sat beside him. 'He has two faces.'

'OK,' Sarah said. 'Can you draw him for me?' She glanced at Maggie who had her back turned, but Elliott knew she was listening in. 'If it's not too scary, that is.'

Within a few minutes, Elliott had sketched an image of a dark figure in a cloak. But there was a shadow falling over his face. He tried to explain to Sarah that the Midnight Man's two faces was something he *felt* rather than *saw*.

'You're doing great,' she said, taking the picture and putting it in her bag. 'If you think of anything else will you let me know, Elliott? Any time. We have all our best officers looking for Jahmelia. I'm sure we'll find her soon.'

As Elliott's dinner was placed before him, Sarah stood to leave. 'Oh, I almost forgot, I got this for you.'

She handed an envelope to Elliott and he recognised the WWF panda picture on the front.

'It's to adopt a turtle, mind, not a tortoise, but apparently only one in a thousand marine turtle hatchlings make it to adulthood. I reckon they need our help, don't you?'

Elliott's eyes widened as he carefully read the letter stating that a turtle had been adopted in his name. He'd receive a cuddly toy, a welcome pack, regular updates and more. 'Thank you!' he said, almost sending his dinner flying as he jumped from his chair to give Sarah a hug.

'Sarah, you shouldn't have,' Maggie said, but like Elliott, she was smiling too.

'Goodness, you're more than welcome,' Sarah laughed.

'C'mon, dinner!' Maggie said, ushering Elliott back to his chair. 'We'll look at the website after and find out more.'

Elliott sat back down and spread the letter next to his plate so he could read it over again. Marine turtles opened up a whole new world of facts to learn. For the first time that day, he felt happy inside. The scary man with the two faces was gone, for now. It was turning out to be a good day.

39

Elsie shifted in her bed. She just couldn't get comfortable. The mattress was so hard it felt like sitting on a dining table. It was with some pride that the doctors had showed her around their new 'obesity clinic'. A room with special scales and machinery, and down the corridor, a reinforced bed. It was no coincidence that Irving had funded the new wing. He was pre-empting any bad publicity should their relationship make the press. Now Elsie was their 'star patient' and staff were excited to work with her. Things sure had come a long way in the last few years. If she wasn't so darn worried about her son, she might have felt real hope. It was nothing short of a miracle that she'd survived her tumble down the stairs, let alone come out of it virtually unscathed. She'd had the wind knocked clean out of her and had gained a bump on her head the size of an egg.

Speaking of eggs . . . Elsie's stomach rumbled. What she wouldn't give for a Cadbury's Creme Egg right now. Her eyes narrowed as she gazed at the pink meal replacement drink which the doctors had offered after advising her about losing weight and meal plans. But she was one of the lucky ones. Her health insurance and this swanky new wing afforded her the best of care. Her mood brightened as she heard the click of heeled shoes in the hall. It was Sarah. Was she here to ask about the so-called Midnight Man? A flutter of fear swept through her. Just when things were working out . . . She recalled Christian's face as he found her on the floor. How he'd squeezed her hand before the ambulance took her away. Whatever she'd seen in his room, Christian wasn't capable of hurting those girls, she was sure of it. From now on, she would be putting him first. She would start by putting Detective Sarah Noble straight. It was time for Elsie to be a proper mother to her son.

40

Sitting in her car, Sarah sighed in contentment as she unwrapped her Big Mac. She'd promised herself numerous times that she would kick her junk food habit into touch. Seeing Elsie in the obesity clinic yesterday had certainly provided her with enough inspiration to maintain a healthy diet. She had even done an online shop and filled her fridge with healthy food. But that was all well and good as long as she could physically get home to cook it. Today, work had been manic as Sarah spoke to residents of Slayton and chased up every dead-end lead. Her eyes were dry in their sockets from watching hours of CCTV downloaded from cameras in town. No stone was to be left unturned, but much of it felt like a waste of her time. Now it was gone four thirty and she hadn't eaten all day. She closed her eyes, savouring each bite as the smell of freshly cooked fries filled the interior of her car. The windows steamed around her, cocooning her in her own little world. Tomorrow she would go full kitchen goddess and batch-cook lots of healthy food.

At least her hospital visit had been fruitful in more ways than one. Seeing Elsie so positive about her future had brightened her day. Her thoughts floated to Elliott. Seeing the boy and his mum happy had been heart-warming too. She wanted to be a part of Elliott's life, not just the police lady who questioned him, but first she had to put things right. The hooded image he'd drawn of the

Midnight Man could have come straight out of a comic book. Maybe it was time to just be Elliott's friend.

She turned down the car radio as a news reporter commented on how little information the police had released. 'Everyone's a critic,' she murmured, sipping her Diet Coke. Social media was flooded with #FindJahmelia, and the private Facebook group had grown. Blackhall Manor had gained a fresh wave of attention and new members were joining from all over the world. Sarah hadn't felt the need to participate herself yet. She didn't know where Richie found the time, and she couldn't fathom his fascination with her family's history . . . but there was too much going on right now for her to dwell on the past.

She turned on the ignition and activated the car fan. There wasn't much left for her to do today apart from see Gabby again. The office dynamics were guaranteed to change now her sergeant was pushed out, which was why Sarah was happy to spend the day out and about. Yvonne would lord it over everyone, as if she was the chief constable instead of acting sergeant. Still, Sarah gave her some grudging respect. She was managing the influx of work with apparent ease. She had the makings of a good sergeant if she wasn't so bloody obnoxious all the time.

Sarah hadn't told Elsie that an arrest package was being put together to bring Christian in. Officers were taking their time and doing the groundwork. They only needed suspicion of a crime to carry out an arrest, but the difficulty arose later with persuading the Crown Prosecution Service that they had enough evidence for a charge. The CPS would only approve cases which had a realistic chance of conviction in court. Timing was everything. Wait too long to arrest and they were at the risk of losing vital evidence.

Move too quickly and they might be underprepared and fail to get a charge. Sarah wasn't privy to every facet of the investigation but the team were doing everything in their power to bring Jahmelia home. So was she, even if some of her movements were off the radar. The irony was, she felt less sure of Christian's guilt now, since she'd spoken to his mother. After cleaning her hands with an antibacterial wipe, Sarah drove out of the McDonald's car park. Her shift was almost over and she knew where she had to go.

She had received Gabby's call just as she was leaving the hospital. As always, it was blunt and to the point. She wanted Sarah to act as her go-between. Gabby wasn't allowed access to the investigation, but Sarah could give her an insight into how things were being handled. Sarah didn't mind being put in an awkward position if it meant helping Gabby out. Time was slipping through their fingers. A huge push had been made in the search for Jahmelia, and police dogs had tracked her scent to the local playground. It seemed she'd snuck out to meet someone – the question was, who? Her parents' heartfelt press appeal was heavily featured in the media and online. DI Lee was doing a good job of drafting in specialist teams to help. From profilers to flyovers, he had requested it all. Reported sightings were trickling in but none had borne fruit so far.

Having gone off duty at the station, Sarah headed to Gabby's flat. The renovated four-floor townhouses were situated in Upper Slayton and built with professionals in mind. It was the go-to place for out-of-towners when it came to renting. Sarah had viewed them herself when she and David returned to Slayton. In the end, they rented the old post office cottage on the corner. One of her earliest memories was of her mother lifting her up to the red postbox to mail a letter. If she was lucky, on a sunny day they would buy an ice cream in the post office shop and eat it on the way home. Powerful emotions were invoked each time she caught the scent of the wisteria in full bloom. It was hardly any wonder she had been drawn to the place.

Thoughts of the past dismissed, Sarah parked her Mini next to the pavement and wrenched up the handbrake. The car was getting on in years and would soon have to be replaced. 'Not yet though, old girl.' She patted the steering wheel before glancing up at the window where Gabby was standing. She raised her hand uncertainly, but Gabby turned away. Her face was so gaunt, she could have been a ghost.

Sarah pressed her finger against the buzzer and waited for the door to click open. The stairwell was clean but cold and she smiled at a young woman as she passed her on the wide landing. She counted the numbers. At the end of the hall on the fourth floor was Gabby's flat.

'Hello?' she said, pushing open the front door which had been left ajar. The room was bright and spacious, with high ceilings and big windows behind plantation blinds, but as she entered she wondered if she had wandered into the wrong apartment. Clothes were draped over furniture, piles of newspapers were stacked on the table, and cardboard boxes filled every corner of the room. Gabby's walls were a stark eggshell blue throughout – no family photos or framed prints to give the room some character. It looked almost as if she'd been burgled, and what they hadn't taken they'd left in piles. Sarah's gaze roamed over the cream sofa which was littered with paperwork and 'Missing' posters of Jahmelia. The flat wasn't dirty, but it *was* a chaotic mess. It was a shock to see the state that such a competent, well-groomed woman was living in.

'Tea or coffee?' Gabby's voice rose from a kitchen just off the living room.

'Whatever you're having, milk, no sugar, thanks.'

'Make some room on the sofa,' Gabby said a minute later, carrying the cups in. Dark shadows beneath her eyes suggested sleep had been a stranger, but Gabby was still smartly dressed in a designer shirt and jeans.

'How are you doing?' Sarah said, after quickly updating her on the case.

As she sat across from her, Gabby's frustration was evident on her face. 'I'm not doing, that's the problem. I'm sitting. I'm pacing, I'm screaming at the television. I'm hounding Bryony for updates when *I* should be the one updating *them*! But I'm not *doing*. I should be in the office with the rest of the team. Both of us should.'

'Then go there,' Sarah said. 'Tell the DI you want in.' Sarah hadn't spoken to Bernard lately because he was so wrapped up in the case.

'I can't,' Gabby exhaled a terse sigh. 'He won't let me near the place. As for your acting sergeant . . .' She rolled her eyes. 'She thinks her shit's custard, that one.'

As she sipped her tea, Sarah bit back her smile. She could have told her about Yvonne's condescension this morning but decided to hold her tongue. One stirrer in the office was enough.

'I shouldn't have said that,' Gabby quickly followed up, her professionalism winning through as ever. 'Yvonne's doing her best. It's just frustrating . . .' Her gaze roamed to the window. 'I don't have a right to sit here in the warmth, not while Jahmelia is out there.' The low drone of a cello vibrated through the walls, and Gabby rolled her eyes in response. 'That's George. He practises for two hours every day.' She sighed wearily. 'It doesn't usually bother me because I'm always at work.'

'Jahmelia's still alive,' Sarah blurted out, leaning forward, cradling her cup. 'That's what Elliott told me.'

'Did you get anything else out of him?' Gabby didn't seem encouraged by the news, probably because she didn't have faith in Elliott's insights.

'Only that she's somewhere dark and cold, that smells bad. She's not in Blackhall Manor. Police have scanned every inch of that place.' Thermal imaging was quicker than physically ripping down the walls.

The cello practice continued. The musician was obviously talented, and the sweeping sounds were a comforting backdrop to their words.

'They've checked every derelict building in Slayton,' Gabby replied. 'They're drafting in extra teams to widen the search.'

Sarah's eyes flicked to the windows as shards of rain pelted the glass. The inclement weather would not help the search. 'She could be in Christian Abraham's car. He reported it stolen after Angelica disappeared.'

'Bernard said they're planning on bringing him in.' Gabby's brown eyes searched Sarah's face for answers. 'You've met him. Do you think he's capable of something like this?'

'Maybe,' Sarah said, feeling a surge of pity for the woman before her. 'But it's not sitting right with me. He found Libby. He called the police.' She rested her cup on a pile of books next to her feet. 'Angelica was his half-sister . . . Why would he want to hurt her? His father's supporting him financially. It doesn't make sense.'

'I hope it was him,' Gabby replied. 'Unless Christian talks, we'll never find Jahmelia. The game stops here.'

'The game doesn't stop until the Midnight Man says so,' Sarah thought aloud. The image of the players floated into her mind. The twins, each holding a candle. Angelica exploring Blackhall Manor, treating it all like a joke. Libby and Jahmelia, peer-pressured and putting on a brave face. What on earth had possessed them to play the Midnight Game? As Sarah looked at Gabby's face, her expression relayed that she was also deep in thought. They sat, allowing the cello music to wash over them from the other side of the wall. It was the saddest, most expressive piece of music Sarah had ever heard.

'Beautiful, isn't it?' Gabby said, her eyes heavy with unshed tears. 'He's very gifted.'

'He is.' Sarah held her gaze for a moment before looking away. It was hard to see so much pain. 'Do you need a hand unpacking?' She sipped the last of her tea. She could spare a bit of time to help out.

Gabby snorted. 'I've been here months, Sarah. If I had any intention of unpacking, I would have done it by now.'

'Right. Of course. Well, in that case, I'd best be getting off.'

Gabby tilted her head to one side, as if struck by a sudden thought. 'Don't you think it was odd, Irving turning up at the town meeting like that?'

'All in the name of Mammonism.' Sarah's voice was cynical and she took in Gabby's questioning look. 'The greedy pursuit of riches tantamount to devotion.' Her eyes fell on an old Missing poster of Angelica which was lying on the rug at her feet. 'I feel for him, I do. But there's a time and a place for talking business and that wasn't it.'

'Your English teachers must have loved you.' A sad smile rose to Gabby's face.

'Not when I was the one correcting them.' Sarah chuckled.

'Right, well, I'm going to do a lap around Blackhall Woods. Where did I leave my trainers?' Gabby bent to look beneath the sofa.

'And I'd better get going.' Sarah picked up her bag from the floor.

'Before you go,' Gabby rose, 'I know I read you the riot act when you came to me about Elliott.' A pause. 'I stand by my guns. But . . .' She rubbed the back of her neck. 'Thanks for speaking to him.'

'No problem,' Sarah said, sweeping her fringe out of her eyes. 'Anything you need, just ask.'

As she opened her car door, she felt Gabby's gaze on her as she stared out the window of her flat. She was a picture of isolation. Why wasn't she with her daughter? Why was she living alone? Sarah vowed anew to do what she could to help Gabby find her granddaughter. But it wasn't Elliott she needed to talk to. It was the Midnight Man.

41

Twilight fell softly as grey clouds rolled across the landscape. After a day of icy showers, a frosty snap was forecast. At least Sarah's cottage was toasty warm. It didn't feel right, being cosy at home when the rest of the team were working around the clock. Progress had been made. She had unearthed CCTV footage of Christian's car driving to Libby's house. The same car was captured in the area the night Jahmelia disappeared. But the image was grey and grainy, not giving up the identity of its driver just yet. Sarah knew she should be happy about the evidence, but she still felt like a dog chasing its own tail.

Yvonne seemed determined to keep Sarah out of the investigation. Only now could Sarah see that most people in the office tolerated Yvonne rather than liked her. At least she had one ally at work, and Richie had promised to text her with any big updates regarding the case. Pulling off her Marigolds, Sarah shoved them in the cupboard under the sink. Her house was the cleanest it had been in months. Gone were the pizza boxes and biscuit crumbs, and the wine stain had been scrubbed out of the rug which was now a shade lighter than before. She picked up Sherlock's food bowl and shook the kibble at the back door. It wasn't like him to stay out so late.

'Here, puss puss. Where are you?' Nothing. Strange. The company of a disgruntled cat was better than no company at all. Her husband's voice was fading, and not before time. She wondered if Yvonne would make a meal out of Sarah's link with Blackhall Manor, when the truth came to light. She'd given her enough gossip for now.

She poured herself a gin and tonic before opening up her laptop. Microsoft Word flashed up on the screen. She didn't remember leaving that open. In fact, she hadn't typed anything worthy of it in a very long time. As she clicked to shut it down a box appeared asking if she wanted to save the document she'd been working on. *What document?* she thought, about to click 'No', when she paused. Maximising the unsaved document, she began to read.

Dear **INCOMPETENT LOSER**

It's been interesting, watching you stumble from one disaster to another. As you amble into your office in your ill-fitting suit and cheap perfume, you could not look any more out of place if you tried. And it's not as if things improve when you open your mouth to speak. Have you seen the way your colleagues' eyes roll when you force your opinion on them? You're there out of pity, you know that, don't you? Why don't you have some self-respect and leave?

They don't want to hear your theories on the Midnight Man, Sarah. Do yourself a favour and leave them out of it. This is between you, me and Blackhall.

It's waiting for you. Deep down, you know you have to return. Hasn't enough blood been shed? It doesn't want Jahmelia, or those other silly girls. It wants you. You can knock it to the ground if you want, but its essence will remain. The game will be replayed until you answer the call. There's no shortage of candidates in Slayton . . . More teenagers can die. More innocent lives be ruined. That is, until you come home.

It's not as if you have anything to live for. Even your cat has left you. He's doing fine, by the way. I suppose you could go on talking to your husband, but he took the wise route out some time ago. So come, finish the game. You never know. You might even win.

I'll be in touch with further instructions. Remember, I'm watching. If you share this with anyone, Jahmelia will die, and the game starts all over again.

The Midnight Man

A sick feeling encompassed Sarah as a cold realisation drew in. Someone had typed this on her computer. In her house. As for Sherlock . . . had he taken him? Not Sherlock. She loved that miserable little bastard. Her eyes snapped away from the screen. 'Sher-lock!' The word echoed around the stillness of her home. 'Here, puss puss . . .'

Nothing.

Her shaking hand found her fringe as she imagined the intruder sitting at her laptop and spouting their bile. They were fearless, which made them dangerous. Part of her wanted to grab her car keys, leave this place and just drive. But she was rooted to the spot, just as she had been in the wardrobe of Blackhall Manor decades ago. Minutes passed as she stared at the screen, unconsciously tugging on her fringe. Should she call the police, or would she be giving Yvonne a bigger stick to beat her with? She could almost hear her condescending voice. Sarah was recovering from a breakdown.

There was no sign of forced entry in her home. Sarah could have written this herself.

She sat in the creeping silence, digesting the words on the screen. '*I suppose you could go on talking to your husband, but he took the wise route out some time ago.*' Each word was like a stab to the heart.

Her limbs jerked in fright as a motorbike backfired outside her home. This cottage was the one place in the world where she used to feel safe. Despite what happened to David, despite everything. It had been her haven, her hideaway. Part of a happy childhood memory. Now, she dreaded walking inside the door. The intruder had been right about her cat. He was also spot on about work. He seemed to see right through her. As she'd feared, Gabby had been wrong about the first letter. This was real, and it couldn't be any more personal. Had he taken those girls just to lure her in? Whoever the Midnight Man was, he knew her. He also knew about her husband.

Sarah allowed herself to visit the moment when her life, which she had so carefully rebuilt, came crashing down once more. She remembered the rain hammering like nails on the roof of her car as she drove home. Her planned day of shopping had been a total washout and she'd come back early with some goodies from the bakery for later on.

David's car was on the drive, and she'd been surprised that he wasn't at work. Calling his name, she entered the house, but there was no response. It was only when she placed her food shop on the kitchen counter that she saw the garden shed light was on. David called it his 'man shed', a place to watch the footie with a small TV and a mini fridge with some beers. With his job, he needed to decompress. But why was he in the shed when he'd had the house to himself? Holding her coat over her head, she ran down the muddy garden path, almost slipping on the way. 'David?' she'd called, pulling on the door. The light was still on, but there was no response. He usually answered before she reached it. She remembered peering in through the window. It was so high up, she'd had to stand on a bucket to see in.

By the time the ambulance came, she'd smashed a pane of glass and was trying to climb in. She hadn't noticed the blood running in rivulets down her hand as she tried to get to him. It wasn't to undo the clear plastic bag he had placed over his head. It was to save him the indignity of being found dead with his trousers undone. Back then, she couldn't make out what he'd been looking at on his computer as he suffocated. But the police did. They also saw the piles of images featuring underage boys and girls. There was nothing. No explanation. Just a shed full of porn.

The shock of it had hit Sarah with the force of a truck and made her question everything. She was twelve when they first met, and he was several years older. As she aged, the distance between them had grown. Perhaps he had always been a predator, but she hadn't allowed herself to see it. She relived the pain of both loving and hating someone at the same time. Like her father, he'd betrayed her without warning. She had had no idea, but had felt the shame of people's stares ever since. How could she not have known? He hadn't even meant to kill himself out of guilt for what he'd become. He'd been playing some kinky game. So why hadn't she been able to let him go?

When he first spoke, she knew he wasn't there. The voice that chipped away at her self-confidence may have sounded like her husband, but in reality, it was hers. 'Don't forget to buy some kitty litter.' That was the last real thing she said to him the day he died. It would have been funny if it wasn't so tragic. The idea of being on her own again had been too much to bear. No wonder she had lost the plot and had to be escorted out of work. Talking to David at home was one thing, but having full-blown conversations at work . . . her cheeks burned at the thought.

Sarah shook away the last threads of a memory she was ready to leave behind. It was time to reclaim her life. Not just from her husband but from Blackhall Manor too. The Midnight Man was coming, according to the letter before her. Sarah slammed down the lid of her laptop. Too many people had suffered. If it came down to her or Jahmelia, then she would not run away.

42

I pressed my ear against the boot of the car. Nothing. Was she even alive in there? My nose wrinkled as a faint whiff of bodily functions rose from the crack where the seal had gone. I didn't want to open it. Blood I could manage, but the image of Jahmelia smeared with tears, snot and faeces was enough to make me keep the boot closed. She may be just a kid, but her shit sure didn't smell of bubblegum. She had enough water to survive, assuming she could open the bottles with her hands tied at the front. She could bang and kick all she wanted against the rusted ice box, but nobody was coming, not out here.

Still . . . I should know if she was alive or dead. I looked over my shoulder. Clenching my hands into fists, I brought them down on the rusted metal, a smile creeping to my face. There was movement. A weak cry of despair. 'Help! Please!' Jahmelia croaked from within. But her movement was feeble. I imagined popping the boot. Her relief as she was enveloped by a whoosh of cold air. The gratitude the town would bestow upon me when she was found – not to mention the hefty reward. A small part of me could be satisfied with that. I had taught these girls a lesson. They would never be the same. But would I? I couldn't go back to the way things were. It was never about their deaths. It was the relentless compulsion to right a wrong. The more time I spent in Blackhall Manor, the more I understood the truth. I had never held so firm in my beliefs as when I lay beneath its roof. I couldn't give up on what I'd planned to do with Slayton's biggest loser cop.

A small, miserable groan echoed from the boot of the car. Jahmelia hadn't eaten and she was scrappy already, but she should survive the night. Not that I cared either way. I walked down the foggy path, kicking stones ahead of me. After what happened with Libby, I'd wanted to finish Jahmelia that night. The trick was to hold the blade firmly but gently against the skin, with slow, even pressure. I thought about Sarah's cat. A little bit of practice couldn't do any harm.

My plan had always been to kill off each player, leaving Sarah until last. But now the twins weren't at home, I didn't have anyone left to take. Police and press were hunting me, and time was a luxury I no longer had. My knowledge of Slayton's back roads had saved me from the roadblocks and police questionnaires. Part of me enjoyed being under their nose, but I could not contemplate getting caught. To the villagers of Slayton, I was an accepted member of the community and I had earned their respect.

I slipped out a strip of tablets from my jacket pocket. Popping two from the foil, I slid them in my mouth. This was bigger than all of us. Whatever the cost, I would see it through.

43

Sarah sat on the sofa, cradling a mug of tea. A repeat of a KCOM News report was on the local television channel. A young blond man with a red nose appeared half frozen as he stood outside Slayton police station. A bunch of disgruntled townspeople had gathered in the search for answers. People were scared. They needed someone to blame. As the reporter listed the police's perceived failings, he seemed more than happy to join in. Such pressure would ensure an arrest. The public needed to see results. She switched off the TV just as an image of Angelica flashed up on the screen.

Sarah had been the same age when her family was murdered. Was that why the Midnight Man had chosen them? What sort of agenda did he have? And what did he want with her? The question gnawed at her constantly, an unnerving hum in the background. As the room fell into silence, she glanced at Sherlock's empty chair, feeling guilty for worrying about her cat when there were parents in Slayton going through a living hell. Resting her mug on the coffee table, she turned over the page of the photo album she had borrowed from Maggie. Sarah didn't have many mementoes of the past, but tonight she was not reminiscing. She was looking for clues.

She scanned the photos, picking up things she had missed the first time around. Simon Irving, looking as arrogant as ever with his sweatshirt tied around his neck. Elsie, with her chubby cheeks and homemade clothes which made her look out of place. To think, what had gone on between her and Irving. It made Sarah uneasy in her seat. Switching her focus, she traced her finger over the image of her and David. The pain she felt at seeing her husband's picture didn't seem as raw as before. Next to her was Maggie, looking gorgeous in a T-shirt and red shorts, and towering above them both was Lewis, sporting floppy hair and his lopsided grin. He had a look of Elliott about him. With his long lashes and dark hair, she could see the resemblance now. But there was another dark-haired person in the background that she hadn't noticed the first time around. Was that . . . ? She peered at the image, wishing she could enlarge it. It was. Richie was standing in the background, clean-shaven and youthful, his motorbike jacket held over his shoulder with one finger. Half the town must have attended the outdoor cinema that night. She flicked through the rest of the photos, seeing who else she recognised. Even her DI, Bernard Lee, had turned up with his other half. He was a lot slimmer back then, but she'd recognise him anywhere. The album was a feast of memories and she felt sure the answers were in the past. They had to be. But who would hate her enough to want to make her life hell?

She flicked on the kitchen light, her heart heavy as she took in Sherlock's untouched bowl of food. Tomorrow, she would make up some posters and put them around town. Pressing her hand against the back door, she double-checked that it was locked. The hairs prickled on the back of her neck. Her house was beginning to remind her of Blackhall in the early days. She was spooked by every shadow. Dreading going to bed. She should be relieved that they were progressing Christian's arrest but while she appreciated

Richie's updates on the case, she couldn't reconcile the letters as having come from Christian. Her colleagues didn't have the full picture. Tomorrow she would bite the bullet and tell her DI about the letter on her laptop.

Sleep came quicker than Sarah had expected, her dreams haunted by a cloaked figure in black. She was back in Blackhall, running to Robin's room in a desperate attempt to save him. But his door-knob turned into a candle and melted away in her hand. As the cloaked figure approached, she was enveloped by a sense of knowing. That was when she caught a glimpse of his face. Gasping for breath, Sarah sat bolt upright in bed. Bathed in sweat, she untangled her feet from the sheets. It was just a dream, wasn't it? It couldn't possibly be true. But her hammering heart felt real enough. She peered around the room, searching every corner for a shadow. Had he been here? Switching off her light, she checked the time: 3.33 a.m. Rubbing her eyes, she shook off the nightmare. Was this how Elliott felt? Her dream had been so lucid. She'd heard the thud of heavy footsteps, felt the Midnight Man's breath on her neck. But it was the sense of recognition that bothered her the most. It felt stronger than any dream. The person behind the hood was someone she knew well. It compounded her instinct that they were hunting the wrong man. She looked at the clock again, remembering that 3.33 was when the Midnight Game was meant to end. She swung her feet out of bed and pulled on her dressing gown.

Satisfied the house was safe, she settled down with her laptop and searched for the Midnight Game online. Here, in the dim light of her lonely kitchen, Sarah found answers. All this time, she'd assumed the game was just a façade. But now as she read the

245

steps, they began to resonate. The game was played in a dark creepy building, where players knocked on a wooden door at midnight, inviting the dreaded figure in. Memories of Blackhall Manor rose in her mind. The power had been out the night her family died. If your candle extinguished it meant the Midnight Man was near. Sarah recalled waking at midnight as the first boom of gunshot filled the air. Tears pricked her eyes as she read the rules of the game. If the player couldn't relight their candle within ten seconds, they had to make a salt circle and stay in it until 3.33 a.m. A sad sigh left Sarah's lips. There had been no salt circle to protect her family on the night they died. She swallowed back her tears as she read on. '*If you are unsuccessful in your actions the Midnight Man will create a hallucination of your greatest fear.*' Sarah tugged her fringe. Her greatest fear was revisiting Blackhall Manor. Then it hit her. The killer had involved her from the start, but only now could she see to what extent. 'It's about me,' she whispered, her words brittle with shock. 'It's all been about me.'

44

After taking a seat in the DI's office, Sarah waited for him to come off the phone. The air was warm and stuffy, carrying a lingering smell of coffee and stale breath. It reminded her of her probationer days, sitting in a smelly office, waiting for a progress report. She wanted to crack open a window, just as she'd had the urge to back then. But as she sat before her senior officer, her bottom felt glued to the chair.

Being the oldest in her intake, she had always stuck out like a sore thumb. Unlike the younger trainees, she'd enjoyed hours of daily study and relished the weekly written tests. It wasn't that she was a swot, she was just so bloody grateful to be there. Being a police officer was her lifelong dream. But her husband hadn't shared her enthusiasm. 'You've been through enough trauma,' he used to say. 'Why would you want to take on anyone else's?' But it wasn't about taking on more than she could handle. It was about making her survival mean something. Today she needed to make her DI listen.

She'd kept her head down during police training and worked through each challenge as it arose. Now, more than ever, Sarah knew she had done the right thing. She would make it as a detective, if she was given half a chance. She would start by finding the Midnight Man. She already had her suspicions, but she could not say them aloud. Not until she had proof. If her suspicions were proved right, the identity of the killer was a bombshell which would cause tremors far and wide. She returned her attention to Bernard as he came off the phone.

'How are you doing?' he said, in his usual jovial tone. Her gaze fell to the paracetamol packet, and the empty coffee cups. He looked tired, and she could see the pressures of the investigation were taking their toll.

'All ship-shape,' Sarah pre-empted his usual question about her mental health. She didn't want to be here, wasting his precious time when Jahmelia still hadn't been found.

'I hear you've been going solo, making visits to our number one suspect.'

Sarah's eyebrows shot up. Was he talking about Christian? His comment came as a surprise. Bernard interlocked his fingers and rested them on the desk. 'There's nothing wrong with you wanting to paddle your own canoe, but it's early days for you. Don't take on too much.'

Sarah looked at him quizzically. 'I'm not with you. Everything's fine as far as I'm concerned.'

But her DI gave her a look which suggested otherwise. 'One of your colleagues has expressed concerns.' The clock on the wall ticked loudly as Sarah absorbed his words.

'Yvonne.' A tight smile rose to her face.

Bernard didn't deny it.

'She's a bully, you know that, don't you?'

Bernard's chair creaked as he leaned forward, his voice deep and mellow. 'If you're raising a complaint of workplace bullying, I'll have to take this further.'

Sarah shook her head. 'It was an observation, not a complaint.' She hadn't come here to talk about Yvonne.

'We had a long chat about you,' Bernard continued. 'I furnished her with details of your background.' He raised a hand as Sarah took a breath to complain. 'It's all out in the open now. It's for the best. I wanted a united front all round.'

Sarah swallowed down the bile rising up her throat. So everyone knew who she was.

'Yvonne is a fine detective. I'd rather you work with her than against. Keep your feet on the ground, that's all I'm asking. And don't be afraid to ask for help.' He looked at Sarah thoughtfully. 'Isn't it time you thought about getting rid of Blackhall Manor anyway? It's nothing but a millstone around your neck.'

'Maybe . . .' she said. The feeling of unfinished business lingered. She opened her mouth to speak but the words would not come. Bringing up the letter now could backfire massively. Would he think she had written it to begin with? Given his 'long chat' with Yvonne, Sarah didn't stand a chance of being taken seriously. If she had a physical letter they might believe her . . . but something written on her laptop, with no sign of forced entry into her home? She could be kicked off the team. Bernard's view of her was tainted, at least until she proved she was perfectly sane.

'Champion,' Bernard said, oblivious to her inner torment as the phone on his desk rang.

'See you later then,' she said, before leaving the room.

Sarah paused outside her DI's office as she kept her annoyance in check. *Keep your feet on the ground indeed.* The bloody cheek of it. It wouldn't surprise her if Yvonne had implied she'd made the first letter up. As for the second . . . she would keep that to herself. Bernard saw her as broken, rather than someone who'd had the strength of character to get out of the hole she was in. *What doesn't kill you gives you coping mechanisms,* Sarah thought. She would prove them all wrong. If the Midnight Man wanted her to play the game then she was ready for him. It didn't mean he would win.

45

Today, Sarah joined her colleagues with renewed determination. She was too immersed in the case to be nervous anymore. She rested her bag on her desk. It contained a new planner which mapped out her week. A small thing, but a sign she was getting her life together. Today's word of the day had stuck in her mind – concatenation – a chain of events. The problem was, while she was focusing on the chain of events concerning her letters, her colleagues were determined to nail Christian Abraham.

'Good news,' Yvonne said, her head rising from behind Gabby's computer. 'With the evidence stacked against Abraham I'm confident we'll get a charge.'

'That's great,' Sarah replied, taken aback as her acting sergeant updated her. It wasn't like Yvonne to keep her in the loop.

'Tell that to your face.' Yvonne eyeballed her as she stood. 'You're not still chewing yourself up over Elsie's journal, are you? Book it in to Property and attach it to the case if you're so concerned.'

Sarah nodded, thin-lipped, as she waited to sit. She missed Gabby. She'd been texting her regular updates but she wanted her at the helm. She opened her drawer and pulled out a clean mug.

'I thought you'd be happy about the arrest,' Yvonne said, her perfectly arched brows rising. 'Christian Abraham's fingerprints were found in both Libby and Jahmelia's houses, plus we've got his car on CCTV.'

Sarah knew about the CCTV, given she was the one who viewed it. 'The driver was wearing a bally, wasn't he?' She stood with her mug in hand, unable to hold her tongue. Thanks to Richie texting her updates, she was up to speed on the case.

Yvonne nodded. 'We found remnants of a balaclava being burned in his back yard.'

Sarah could see where she was coming from. She could testify about the fire on the day she called around. On paper, it seemed a strong case. But she could no longer equate the shy, awkward gamer she'd met with the Midnight Man. She resisted the urge to point these things out. If Yvonne was willing to make an effort, then so should she.

She undid the top button of her shirt. The office was like a furnace. It was either stuffy from the radiators pumping at full blast or freezing as winds of *Game of Thrones* proportions flooded in through the open windows. She was about to walk away to make herself and Richie a cuppa when Yvonne stepped closer to her. For once, her voice was low.

'The letter you got makes more sense, now we know who you are. And I'm sorry if I didn't give you the warmest of welcomes. I hope we can wipe the slate clean.'

She looked at her so earnestly that Sarah forced a smile. 'Of course.'

'Good. Because I've been talking to Bernard and we've both agreed you should be more involved in the case. I want you to observe Abraham's interview. So log in, check your emails, and make yourself a coffee. Richie will be interviewing in twenty minutes or so.'

'Thanks,' Sarah said. '*Both agreed*', *my backside*, she thought as she walked to the communal kitchen. It was obvious Bernard was pulling the strings. Yvonne was only nice to her because the DI told her to be. But that was fine by Sarah. She needed all the help she could get.

Sarah followed Yvonne to the recently decorated monitor room. It wasn't much bigger than a broom cupboard, with slate-grey carpet tiles replacing the worn-out blue. Magnolia walls brightened the windowless space, which was big enough to house a desk, computer monitor, telephone and three chairs. It wasn't like on TV crime shows with the benefit of a two-way mirror and speakers, but it was an effective way of observing an interview from another room. A microphone and earpiece were also available, should the person monitoring wish to communicate with the officer holding the interview. Today, Richie was interviewing.

Yvonne flicked on the lights.

'I'm surprised Gabby hasn't been in,' Sarah said, pulling the swivel chair back from the desk. She thought her sergeant wouldn't be able to keep away.

'We haven't told her that we've brought him in – not yet. We don't need her interference, she's been a real pain in the . . .' Yvonne seemed to remember her audience. 'Anyway, we'll update her after the interview. Hopefully we'll have some good news then.'

A flutter of butterflies rose in Sarah's stomach as she watched the empty interview room through the desktop computer. She wanted to be in the heart of the action, but monitoring was a step up from knocking on doors. 'It's a shame we couldn't have observed him to see if he would lead us to Jahmelia.'

Yvonne didn't disagree, but Sarah knew obtaining permission for undercover surveillance would tie them up in red tape. As Yvonne stood over her, the sweet scent of her perfume filled the air.

They watched the monitor as the interview-room door opened and Abraham was led inside. Sarah's spirits lifted as Richie appeared with Christian. *This should be interesting,* she thought. In their shirts and ties, they could have both passed as police officers. But at a closer look, Richie carried himself with confidence, while Christian's face was pale, his head bowed. Given it was such a serious offence, Sarah was surprised to discover Christian had declined free legal advice. This was a first account interview and the decision had been made for Richie to take the lead. A younger officer sat next to him and readied himself to make notes. Interviews for serious offences could go on over the course of days, provided they could get an extension past the permitted twenty-four hours. The purpose of this interview was to obtain a quick and dirty account of Jahmelia's whereabouts. The rest would come in time. Richie began with the usual preliminaries of cautioning the suspect and ensuring he was aware of the offences he was arrested for.

'Enjoy,' Yvonne said, heading towards the door. 'I've got an interview of my own to make. Update the system straight away if he coughs it.' A 'cough' was what they called a confession, although Sarah couldn't see that happening anytime soon.

Sarah watched as the door clicked shut. *That's some personality change. Bernard really must have gone to town on her.* Perhaps she wasn't the only one to mention her bullying behaviour. She wouldn't put it past Richie to have had a word. Sarah relaxed in her chair, engrossed in the interview. Preliminaries over, Richie began with open questions. Each one was met with a grunt or a shake of the head.

Rolling up his shirt sleeves, Richie pinned Christian with a gaze. 'The evidence is mounting up against you, Christian. It's better for you if you come clean. Where is Jahmelia?'

Christian opened his mouth but seemed to think better of it and snapped it shut again. Richie wouldn't disclose all the evidence they had against him just yet. That would come later.

'I'll ask you again,' Richie pressed. 'What have you done with Jahmelia? Because we've got teams of officers scouring the area. It's better for you if you tell us where she is.'

Sarah was well versed in interview techniques, it was her favourite part of training. But she couldn't see Yvonne unleashing her upon a suspect anytime soon. It was good to watch Richie in action. She had warmed to him since she'd got to know him, but he wasn't making much headway with Christian yet. She watched as Richie turned his laptop. It displayed images of Christian's car on CCTV, taken at the gated community where Libby lived.

'That wasn't me,' Christian said dully. 'My car was stolen.'

He picked up a disposable plastic cup of tea that Richie had brought in for him. His face soured as he took a sip. Sarah didn't blame him. Custody tea was made with cheap tea-bags, powdered milk, and tasted like lukewarm dishwater. Beneath the table, his knee bobbed as nerves seemed to set in.

'We have your fingerprints in Libby's home. Jahmelia's too.' Richie remained cool. 'Can you tell me how they got there?'

'I'm an estate agent,' Christian said quietly, staring at the plastic cup. 'I've been in lots of homes.'

Sarah watched him closely. He was nervous, but she sensed he was telling the truth. The image of the car they had captured on CCTV showed the driver had been wearing what appeared to be leather gloves. She rubbed the back of her neck. This wasn't going well.

Richie picked up a clear plastic bag from the floor. 'Then why did you burn a black balaclava in a barrel at the back of your home?' He pointed to the photo of the CCTV image of a man in a balaclava driving his car. Richie reeled off the exhibit number for the benefit of the recording as he waited for Christian to reply. All Christian had to say was that he was burning some old clothes. Lots of people owned balaclavas. It wasn't strong enough evidence to pin the crime on him. But Christian was glaring at the bag, his lips parted in surprise.

'I . . . I don't know. That's not mine.' He looked at Richie. 'Mom's in hospital. I was clearing the house of some of her old clothes.'

'Well, I seized it myself from your back garden,' Richie replied.

Officers had attended after the arrest and carried out a complete search. It was fortunate the item hadn't burnt away completely. But it was the look on Christian's face that had come as a surprise.

'I swear . . . I've never seen it before,' Christian reiterated, beginning to gnaw his thumbnail.

'I'm now showing you exhibit DR02.' Richie picked up another exhibit bag from the floor. 'An ivory-handled knife, found in your bedroom. Believed to be the same murder weapon which ended Angelica Irving's life. Is this yours?'

'No!' Christian's voice broke mid-way as it echoed around the room. 'It's not mine. I've never seen it before.'

'Then I would also like to bring your attention to these photographs of Elsie Abraham's injuries.' Again, Richie reeled off the exhibit numbers. 'Did you push your mother down the stairs?'

Christian shook his head vehemently. 'No! I love my mom. She fell down the stairs when I was at work. Ask her.'

'Did you kill Angelica Irving?' Richie fired another question.

'No!' Christian's response was louder this time. Sarah squirmed in her chair as she watched the interaction. If Christian was lying, he was putting on a hell of a good show. He looked as if he was about to cry.

'What have you done with Jahmelia?' Richie continued, before being stalled by the knock on the interview-room door. Sarah peered at the screen as the door opened. People weren't meant to interrupt interviews like this. Sarah recognised the officer from the custody block. He introduced the solicitor who stood behind him. He did not appear best pleased. Richie paused the interview as he dealt with the interruption. It seemed Simon Irving had hired legal advice. There would be no confession today.

46

Elliott didn't like the woman with the drawn-on eyebrows. She told him to call her Yvonne, and she said she was Sarah's boss. She acted all nice to Maggie, but she had sharp edges and cold eyes. She looked at Elliott warily, as if he was going to jump out at her and take a bite. They'd had to leave school during lunchtime to come and see her in the police station. Sitting on the sofa, he gazed around the room. This was a different part of the police station, Yvonne explained. He wasn't in trouble. He was just being helpful and this was the place where victims and witnesses came to speak.

Except there were cameras in each corner of the ceiling watching him. Elliott squirmed, feeling the heat of their gaze. At least his mum was sitting beside him. He scooted up closer to her on the squishy blue sofa. She put her arm around his shoulders and gave him a squeeze. The room was cold, and he shrank his hands up into the sleeves of his jumper. There were pictures on the wall and flowers on a table, but it didn't feel homely. It felt like he was on stage.

'You're not in any trouble,' Yvonne said again, crossing one leg over the other. 'We just want to ask you a few questions.' Yvonne had already told his mummy that they had rested someone, although Elliott wasn't entirely sure what that meant. At least they were trying to find Jahmelia, and that meant talking to everyone she knew.

And so the questions came. How did Elliott know about the Midnight Man? How did he know where Angelica had been buried? Who told him? Had someone put him up to it? Did he know where Jahmelia was? Had he heard them talking when they were babysitting? Had anyone told him to keep a secret? On and on, the same questions in different ways. But Yvonne didn't seem to like his answers, as she kept asking more. 'So nobody mentioned the Midnight Game to you? Are you sure?'

Elliott sighed. 'I'm sure.' His throat was scratchy and he was tired of talking. He just wanted to go home.

'Yeah, yeah,' she replied, without really listening. 'So how *did* you know about the Midnight Man, Elliott?'

'I dreamt it,' he said again. She wouldn't understand if he told her about the pictures that filled the spaces of his head. He stared at his school shoes. While other kids thought about computer games, he had flashes of feelings and pictures that he could not understand.

He hadn't realised that he'd been rocking until the detective asked if he was OK. He looked at her with curious eyes. She had darkness in her too. Maybe they were all fighting their own demons.

A rush of blood painted Yvonne's cheeks as she looked away.

'We need to get back to school,' Maggie said. 'He's answered all your questions.' Elliott was glad his mummy was there to stand up for him. He didn't want to think about Jahmelia. He wasn't sure that he'd see her alive again. If he did, she would be like Libby, not the same. Like one of his puzzles but without the best pieces. Blackhall Manor took the best from everyone who went there. He looked around the room, past the people and past the walls.

He could feel Jahmelia sleeping now, dreaming of a family she may never see again. Outside, a police siren blared, making him blink thoughts of her away. Yvonne was still asking questions, as if Maggie hadn't spoken up at all. 'I don't know where Jahmelia is,' he answered when the detective asked about her. 'Somewhere dark. And small. She's cold and thirsty and it smells . . .' He lifted a finger to his nostrils as the stench became too much. 'Smells bad. Like poo.'

'Yeah? Go on . . .' Yvonne smiled as she scribbled on her notepad.

Elliott tried to chase the thought but it was gone. It was more than he'd meant to say. Maggie squeezed his shoulder a little tighter this time. She always told him to keep things to himself, but he really wanted to find his friend. Then all of a sudden a thought entered his mind which made him sick with fear. *If you tell, you'll go to hell.* When the Midnight Man was finished with Jahmelia, he was coming for him.

'You did great,' Maggie said, as they walked out to the hall. She drew him close like she could feel his worry. 'How much longer will the police be in our house?' she asked Yvonne.

'Not long,' Yvonne replied, bouncing on her heels as she walked with them down the hall. 'But we appreciate you giving us permission for the search.' All residents in Slayton were being visited by the police in case Jahmelia was hiding out somewhere. Elliott stole a glance up at Yvonne, but she would not meet his gaze. The hallway was long and bright, with posters on the walls.

'I hear you're a friend of Sarah's,' she continued. 'Sarah Noble. She's been telling us all about you – and Elliott.'

'I've known Sarah since school,' Maggie answered.

'Yeah, yeah,' Yvonne replied.

Elliott scratched his nose. Yvonne said 'yeah, yeah' a lot. It meant she wasn't really listening at all.

'Sarah's only a statement taker, barely out of probation, in fact,' Yvonne continued. 'But she does her best, bless her.'

'I'm sure she's a very capable officer,' Maggie replied, as they got to the door.

'Oh, what am I like?' Yvonne smiled, in no hurry to let them out. 'I've spoken out of turn. Sarah's a great little officer. She's very pragmatic. Doesn't believe in all this superstitious nonsense. She's always said that there's a logical answer for Elliott's behaviour.'

'And what do you mean by that?' Maggie's voice grew sharp. 'Because I don't like your tone. It's bad enough officers are traipsing through my house . . . Elliott's done nothing wrong.'

Yvonne's hand touched her mouth. 'Oh my goodness, I'm so sorry, Mrs Carter, I didn't mean to offend you. Elliott *has* been helpful. We're all so worried about Jahmelia. If we've seemed . . . aggressive with our methods then I apologise. If Elliott was missing, we'd do the exact same. Please don't take it personally.' She flashed them both a smile before opening the door.

Elliott blinked in the sunlight. Felt his mother relax a little next to him as she spoke. 'Of course. I understand.' But Yvonne had been mean about Sarah. He could see it on her face when she spoke. His schoolteacher, Miss Grogan, said if everyone was kind then the world would be a happier place. Elliott liked Miss Grogan a lot.

As his mother ushered him into the car, Elliott took her by the hand. 'I don't like that police officer. She's not a nice lady,' he said.

'Yes, seems that way,' Maggie replied as Elliott strapped himself in. 'But don't you worry about it, sweetheart. You've done all you can for Jahmelia. I'm sure they'll find her soon.' She closed the car door before he could answer. Elliott chewed on his bottom lip. Had he done the wrong thing by speaking up? He would talk to Sarah. She would help find Jahmelia. Because something told him she was the only one who could.

47

Sarah dropped a tuna sandwich onto Richie's desk. She had gone on a four o'clock sandwich run to the new bakery in the centre of town after finding out some of her colleagues hadn't eaten all day. But the new owner, Lisa Davis, had given her a grilling before she left, pressing her for details of the case. Sarah had listened patiently before offering reassurance, telling her not to believe everything she read in the press. It felt good to be back in the office. To feel like she finally belonged. The revelation of her identity, something she had always feared, had gained her a quiet acceptance.

'Thanks for this.' Richie twisted the lid off the bottle of Diet Coke that she had also deposited on his desk.

'How's it going?' she said, glancing over his shoulder as he tapped his computer keyboard. She squinted, trying to read the Word document on his screen. But as he spun his chair around to face her, she quickly averted her gaze.

'Slowly,' he replied. 'Thanks to his super-duper lawyer, Abraham is now answering "no comment" to everything.' Richie nodded towards Yvonne. 'How's she treating you?'

'She's been strangely nice, now the cat is out of the bag.'

'Nah.' Richie swigged his Diet Coke. 'She's keeping the DI on side.' He tilted his head in Sarah's direction. 'What's the deal with you and Bernard?'

Sarah's gaze narrowed. Had Richie been speaking about her to the DI? 'There is no deal. He played golf with my husband. They were friends.' She scanned the room. Everybody else was getting on with their work. Yvonne left the office, paperwork in hand.

Sarah leaned against Richie's desk. 'Why are you asking about the DI?'

'I'm just figuring things out. He's very protective of you, isn't he?'

Sarah's eyes widened. 'We're not carrying on, if that's what you mean.' She spoke in a harsh whisper, mindful of her colleagues.

'None of my business if you are.' Richie raised his hands in the air.

'Then why ask?' She took the chair next to him, her voice low. 'Is that what people are saying? Did you speak to him about me?'

'Sarah,' Richie smiled. 'Chill. Nobody's saying anything. I'm just trying to get a handle on the DI. He plays golf with Irving too. They're pally, from what I've heard.'

Sarah's frown deepened. 'What are you getting at?'

Richie returned his attention to his sandwich. 'Nothing. He's probably part of some old boys' club.'

Sarah watched as Richie chewed, a faraway look on his face.

'You're one of those conspiracy theorists, aren't you?' she said, thinking of his interest in the Facebook group. 'I bet you believe in UFOs.'

Richie laughed. 'There's nothing wrong with getting to the truth.' He wiped his mouth with the back of his hand. 'I just can't figure out why our DI has taken such a liking to you.'

'Geez, kick a girl while she's down, why don't you?'

'I don't mean it like that.' He scrunched up his sandwich wrapper and threw it in the bin.

'Not everyone has an angle.' Sarah returned her glance to the document Richie was putting together post-interview, keen to change the subject. 'You think CPS will give you a charge?'

'We've got a strong case against Abraham, especially after finding the knife in his room. But find his car, and I think we'll find Jahmelia – that's if he hasn't buried her somewhere already.'

'She's still alive,' Sarah said. 'At least, for now.' She shook her head. She couldn't imagine what Gabby was going through. All day, she'd been texting, and Sarah passed on updates when she could.

'You sound confident.' Richie rubbed his beard. A look passed between them. 'You know something, don't you?'

Sarah's gaze flickered around the office. 'Maybe,' she said. 'But I can't tell you. Not yet. I've got a line of communication open and I don't want to blow it.'

'With who?'

'You wouldn't believe me if I told you. There's more to this than meets the eye.'

Richie regarded her with interest. 'Tell me.'

A beat passed between them. Could Sarah trust him? Maybe two heads were better than one. 'All that stuff . . . the balaclava that didn't burn, the knife. The CCTV of Christian's car. It's too convenient. Sure, Christian's a bit of an oddball, but doesn't that make him the perfect candidate to set up?'

'I don't know . . .' Richie paused for thought. 'Seems prima facie to me.'

'And that doesn't bother you?' Sarah said. Not all cases were open and shut.

'For every argument, there's a counter-argument,' Richie replied. 'Irving was a complete bastard to Christian's mother and barely acknowledged him as a son . . . Killing Angelica could have been Christian's way of getting revenge. You should see the computer games he plays. The guy isn't right in the head.'

Sarah had been ready to disclose the Word document but his last sentence gave her pause. It wasn't that long ago people were saying the same thing about her. Having mental health issues didn't make you a murderer, but it did make people view you through a different lens. She thought her response over.

'Whoever it is hates me with a passion. You saw the letter on the system, didn't you? They're using Blackhall Manor as a tool to get to me. If you dig deep into the Midnight Game you'll see it's directed at me. Why choose Blackhall Manor? Why choose a fourteen-year-old girl? And why involve me?'

But Richie was looking at her blankly. He didn't understand.

Sarah sighed. She wasn't opening herself up to further ridicule. 'Just don't be blinkered to other explanations, that's all I'm saying.'

'Alright!' Richie brushed the crumbs off his desk. 'I'll keep an open mind.' But his gaze lingered, and she could see there was something else on his mind.

'What is it?' Sarah said, noticing his expression change.

'It's about Blackhall Manor. I've been waiting for the right time to tell you.'

'Now is as good a time as any.'

Richie nodded towards their DI's old office.

266

'The confessional?' Sarah's heart skipped a beat in her chest. 'What's so important you want to drag me in there?'

'C'mon,' Richie said, rising from his desk. Sarah followed him in. The narrow room was lit by a fluorescent light and flanked by walls of files either side. She rubbed her damp palms against the back of her trousers. Whatever this was, it wasn't good.

Richie's face was a picture of awkwardness and concern. She was getting to know his expressions and learning to read between the lines. This wasn't about Christian. This was personal. She watched him clear his throat as he stood with hands on hips.

'You know the crawlspace in Blackhall Manor where Libby was held?'

'What about it?'

'The search team found a gun silencer covered in cobwebs. It's not related to this case.'

'Go on.'

Richie took a step towards her. 'Sarah . . . it looks like it's been there years. CSI found fragments of blood on it. It's been sent for testing.'

'Oh God,' Sarah said softly, feeling like she'd been punched in the chest. This was relating to her family's case. This was in connection with their deaths. But her father didn't use a silencer. That much she knew. She forced herself to stay calm. Richie's hand was warm as he touched her arm.

'Are you OK?'

Needing to distance herself, Sarah took a step back. 'Whose blood?' she whispered. 'You know, don't you?'

Richie shook his head. 'Not yet. But it fits the shotgun that killed your family.'

Sarah stared into space, the words a blur as she processed the news. 'I heard each one of those shots ring out. They were like thunder. The only shot I didn't hear was my father's.' Her cheeks were burning now. The last thing she wanted was to make a scene, but the memory flooded her mind. 'My ears were ringing after he shot through the wardrobe. My vision was blurry with blood. But I remember lying there, my eyes half open as the police came for me. I should have heard something when my dad turned the gun on himself.'

'We don't know anything, not until the results come back.'

'Who's authorised the testing?'

'Bernard. He's fast-tracked it. He asked me to break the news.'

Sarah nodded in understanding. So that's why Bernard had called her in to see how she was doing. It was also why he'd instructed Yvonne to go easy on her. But as well as he knew her, he hadn't been able to break the news himself.

'Five o'clock, Ms Part-Timer – home time!' Yvonne's high-pitched voice broke the moment as she stuck her head in. Some things never changed. She took in Sarah's face and paused. 'Everything OK?'

'Yes,' Sarah said. But her hands were shaking. 'Thanks for letting me shadow you, Richie, I'll leave you in peace now.'

'Are you sure?' he said. 'Because if you need to talk . . .'

'Nope, all good here. Have a productive evening.' Forcing one foot before the other, she grabbed her coat and bag.

She needed to get away. She needed time to think. All these years she had blamed her father. What if it was his blood on the silencer? He could have been murdered first . . . his so-called suicide staged. That must be what Richie was thinking. She saw it written on his face. As Sarah pulled on her coat and left, theories ran wild in her mind. If her father wasn't responsible for the murder of her family, then who was?

48

Maggie sat next to her husband's bedside, just as she had done every week for the past year. It was a long and painful process, watching him battle with his illness and she wasn't sure how much longer she could do this for. As always, she masked her feelings as she talked to Lewis, who stared vacantly at the wall.

'And Sarah adopted a turtle in Elliott's name. Honestly, you should have seen his face. He was so happy. Anyone would think she'd brought it in and physically handed it to him.' She smiled at the memory. 'Now all he talks about is turtles. He's been learning all the facts and even drew up a chart comparing turtles and tortoises. I told him he should get a job in a zoo when he grows up. You know what he said?' She squeezed her husband's hand, knowing better than to expect a response. 'He said he wants to be a marine biologist. Isn't that great?'

But Lewis's hand remained limp, his gaze vacant.

Maggie swallowed back the tightness in her throat. She had already told him about this morning's interview, and how brave Elliott had been. If anything, the investigation had provided her with a talking point. Telling her husband about every facet of her life was better than sitting in silence, listening to the clock tick away each long minute in his company. What she'd give for his support right now. She thought about Yvonne and the way she had spoken to them in such a patronising tone. Recalled the way her face had soured when she spoke Sarah's name. How she had looked at Elliott, physically shuddering when they first met. Someone should bring her down a peg or two. She walked to the window and stared out into the car park.

'Not much of a view, you'd think they'd give you better for what it costs to keep you here.' But there were trees nearby, and sometimes birdsong. Not today. Today everything felt cold and bleak. All the rain from the last week was beginning to turn to ice. Winter was coming and it was biting down hard. She glanced at the skeletal trees, enveloped by a shroud of mist. 'I'd better not stay too long,' she said. 'The fog is coming down.' Returning to her chair, Maggie crossed her legs. Sarah coming into her life felt like a chance for a new start. She should never have doubted her friend.

Sarah had once asked Maggie if people in Slayton were cursed. How could she tell her that she sometimes wondered if karma was knocking at her door? Maggie was not the true friend that Sarah thought she was. But she had paid for her misdemeanours, hadn't she? With her husband's prolonged illness, and her son the way he was. She thought of Elliott and how easy he found it to talk to his new 'Auntie Sarah' as he had begun to call her. They had quickly forged a bond and Sarah made him happy. How could she take that away from him? As for Sarah – Maggie knew she saw a little of her brother Robin in him. If she found comfort in their friendship then where was the harm? Maggie's white lie had been so many years ago. But what started off as a snowball had now become an avalanche. Would Sarah forgive her when she discovered the truth? She needed her friend in her life. Being an army wife had been hard. She'd gotten used to Lewis's long absences over the years, but now it felt like he would never come home. She couldn't face the future with just her and Elliott. She needed her friend's support.

'I miss you,' she said, returning her attention to her husband who hadn't moved an inch. 'I wish you could tell me what to do.' But all she heard was the rattle of a medication trolley passing their door and the tick of the clock on the wall.

49

His fleece blanket wrapped around his shoulders, Elliott sucked the last drop of liquid from his Teenage Mutant Ninja Turtles water bottle. Mummy didn't like him drinking at bedtime in case he wet the bed but it didn't come close to quenching his thirst. He needed to speak to Sarah, but he was meant to be asleep. Jahmelia needed his help. Time was running out, and the Midnight Man was getting closer. He could feel him in the shadows, waiting and watching. But the world was so big, and Elliott's voice was so small.

Maggie had been quiet since coming back from visiting Daddy. When Elliott told her the sandwich she toasted was empty, she looked like she was going to burst into tears. Now, her voice was rising from the hall as she spoke to someone at the front door. Elliott strained to hear. It was Sarah!

'You're out late,' Maggie said, allowing her inside. 'I was just about to go to bed.'

Elliott's face scrunched in disapproval at the lie. Mummy wasn't going to bed, she had just opened a bottle of wine. He saw it on the coffee table next to her glass when he sneaked into the kitchen to refill his water bottle.

'I was worried,' Sarah replied. 'You weren't answering your phone.' Sarah took an envelope from her bag and handed it to Maggie.

'You know how I'm always entering crossword competitions? I won some Benetton vouchers. I thought you could spend them in Benetton Kids. They're a bit too colourful for me.'

'Thanks,' Maggie said flatly, taking the envelope from her hand.

'Is everything OK?' Sarah said, her brows knitting together.

'Sorry,' Maggie sighed. 'I'm tired. It's been a long day. You're too generous, Sarah, I don't deserve your friendship. I . . .' The words hung in the air. Maggie bowed her head. 'Sorry.'

'For what?' Sarah said, touching her arm. 'It was just a crossword competition. It only cost me the price of a stamp.' A beat passed between them. 'Want to talk? It looks like something's bothering you.'

But Maggie shook her head.

'Have you been to see Lewis?' Sarah said softly. 'Is that what's wrong?'

Elliott watched. Sarah was per-cep-tive. Like him. He only knew the word because Miss Grogan used it with him all the time. She said that it was a good thing, and it made him care a lot. Elliott had wondered if Miss Grogan had been per-cep-tive too.

He watched as Maggie nodded. 'I went to see him this afternoon. It's hard . . . you know? I miss him. But I don't know how much longer we can go on like this.'

'Then how about I take over his hospital visits for a while? It must be tiring, juggling your visits to Benrith with caring for Elliott.'

'Oh, no, I couldn't possibly expect you to . . .' Her hand went to her wedding ring and she began to twirl it on her finger. 'I mean, I wasn't getting at that. It's not as if he'll be able to talk. Most of the time he doesn't notice I'm there.'

'I'm a very good wheelchair pusher,' Sarah comforted. 'We could go together if you prefer, wrap him up warm. Wheel him around the grounds. I used to wheel Grandad Noble everywhere. Great for toning your arms.' Sarah winked.

'No, honestly, I . . .'

'Come on.' Sarah's smile was as warm as the sun.

'OK. I'll talk to the hospital. Clear it with them first.'

Elliott sucked his bottom lip. Maybe he could go too. Sarah would make everything alright.

Sarah glanced down the hall, a brief smile touching her lips as she caught him staring at them both. He ducked behind his doorway before his mother told him off.

'I see you, Elliott,' Maggie said. 'Come on then, thank Sarah for the vouchers and get back to bed.'

Elliott didn't need to be asked twice. 'Auntie Sarah!' he called, his feet thumping against the wooden floorboards as he ran to her.

'Hey there, little man. Are you OK?' Sarah beamed.

Elliott tugged on her arm before cupping the side of his mouth. He didn't want to say this in front of his mummy. She was upset enough as it was. Sarah looked to Maggie, who took the hint without being asked. Allowing them some privacy, she walked a few steps down the hall. He wished he could explain what had taken root inside him. Jahmelia was past being cold, or hungry, or feeling anything at all. Her eyes were closed, and she had no more tears to shed. She was still alive. But not for very long. Her light was growing dim.

'Please. Find Jahmelia,' Elliott whispered, as Sarah bent to his level. 'It's too cold outside. Tomorrow is too late.'

As Sarah met his gaze her eyes were shiny with tears. 'I'm trying, but I don't know where she is.'

'You will. Soon.' Taking a step back, he looked at his mother then back to Sarah. 'Thank you for the vouchers. You need to go home now.' Only then did he realise that the darkness he'd felt wasn't around him. It was coming for Sarah. That was all he knew. But Sarah was brave like Daddy. He hoped she would be OK.

'Elliott?' Maggie returned, resting a hand on his shoulder. 'Are you alright?' As he turned to his mother, he inhaled a breath of icy night air.

'I'm OK now, Maggie,' he said. He hugged her goodnight and said goodbye to Sarah. The pain of the scary feelings surrounding Jahmelia had faded. She would be found by tomorrow. The Midnight Game would soon be over. He hoped she would be alive.

50

Sarah flicked on the light switch, peering down her long, lonely hall. Still no sign of Sherlock. A lump rose in her throat. A feeling of gloom told her he was never coming back. As for Jahmelia . . . Elliott's message had been given with such a sense of sincerity, that she had indeed come straight home. Unwrapping her new scarf, she hung it with her coat. Her hair was damp from the thick blanket of fog which had settled over Slayton. This wasn't a night to be outside. As she looked into the hall mirror, Sarah saw her mother's eyes staring back at her. Only now could she see the resemblance. At times like these, the absence of her family caused her physical pain. She touched her own reflection. What she'd give for one more moment with her mum. To hear the sound of her voice. The touch of her kiss . . .

Her phone beeped with a text. It was Richie, and she was grateful for the distraction. Her job had become a lifesaver in so many ways.

Extension granted to keep Abraham in custody. Still going no comment. He's bedded down for the night. More interviews in the morning.

Sarah's fingers pecked the screen as she drafted a reply.

Thanks for the update, see you early doors.

Tomorrow the onus would be on finding Jahmelia's whereabouts. Police weren't allowed to keep repeating the same questions in further interviews and there were only so many ways you could rephrase them. Elliott had seemed so sure when he said tomorrow was too late. She looked at her watch, a feeling of helplessness washing over her. It was late and she had explored every avenue. She didn't have long left. Should she go to Blackhall? She shrivelled at the thought.

She bent to pick up the junk mail from a pile on the floor, stopping when she came to a small black envelope. It felt tainted in her hands. That hadn't been there before. She knew it was an invitation before she opened it.

'Bring it on,' Sarah said, but her words were hollow as she read. *Tonight. Blackhall Manor. Midnight.* She turned the card.

If you tell, you'll go to hell.

The flow of adrenalin started as a tremble in her legs, increasing her heart rate and redistributing her blood.

'Tell me what to do,' she spoke aloud, but no response came. 'Oh you desert me now, you bastard. All this time you've been hanging around and the one time I need you . . .' A sob caught in her throat. Her husband was long gone. But an imaginary voice had been better than nothing at all. She had to find Jahmelia, but that meant returning to Blackhall Manor. This man was no serial killer. All this had been for her. He could have murdered Libby and Jahmelia's brothers, who were both wearing headphones when he entered their homes. Instead, he'd barricaded them in their rooms with a chair. As for Sarah . . . she lived alone. He had been here more than once. He could have finished her off when she was asleep. There was something much bigger to all of this. A sense of returning to past wrongs. Only by killing her, could the Midnight Man complete the game. Maybe he knew she was nearly ready to flatten the Manor. And she would. By God, she would. But first she had to get Jahmelia back. The rules of the Midnight Game played in her mind as she prepared to leave.

Rule one: Stain some paper with a drop of your blood next to your name.

Rule two: Turn off the lights at midnight, leave the paper at the front door and knock twenty-two times. Open the door. You have invited the Midnight Man in.

Rule three: Relight your candle. You must avoid the Midnight Man until 3.33 a.m. If your candle extinguishes, it means the Midnight Man is near. If he finds you, you will die.

'Get your shit together,' Sarah told herself as she packed a rucksack. The thought of revisiting Blackhall Manor made her stomach churn. The weight of her stab vest offered a little reassurance as she tightened the Velcro straps. She tugged her coat over it, covering up the fluorescent police badge on the back. She had an idea of who she was meeting, but she didn't want it to be true. Because there was something else that Elsie told her in the hospital. Christian had needed support growing up. It had come in the form of the big brother scheme. It was something social services made use of when dealing with boys who needed a male influence in their life. For Christian, the scheme had worked well. His 'big brother' met him regularly, providing guidance and support. According to Elsie, he'd looked up to him as a teen. Had their friendship been reignited? Was Christian an unwilling accomplice to the Midnight Man's crimes? It would explain how he had gained access to her home and Christian's car. But evidence had been planted. Had the Midnight Man turned on him? Sarah hadn't shared her suspicions as she didn't know his motives. But also because the person she suspected was her friend. A man with two faces. One good, one bad.

As she drove down the lonely track to the house, she waited to hit the pothole which signalled her arrival. But this was years later and the bump did not come. Brambles scratched against the metal of her Mini as it juddered along the bumpy path, and she flicked on her wipers as a thick mist enveloped her. She turned on the car heater, only to be rewarded with a blast of cold air. The sight of Blackhall Manor from a distance had been enough to raise a chill on her skin. Now she was frozen to the core. It wasn't just the house. It was the memory of her family. All these years she had blamed her father for taking her family away. Now she was not so sure. Perhaps it was time for the ghosts of the past to be set free.

Pulling on her car handbrake, she stopped at the tall wrought-iron gates. They gaped open in a chasm of darkness, the thick padlock that usually secured them hanging from one gate. The Manor loomed above her, cloaked in mist. 'C'mon girl, we can do this,' Sarah whispered as the engine rumbled in protest at having to take the hill. Curling her fingers around the freezing steering wheel, Sarah negotiated her car up the weed-choked path. The house seemed as big as ever, its cracked windowpanes gazing down upon her with black, soulless eyes. Sarah parked her car ready for a quick getaway. She prayed Jahmelia would be with her when she left.

Tense with trepidation, Sarah approached the door. She imagined Angelica and the other girls pricking their fingers on a piece of card next to their names. She wasn't playing the game. She was here for two reasons. Reasons worth risking her life for. To find her tormentor and to bring Jahmelia home. But there was no power in the building, so she would use a candle and give the illusion she was playing the game. Her actions were robotic as she lit the fat white candle, because her thoughts were firmly on the house. She was in there, somewhere. Her fourteen-year-old self. She was still up in that wardrobe. Only the wardrobe wasn't there anymore. She wandered into the house, and had a sense of things scurrying around her feet. The smell of rotting upholstery assailed her nostrils and for a fleeting second she thought what a shame it was to see the place fall apart like this. Above her, bats skittered in the rafters, and her candle flickered as a door upstairs slammed shut. Sarah stood, entranced, as the ghosts of the past returned.

She was a child again, returning from trick-or-treating with her gran. Her uncle's car was on the drive. His mediation had failed. Robin, in his Batman costume, on a sugar high as he clutched his Halloween spoils. The scent of lavender as Sarah gave her mother a hug. Her father's weary, smiling face as he said goodnight. Her eyes rested on a salt ring, disturbed by the boot prints of the police officers before it was released as a scene of crime. To her left, was a splintered hole in the wall where Libby had escaped. What had possessed Angelica and her friends to come to this awful place?

On Sarah walked, to the wide staircase, tentatively moving up each step. It creaked, as if in acknowledgement. Her hand hovered over the banister. She did not want to physically touch anything. Slowly, she climbed, wary of the rotting steps. A feeling of coming home descended as instinct guided her up the stairs.

51

I watched from the secret crawlspace, a deep sense of satisfaction washing over me. Everything was coming together. It surprised me, what I was capable of. Finding the right crawlspace had been instinctual. Blackhall revealed itself to the special few. It was why Libby couldn't open the panel which would have granted her an easy freedom. It was a privilege to be part of something bigger than myself.

Depression was my constant companion – the black dog that never left my side. I masked my true feelings with jokes, caring for others to take the onus off myself. In the beginning, the big brother scheme was as much for myself as anything. Helping others took the focus off my own pain. Then I met Christian, a sad, insecure little boy with responsibilities beyond any normal ten-year-old child's. With few male figures in his life, social workers believed he would benefit from spending some time with me. It felt good to be looked up to.

Before long, he idolised me. I was indeed the big brother he never had. As the years passed, our meetings became less frequent and eventually we lost touch. He'd been shocked to catch me sleeping in Blackhall. Truth be told, he barely recognised me. I wasn't the fresh-faced young guy he'd looked up to anymore. I was reaching middle age, with shoulders burdened by depression. But he said he'd do what it took to see me through. I told him I was working on something very important, and he was happy to help – no questions asked. I think he wanted to repay me for the past. I had to come down tough a couple of times when he tried to back away. But spending time in Blackhall brought him around to my way of thinking and he was happy to loan me his car. It was me who advised him to report it stolen in an effort to cover my tracks.

Then, when Blackhall was crawling with cops, he'd offered to let me stay in his room. I had my own place, but it was good to keep an eye on him. I'd felt bad, planting the knife and the balaclava in Christian's back yard, but I needed to keep the police off my back. I also knew he'd stand a good chance of getting off. Especially when he'd have the best defence that money could buy. Being the son of an Irving brought privileges and that was certainly one of them. But this wasn't about Christian, or the Irvings for that matter. It was about bringing Sarah Middleton back to where she belonged.

I watched her explore her old home, her face gaunt beneath the light of her candle. A quick call from my burner phone would divert the police to Jahmelia. That would keep them tied up for a while. Jahmelia was of no further use to me now. Sarah was the last piece of the puzzle and it was time for her to die. Again.

52

Sarah's heart knocked hard and fast in her chest as she stood on the landing, listening for every sound. Was she imagining the faint whispers? The scratching in the walls? Blackhall Manor had a dark past long before her family inhabited it. The big, grand manor house full of secrets and dread. Tonight, the air was thick and frozen, white breath billowing as Sarah took slow shallow breaths.

'Hello?' she called out, her candle quivering in her grip. She hardly needed the light. Now that she was back here, she remembered every inch of this place. It was buried in her memories, the ties of the past steadfast. But she didn't belong here anymore. The place was toxic. When this was over, she would have Blackhall Manor flattened to the ground. A long, hollow groan swept through the landing, as if in response to her thoughts. Or perhaps it was preparing for battle. *One step in front of the other,* she told herself, as goosebumps rose on her arms.

There was movement throughout the house from every orifice. Bats, mice and insects had made this place their home. She shuddered as she felt a breath of wind sweep over her face.

It was wind, wasn't it?

'Hello?' she called again, every fibre of her being on high alert. She checked her phone. No signal. As she touched her bedroom door the voice of her mother whispered in the air. '*Not my little girl.*'

Sarah froze. It was the echo of a memory, that was all. But was that lavender she could smell? The lightest of touches was all that was needed for the door to creak open. The room was cloaked in darkness, but there was a person-shaped lump beneath her bed clothes. Every horror story she had ever heard came flooding into her mind. But this was *her* story. She had to finish it. She gripped the candle tighter, hot wax burning her skin as she crept towards the bed. Could it be Jahmelia? She did not want to see what was beneath the blanket but was helpless to stop. As she pulled back the cover she felt awash with relief. It was a pillow, blue-black with mould.

Sarah knew she should check beneath the bed but was unable to bring herself to do it. She was just waiting for a hand to shoot out and grab her by the ankle. 'Stay calm,' she whispered to herself, creeping out of the room. Her persecutor wasn't here because that wasn't how the story went. She recalled Robin's partly open bedroom door, and how she'd been too scared to look inside. Her young mind had completed the most horrific of puzzles. By then, she knew her funny, cute, annoying little brother was dead. She had missed him every day since. The newspapers said he had still been cuddling his teddy when he was shot. It was quick and painless. He would not have known. It was a tiny crumb of hope, but she clung to it. What sort of a monster could have ended his life? Sarah rubbed the back of her neck. It felt like the walls were closing in. If evil had a home, it was Blackhall Manor.

She recalled the battle on the landing and how her mother had fought to protect her family. Why were dark forces so prevalent here? Fear sharpened Sarah's senses as the pipes in her father's study rattled in discontent. She swallowed down the grief that had always held her back. But there was something else. A sense of her old life ending. Of fighting for a future which had been denied to her so far. Sweat dampened her palms as she forced herself on.

'Jahmelia?' she called, approaching Robin's room. Her candle wavered, her pulse quickening as she rested her hand on the old brass door-knob. She didn't want to see the evidence of what had taken place there. She started as her parents' bedroom door creaked open further down the corridor. Was Jahmelia in the wardrobe? But police had searched every inch of this place. Besides, there *was* no wardrobe, was there? Yet parts of this house seemed to have been recreated, like a stage set. Sarah swallowed back the tears that threatened. She had never felt so alone.

Turning away from Robin's room, she sensed unseen forces crowding around her as she carried on down the dark passage. She stood before her parents' old bedroom – the place where her childhood ended. *I died here,* she thought, her attention drawn to the wardrobe in the centre of the floor. She recognised it from her grandparents' old room. Someone had gone to a lot of trouble to set the scene. But this time the room flickered with the light of candles melting on the window ledge. What was she supposed to do now? She opened her mouth to call Jahmelia's name, the quiet click of a shotgun making her freeze. She should have known. The stab vest she was wearing would not save her now.

53

'Don't move.' Sarah's heart was heavy as she recognised the voice behind her. She tilted her head to see a black figure in her peripheral vision. He was in character, shrouded in a cloak reeking with a sour, damp stench. It was as if the soul of Blackhall Manor had settled on his shoulders.

'Let Jahmelia go.' She returned her gaze to the wardrobe. 'She doesn't belong here.'

She wasn't surprised at the identity of the so-called Midnight Man. Christian's 'big brother'. She took no pleasure in knowing who it was.

'I called the police when you got here,' he said. 'They're on their way to her now. I'd say most of the police in Slayton are . . . Don't turn around!' he shouted, pressing the gun into the hollow of her back.

Sarah froze, a tremble on her breath.

'Throw your rucksack into the corner, phone on the floor.' She slid her phone from her pocket and did as instructed. Unhooking her backpack from her shoulders, she threw it to one side.

'Where's Jahmelia?'

'In the quarry, in the boot of Christian's car.' The unused quarry was thirty miles outside of Slayton. A perfect distraction for the police. He must have planned this all along. If Sarah managed to call the police now, they would never reach Blackhall Manor in time.

'Get into the wardrobe.' The barrel of the gun jabbed into her back.

Sarah knew how this game ended. She had lost, and the Midnight Man was recreating her greatest fear. Closing her eyes, she summoned her strength as she drew in a slow breath. 'I'm not getting in that wardrobe. Not for you, not for anyone.'

'If you don't, you'll have his blood on your hands.'

Oh no. A thought flashed bright in Sarah's mind. *Please God, no.*

'Elliott's sleeping for now. All nice and cosy in Robin's bed.'

'I swear, if you hurt him . . .' Sarah spun around to face her tormentor and gasped as she saw his face. Her hands flew up in the air as he gripped the rifle and aimed it at her head. Cold fear enveloped her as she met his gaze. She barely recognised the old friend she used to love. His face was heavily scarred and twisted with rage. Wisps of hair poked from beneath the hood, and thick burn scars distorted half his face. His left eye was drooped, the left side of his mouth hanging down. But on the right side of his face she saw her old friend. A man with two faces, just as Elliott had said.

'Lewis. You wouldn't kill your own son. This isn't you. You love Elliott.'

But this wasn't Maggie's husband. Neither was it her old friend. It was his face, his body. But there was something else in him. As he pushed back the hood, it was a shock to see the burns he'd suffered, but that wasn't what made him so frightening. It was the hatred blazing in his eyes. If Blackhall Manor had a soul, then Lewis Carter was its living manifestation.

Sarah hadn't wanted to believe that Elliott's father was capable of murder, which is why she'd called on Maggie – to give her a chance to explain. But her old friend had continued to lie. She couldn't call her out in front of her son. The idea had come when she visited Elsie in hospital and stopped by the burns unit to speak to Lewis. But he wasn't in the hospital burns unit. His physical injuries had been dealt with. He'd been at The Oaks Rehabilitation Centre in Benrith, being treated for clinical depression and PTSD. But Lewis hadn't been committed. As a voluntary patient he could come and go as he pleased. Elliott had sensed a man with two faces – his loving, heroic father and the vengeful man he had become. Elliott didn't recognise his daddy in his visions because half of Lewis's face had been melted away. The physical scars may be healing but the mental scars were raw and exposed. And now he was standing before her, threatening her with a double-barrelled shotgun.

His voice dripped with venom. 'All these years . . . I thought you were dead. Then you come back here like nothing has happened. You didn't even have the decency to tell me you were alive.'

Sarah's heart plummeted as she recognised an emotion she knew only too well. Unadulterated grief. But her friendship with Lewis was so many years ago now. He had wanted to take things further, but Sarah hadn't felt the same way. The other night in her kitchen, Sarah had stared at the photo of them together – Lewis smiling at the camera, his arms thrown over their shoulders as she and Maggie stood either side. It was the way Maggie was looking at Lewis in the photo that had left her feeling unsettled. Had she guessed Lewis's feelings for her? Was that why she'd helped spread the rumours that Sarah died in the wardrobe as a teen?

'Lewis,' she said. 'Maggie was meant to tell you I was OK. I was in no state to reach out myself.' But her words did nothing to dampen the anger that seemed to emanate from Lewis's every pore.

'Bullshit!' he spat. 'She told me you died. I blamed myself for what happened to you. If you hadn't been grounded because of me, you would have been on a sleepover at Maggie's on Halloween night.'

'I didn't know,' Sarah said, aghast. 'How could I?'

Lewis had organised a night out for the foursome in Slayton's old asylum. It hadn't stood out as unusual – lots of teenagers checked out Slayton's abandoned buildings at that time of year. But it was just an excuse for him to get her alone.

It was only today that Sarah revisited that night – shortly before Halloween. She had been excited and nervous to be somewhere so off limits with her friends. But when David and Maggie ran off into one part of the building to explore, Lewis had found her. She still remembered the expression on his face as he made his confession – that he had always wanted, loved *her*. Not Maggie. Sarah's cheeks had burned with betrayal, knowing how her best friend felt about Lewis. She hadn't known what to say when she was saved by the headlights of a car driving up the road. Her parents. They had guessed where she was and were coming to pick her up.

'Don't go,' Lewis had pleaded, touching her cheek. 'Please.'

At fourteen years of age, Sarah couldn't handle such grown-up emotions and didn't have the words to let him down. As her parents' car beeped outside, she was relieved to have an excuse to run away. Her parents had been worried sick, which was the reason she was with her baby brother on Halloween night, instead of out with her friends. Had Lewis taken her silence as compliance? She should have found a way to tell him how she felt . . . that she loved him as a friend but no more. And now Lewis was looking at her with pain which had festered into hatred strong enough to kill.

'I took an overdose, did you know that? Came to Blackhall and swallowed a bottle of sleeping tablets just so I could be with you.'

'I'm sorry . . .' Sarah stuttered. 'I—'

'Then I joined the army to forget you . . .' Lewis interrupted, holding the gun firm. 'But every time I came home, I visited Blackhall, retracing your father's steps . . . wishing I could turn back time.' His breath trembled as he delivered each painful word. 'All these years, I carried the guilt. It ate me up inside. Then you walk back in like nothing happened, married to *David*, without giving me a second thought.'

'I had no idea . . .' Sarah said, looking at the man he had become. His face was slick with sweat. He had withdrawn into a world of hatred and regret.

'Shut the fuck up!' Lewis's words echoed around the room as his finger curled over the trigger. 'All of this . . . it's because of you. It's time you know how it feels.'

But Sarah could barely comprehend his words. She stood, unmoving, her need to protect Elliott forcing her words. 'Lewis, I know you have your reasons for hating me, but leave Elliott out of this. Please. He looks up to you. He wears your medal. This . . . this has nothing to do with him.'

'Get into the wardrobe.' The words weren't spoken but growled. Elliott's safety depended on her cooperation. But Sarah wasn't giving up her life that easily.

'How do I know you won't hurt Elliott?' The thought of the little boy lying in Robin's old room crushed her heart. She couldn't face the pain of losing another child she loved. Talking seemed to be an effort as Lewis spoke between clenched teeth.

'Because that's not how the game goes. You shouldn't have survived.'

'But you've framed Christian for the murders. If you hurt me, they'll know it was you.'

'It was never my intention to let Christian go down for this.' Lewis clenched his gun, flecks of spittle forming in the corners of his mouth. 'I was just buying time. They'll know who it was soon enough.' It was then that it struck her. He didn't care about killing her because he had no intention of going on. He wanted to die, and to take her with him, just as he believed her father had planned.

Cold steel grazed her neck as he pressed the gun to her head. 'Get in, or I'll shoot you as you stand.' He leered at her. 'I'll make it like before. You stand a fair chance. You might even make it out alive.' She could hear the smile in his voice. The anguished pleasure he was taking from this.

'You think you're fixing a blip in history because you're stuck in a loop,' she said. 'My father didn't kill his family. You've got it all wrong.' The walls seemed to judder around them as the corridors filled with the clicks and chatter of bats.

'You're lying!' he roared, the flame of dancing candlelight reflected in his eyes.

'The search team found a silencer hidden in the walls of the house,' Sarah replied. 'It has my father's blood on it. The whole thing was a set-up.' The test results may not have come back, but she knew in her heart it was fact. She turned to face him for a second time. Silence grew wide between them. 'Please. Don't do this.'

Sarah watched his eye twitch. A flicker of recognition. 'I can shoot Elliott, or you can take your chances with the wardrobe. When I get to five, I'm pulling the trigger. One . . . two . . .'

'Alright!' Sarah forced herself to open the wardrobe door. Like the rest of the furniture in Blackhall, it was riddled with woodworm – eaten as it stood. Wire hangers jingled and memories of the past wrapped themselves around her . . . How her father's old coats had brushed against her, and her mother's dresses carried the faint scent of her perfume. She tried to focus her thoughts as they wavered between past and present. Lewis let Libby go, and seemed to have released Jahmelia. He might do the same for Elliott, his own son. He had kept his word in the past, and it was her death he cared about. Right now, it was the only hope she had.

Climbing into the wardrobe, she listened as the lock in the door clicked shut. Dust rose from the base and she pinched her nose as she ingested a sneeze. At the back of her mind, her body's sense of self-preservation screamed. Why was she complying with Lewis's demands? Why had she come here unarmed? A sense of resignation washed over her. Perhaps this was what her life had been leading to all along. She wasn't a religious person, but as she sat in the wardrobe, she felt the presence of her family nearby. It was why she'd stockpiled the pills in her bedside table. After David's death, life had got too hard. How easy it would be to just close her eyes and succumb to it all. The cramped space was dark, apart from the tiniest chink of candlelight through the keyhole. This time, she didn't look out. Sitting in the darkness, Sarah pulled her knees close to her chest. She blinked, adjusting her vision as she took in movement around her. In the darkness, white moths fluttered, gently touching her hands, her legs, her face. How was she seeing their downy wings? They appeared out of nowhere, like messengers of light, the soft beat of their wings invoking a sense of peace. She wasn't afraid. Her family weren't gone. They were waiting for her. Whether it was now, or in decades to come, she would see them again.

Curling into a ball, Sarah pushed her hands over her ears as the booming thunder of a gunshot filled the air.

54

'I'm coming!' Maggie called, drunk from sleep. She stumbled out of bed, shoving her arms into her dressing gown. Silence. Had she dreamt her son's cries? 'Elliott?' she whispered, creeping down the corridor. She paused at her son's bedroom door. The clothes were pulled back from his bed. It was empty. She glanced out his window. All she could see was thick white fog. Twelve minutes past midnight. Where was he?

A noise rose from the kitchen. 'Elliott?' she said, making her way downstairs then silently entering the room. Her hand rose to her chest. Her son was standing at the locked back door, a statue in the moonlight as he stared into the night. 'Elliott!' she rushed towards him. 'What are you doing? Are you OK?'

'Sarah's in trouble. She's with the Midnight Man.'

Maggie's mouth gaped open in horror as she took in her son's tearful expression.

'Is she in trouble like Jahmelia?'

Elliott nodded. His eyes were dark and full as he stood, cold and rigid in the dark.

She wrapped her arms around him and he clung to her as she picked him up. 'Are *you* OK? Oh my sweet boy.'

'I saw him, in my dreams,' he sobbed, as his mother cradled him. 'His face was like this . . .' He pressed his palm to his cheek and dragged the skin down. 'But he had two faces. He looked like Daddy too. They're in B-Blackhall Manor,' he sobbed. 'He wants to fin-finish the game.' He was talking about the injuries Lewis suffered when he ran into a burning building without a thought for himself. Part of him died that day. He'd returned a different man.

'Oh my darling,' she soothed, bringing him to her own bed. 'It was just a nightmare. You can sleep with me tonight.' But her mind was racing. What if this wasn't a bad dream? What if Lewis really had returned? His room was on the ground floor. He was allowed to leave when he wanted. Nobody was keeping him there. She had lied to Sarah about his illness because she was trying to buy herself some time. Her husband had appeared vacant to the outside world – but he was physically capable of moving about on his own. Staff told her to be patient, that he would speak to her in time. What if it was all a game?

The description Elliott gave was clear. He had barely recognised his father because of the scarring on his face. The knot of worry that had plagued Maggie recently twisted in her gut. Was Lewis the Midnight Man? It wouldn't be the first time they had played that game. She thought about the hell of his PTSD and the decline of his mental health. His erratic paranoia and obsessions as he spiralled into depression and substance abuse. She'd been too embarrassed to tell people that her heroic husband had fallen apart – but what did that say about her?

After soothing Elliott back to sleep, Maggie picked up her home phone. It was gone midnight, but Sarah would forgive a late-night call. The phone rang off the hook. Her nerves on edge, Maggie tried her mobile number again. No response. The memory of Elliott's words chilled her bones. *'Sarah's in trouble, Mummy. She's with the Midnight Man.*' She drove her hands through her hair. This was crazy talk. Would the police listen to her? But her son had described a living person, made of flesh and bone. She picked up her phone. Sarah was in trouble. She had to make the call.

55

'I got you.' Richie's voice broke through the confusion as Sarah blinked at the flash of his iPhone light.

'Richie? What's going on?' she said, on a shaky breath.

'You're OK. It's all going to be OK.' Richie extended his arm. The strong grip of his hand was the lifeline Sarah needed as Richie helped her to her feet. The acrid stink of discharged gunpowder fouled the air. She didn't want to let Richie go.

'You're bleeding.' Dazed, she peered in the flickering light at the blood running in rivulets down his arm. A moan rose from the corner of the room. Her legs felt too weak to support her as she turned towards the noise. Lewis was on his back, eyes half-closed, a set of cuffs on his wrists.

'It's just a graze,' Richie looked stunned as he followed her gaze. 'I managed to wrestle the gun off him but the bullet skimmed my arm.' In the dim light Lewis seemed uninjured but concussed.

'Thank God you're OK.' Sarah's eyes danced around the room. 'The moths.' But they were gone. She blinked, coming back to the room, the living, the here and now. 'Elliott! Where's Elliott?' Plucking a candle from the window she headed to Robin's old room. This time there was no hesitancy in opening the door. Shadows danced beneath the light of her flame, but there was nobody there. Nothing but a mouse scurrying into a crack in the wall. She checked each room in turn. 'He was bluffing . . . please let him have been bluffing.' She exhaled a sob-choked breath. 'Elliott's not here.' Her words echoed in the dim landing as she returned to her parents' old room. Perhaps Lewis hadn't been able to go through with hurting his own son. He had been a devoted father, from what Maggie had said. She should have known such bonds were not so easily broken. Shaking his head, Richie took in the scene. 'Our local hero,' he said, his gaze falling on Lewis. 'I can't believe it's him.'

'He had help,' Sarah replied, her heartbeat returning to a normal rhythm. 'He roped Christian in too.' She thought about Maggie's visits. She must have broken the news of Sarah's return to Slayton with David over a year ago. Of her new job, her colleagues, and even the investigation. Everything Sarah had told her must have filtered down. Then using Christian's keys, he'd gained access to her home. No wonder he knew so much about her life.

Richie updated control with his call sign on his police airwaves radio. Blood dripped from his arm onto the wooden floor. 'I'm going code three two with Lewis Carter for the attempted murder of Detective Constable Sarah Noble. Can you get an ambulance over here, the suspect appears concussed.' The rifle had been disarmed and placed next to the door. Sarah's attention was drawn to the vibration of her own phone and she bent gingerly to pick it up from the floor. It must have picked up some signal. It was Maggie. She'd sent a text, after several missed calls.

Everything OK? Elliott had a bad dream and said you were in trouble. He's fine, back in bed. Text me when you get this x

300

Relief flooded over her. Elliott was OK. 'Jahmelia?' she said, turning to Richie.

'We got an anonymous tip-off. She's been found in the boot of Christian's car. Still alive, but critical.'

'That's a relief.' Sarah turned to Lewis. 'Is he going to be OK?'

'I took his legs out from under him with my baton,' Richie said. 'That's when the gun went off. He hit his head against the floor when he fell.'

Still dazed, she helped drag Lewis into a sitting position against the wall. A low groan escaped his lips. He was going to be OK. 'Jeez, what is this thing?' Richie shuddered at the sight of the insects crawling in Lewis's cloak. Sarah smiled. Bugs had been the least of her worries. Blank and bleary-eyed, Lewis's eyes fluttered open. He stared past them in silence as Richie relayed the police caution. The darkness that seemed to invade him had retreated into the shadows, dormant for now.

'Put some pressure against that wound,' Sarah said, pressing a tissue to Richie's arm. 'How did you know I was here?'

Richie guided her towards the window, his voice low. 'Yvonne made me stay behind to man the phones while everyone went to the quarry. Your friend Maggie rang the office. She didn't make a lot of sense at first, but I gathered that she was worried about you. She told me where you lived so I drove by and saw your car was gone. I knew where you had to be . . . I came straight here.' He cast an eye over Lewis. 'I saw the candles in the window. He was taking aim when I got here.'

'I'm glad you did,' Sarah said, explaining the events which had led up to that point. Richie had saved her life. She stared out the window, waiting for the welcome sight of blue lights. Deep down she already knew that the fourteen-year-old girl trapped in the wardrobe for all these years had finally been freed.

'I'm going to clear my father's name.'

'You are?'

Sarah nodded. Only now, through the eyes of an adult, was she able to see what really happened that night.

56

Sarah stared at the man before her as he struggled to take his last breaths. It was hardly surprising that nobody was by his hospital bed. All his life, this man had placed money before family, worshipped advancement over relationships. There was nothing wrong with having ambition, but when you became a shark you ate your friends. That's how it had been with her uncle, John. He was part of a boys' club which covered up his mistakes, portraying him as a generous businessman, someone to be admired. But nobody close to him was fooled. His wife had divorced him years ago and moved halfway across the world. They never had children because he had no room in his life for them. It was probably best.

Sarah had assumed it was grief that had made him this way. His brother was dead. So was his nephew, his sister-in-law and his parents. But now the test results were back. The blood found on the silencer recovered in Blackhall Manor was her father's. A partial fingerprint was also found. It matched the man before her. Sarah's family had died at his hands.

As Sarah dug into his affairs, she always met with a barrier. It was Richie who had helped her unearth evidence over the last four weeks and gained access to computer files which screamed the disturbing truth. He also accessed the phone number of a woman who knew the story first-hand. John's ex-wife, Mandy. She may have moved halfway across the world, but she took Richie's call with the steady acceptance of a woman who had been expecting it all along.

'Are you sure you don't want to do this at home?' Richie said, handing Sarah Mandy's phone number. But Sarah was ready. 'I want him to hear it,' Sarah said. She needed the words to reach the recesses of John's mind. He'd had a long and successful life, but he could take what he had done into the next world. She wasn't letting him off the hook now. Given what Richie had told her, Mandy was ready to confess all. Sarah dialled the number.

Mandy's responses were hesitant, her voice thick with shame. But with a little encouragement from Sarah, she seemed grateful to get it off her chest. 'I'd always had my suspicions,' she said. 'I knew John, and I knew what he was capable of.'

'Then you should have reported it.' Sarah was unable to keep the bitterness from her voice as she took the call on speakerphone.

'I did, anonymously,' Mandy replied. 'But nobody listened. It was hard. I was a lot younger than John and completely out of my depth. He was a monster. I had to get away.'

Sarah's anger ebbed away. She knew what it was like to be blamed for your husband's wrongdoings. To be filled with repulsion. To have a voice that nobody wanted to hear.

'The police were under pressure for a quick conclusion. The councillors, townspeople and businessmen were desperate to put it to bed. Nobody wanted to think they were living where evil was roaming free.'

'I know about the development,' Sarah said. That much, she had found out on her own. 'John wanted my grandparents to sell the land to the Irving family.'

'That's right, but your grandfather wouldn't have it. I remember how angry John was, saying his father was going to outlive them all. John was desperate for money. He was in a lot of debt. He was flash. He couldn't bear to go broke.' A long sigh ruffled the line. 'To begin with, I understood. Your mum and grandmother wanted to sell it too. But your grandad wouldn't listen, and your father said he'd support him, no matter what.'

Sarah nodded. 'And that didn't go down well with John.'

'No. He couldn't understand why his father wanted to keep the place on. But it had been in the family for generations. It clearly meant a lot to him and he was trying to turn it into something good. He told John that he was going to change his will and leave your dad the lot.'

'I didn't know that,' Sarah said, sorrowfully.

'Not only that, but one day your father would pass it to Robin, and it would stay in the Middleton family. John didn't have children. Your grandad knew he'd sell the land off.'

Sarah exchanged a look with Richie. As they sat, side by side, he gave her a reassuring smile. Their friendship had blossomed in the last few weeks. He had been a rock to her. 'All this time, I thought my parents were on the brink of divorce. When Granny said John was there to mediate . . .'

'The only person John was interested in was himself. Your parents were close. Nothing would have parted them. They were a force to be reckoned with.'

'And John? What was he like at home? Did he say anything?'

Mandy's reply was instant. 'He was furious, because the developers gave him a deadline and time was running out. Then a calm settled over him. I asked if he'd made a deal and he said no, but everything was going to be OK. I couldn't see how, with the amount of debt he'd told me we were in. It was over half a million pounds.'

'I don't understand why this wasn't taken into account by the police.'

'Because some mystery investor cleared his debt *before* your parents died. There goes his motivation. John never said anything, but I think it was Eric Irving.'

Sarah nodded at the revelation. Eric Irving was Simon Irving's father. Three times as rich and doubly ruthless, from what she'd heard. 'So the investor could have known about what John planned to do.'

'I honestly believe he did. But Eric Irving was very influential. He had a lot of power over this town. He donated money to the schools, churches, even gave a chunk of money towards refurbishing the police station. He had fingers in lots of pies.'

Like father like son, Sarah thought with disgust as Mandy relayed a long-buried truth.

'I remember John being agitated on Halloween night. He said he was going to have it out with his father, make one last effort to change his mind. He said if he could get your dad on side, then they could persuade their father to let Blackhall Manor go and everything would be alright.'

Sarah sighed. How different things could have been.

'That night he came home, he said he'd done everything he could. Again, he was calm. I thought maybe he was turning a corner. It was only later, when I heard about his debts being paid off, that

I realised for him there was no turning back. The men he owed money to weren't going to be understanding.'

'My mother called my father's name that night,' Sarah said, moving on the narrative. She didn't want to hear about John's motivations because nothing could excuse what he did. 'At first, I thought she was shouting *at* my dad. But it was only when I went back there that I realised she was calling *for* him, not *to* him.' Sarah paused for breath. '"Not my little girl," she said.' An ache rose in her chest as she recalled that night. 'When Mum said, "He's got a gun," she was talking about Uncle John. Then later, when I was in the wardrobe, I presumed Dad was calling my name. His voice sounded different, but I was so panicked, I couldn't think straight.'

Mandy cleared her throat. 'He's a monster. To do such a thing. I had been afraid of him for a long time by that point, but to kill innocent children in cold blood . . .' Her words faded as she caught her breath.

'I think John hid in the crawlspace, then shot your father and hid his body until it was time to stage his death. He knew that house better than anyone. Your grandad was always telling him to stay out of the walls.'

Given what they knew about the silencer, her theory held.

'I remember the funeral,' Sarah said. 'John couldn't look me in the eye. I thought it was grief. But later I came to think he was worried about being found out.' She gave Richie a sideways glance. He was staring at John, his jaw tensed.

'I asked John outright if he did it once,' Mandy said. 'He laughed and said I mustn't speak of it again. It was all so odd. I couldn't bear to live with him after a while, because deep down, I knew.'

'Surely you could have pushed it, made the police listen.'

'I tried. Believe me, I . . .' Mandy's voice broke as she struggled to explain herself.

'Go on.' Rain hammered against the hospital windows. The day was as grey as Sarah's thoughts.

'One night, John went to a function,' Mandy continued. 'It was only a week after the funerals, and I didn't want to go. It seemed wrong, you know? Disrespectful. But if John was grieving then he didn't show it. He went out and I stayed at home alone. I was going to bed when the power went out. I went downstairs to find the fuse box and . . .'

'Yes?'

'I've never told this to a living soul.'

'You can trust me,' Sarah said. 'I just want closure.'

There was a pause before Mandy inhaled. 'The next thing I knew, someone was grabbing me from behind. They blindfolded and gagged me. Tied me to a chair.'

Sarah was chewing her bottom lip. 'Who? Not John.'

'No. He was still at the party. I remember their rough hands. The smell of booze on their breath. I've never been so scared in all my life.'

'What happened?' Sarah wasn't sure if she wanted to know.

'They told me to shut up. They said if I even *thought* about speaking to the police that they'd be back to finish what they'd started. They didn't mention John. But I knew. He'd got himself involved with some bad people. He was in way over his head.'

'What about when he came home?'

'He found me, still tied up. He seemed upset, but not once did he offer to call the police. There was no forced entry. He said I couldn't have locked the back door. But I did. I specifically remembered doing it. That's when I wondered if he'd given them a key. The next day I packed my bags and left. I wanted no part of it.'

As the conversation came to a close, Sarah realised that what passed between them had felt like a confessional, and Sarah had forgiven her. But she would never forgive John, which was why she was here.

A young nurse wandered into the room, checking his stats and giving Sarah a gentle smile. 'He's not in any pain,' she said, her soft voice imbued with empathy. She mistook Sarah for someone who cared. Up until now, the only people who thought about the man before her were the vultures waiting for their piece of the pie. Not only had John recovered from his debt, he'd became wealthy from the business ventures which followed. The nurse didn't know who Sarah was or the circumstances which brought her here. Had she known the danger John was in, she would never have allowed Sarah into the room.

'That was heavy.' Richie squeezed Sarah's hand as the nurse left. 'Are you ready to go?'

'I need five minutes alone with him. Why don't you grab a coffee? I won't be long.'

Sarah felt nauseous at the thought of John in the crawlspaces of their home.

The second Richie left, Sarah leaned over John's bed and whispered into his ear. 'You evil old bastard. You're going to hell for this. I'll never forgive you for what you did. Never.'

Because only now did she know the full story. Today John was paying for his crimes.

57

'Would you like me to dim the lights?' The nurse popped her head in. 'I can get you a blanket if you're going to stay.'

'I'm fine, thanks.' Sarah forced a gentle smile. 'I'm heading off soon.'

The click of the door invoked unwelcome memories as she recalled the sound of the key turning in the wardrobe lock. Folding her arms, she stood over John's bed. The man was a shell of his former self, his eyes sunken, his skin like parchment. Cancer had already ravaged his body. All his money couldn't save him now. Sarah did not know if he could hear her, but she was determined to have her say.

'Mum was ten years younger than I am when you murdered her in cold blood. Why did you leave her until the end?' She shook her head bitterly. 'Did you think she'd run away with you after you killed her children? Is that what it was?' No reply. He was a monster trapped in the body of a frail old man. 'Was it worth it? Because everybody hates you. And you can't take your precious money where you're going.'

Anger flaring, she watched his chest rise and fall. Each breath was taken as if it was his last. 'I can barely remember him,' Sarah continued, as thoughts of Robin returned. 'All I have are blurry old photos. I can see his face, but I can't remember his essence, because I've buried the memory so far down.' She was shaking now, a volcano of emotions. She swiped at the tears blurring her vision. 'You took that from me. You killed an innocent child for *money* then let my father take the blame.' Her lips a thin white line, she stared at the man before her. 'You didn't just kill Robin, or Mum and Dad. Whole family lines were wiped out because of you.' She exhaled a shuddering breath. 'I'll dance on your grave, do you hear me? But not before I make sure everyone knows what you are.' The steady rise and fall of John's chest came to a halt as he exhaled a long, lingering breath. Sarah leaned closer. Was he dead?

Then a sudden, clawing breath as John's chest jutted upwards, his mouth gaping open. Her legs giving way, she plopped back into the chair. 'Oh my God. I thought you were dead!' she tittered, emitting a tearful high-pitched laugh. She tried to imagine what it would feel like, cutting off his air supply. Since finding out about his involvement, she had fantasised about it. Retribution was a drug.

The cold chill of fear brought her to ground as Richie entered the room. 'I shouldn't be here,' she said, reading the concern on his face. 'I'm scared of what I might do.'

'I'll drop you home.' Richie took her by the hand. John's breath rattled. He wasn't long for this world.

'Why do you care?' Sarah said. 'You know what they say about me; I'm bad news.'

'Believe it or not, I like you, although you've dragged me through so much shit I'm questioning my own sanity, never mind yours.' He levelled her with a hard stare. 'Let him die alone. It's all he deserves.'

'But I want everyone to know what he did.' The injustice of the situation made her sick to her stomach, but Richie was guiding her towards the door.

311

'They will. But now I'm getting you out of here. I don't want you blamed when he croaks.'

Sarah allowed herself to be led away. The nurse met them in the corridor. 'Are you OK?'

'It all got a bit much,' Richie said sombrely. 'I doubt he'll see out the night.'

She delivered a slow nod, most likely wondering why they were leaving. 'Is there anyone I should call?'

'No,' Sarah said flatly. 'They're all dead.' The nurse would find out soon enough. But for today, Richie was right. It was time to move on, and she knew where to start.

Sarah was in the hall when she heard the familiar swish of the cat flap in the kitchen. For a second, she imagined another letter and she was instantly filled with dread. But Lewis was in custody. Could it be?

'Sherlock!' she exclaimed as she entered the kitchen. 'I thought you were dead!'

As she checked him over, her cat arched his back responding with a loud miaow. 'Have you been in the wars, me old Sher?' Sarah cooed, as he allowed her to stroke him for once. His fur was matted and dirty and he had lost a little weight, but there was something about his swagger that took her by surprise. Curling his tail around her leg, he pushed his face against her jeans, happy to see her. Sarah stood in surprise as she watched this sudden display of affection. He'd always been so uptight before . . . She laughed as realisation dawned. 'Were you out doing the deed? You dirty old dog. Is that what it was?' Another loud miaow in response.

'You do look kinda pleased with yourself.' Sarah had never got around to getting Sherlock neutered. Perhaps that's what was wrong with him all along.

Opening the cupboard, she took out Sherlock's kibble and emptied some into a bowl.

'And here was me thinking you hated me.' She sniffed away happy tears as she stroked her cat. 'You were just repressed.' She filled a saucer of milk and lay it next to the food on the ground, feeling a sense of satisfaction as she watched him wolf it down. Tomorrow, she would give him a wash, but right now, she was glad of his company.

Sarah opened the fridge door and plopped a cooked chicken breast on top of Sherlock's bowl. 'Just for tonight,' she whispered, as he arched his back in response to her touch. There was a sense of peace as her job, her past, her life all reached a resolution. There was just one more thing left to do.

58

Sarah stood, arms tightly folded as the demolition machinery trundled up to Blackhall Manor. Her breath was frosted and the tips of her fingers were growing numb. She wriggled her toes to keep the blood flowing. Here on the hilltop, you felt every ounce of the cold. At least the photographers and small band of press that had gathered were at the other end of the field. Some of them had braved the wind to capture the final chapter of the story which had haunted Slayton for decades. She did not see Gabby until she was almost standing beside her. Next to her was Jahmelia, in blue dungarees.

'Hey, how are you, Jahmelia?' She was the last person Sarah had expected to see.

'She's been having nightmares,' Gabby replied, as Jahmelia eyed Sarah suspiciously. 'I told her mum I'd take her out for some fresh air.'

'And you brought her here?' Sarah said quietly, frowning.

'Closure,' Gabby simply said. Jahmelia had recovered well over the last few weeks, although it had been touch and go in the first few days. But while her physical scars may have been healing, the mental scars might never fade. And she was not the only one.

Libby had hidden herself away, with her parents arranging private tutoring as she took the term off school. The community was still recovering from the aftershock of the horror story that had begun on Halloween night.

'How did you know about the demolition?' Sarah was dressed casually today, in jeans and a knee-length puffa jacket, watching the press with a measure of distrust.

'Richie mentioned it. I saw your car, figured you wouldn't mind me trespassing on your land.' Gabby and her team had worked hard to get Lewis charged with Angelica's murder, Libby's abduction and Sarah and Jahmelia's attempted murders, among other crimes. After taking advice from a solicitor, Lewis had admitted everything, blaming it on PTSD. It wouldn't surprise Sarah if he gave a defence of temporary insanity when it went to trial. When she remembered his face at Blackhall Manor, it seemed believable. Christian had been an unwitting accessory who had grown frightened of the man he had once looked up to. Sarah hoped he would be spared prison time. The young man had been through enough.

'Trespass away,' Sarah said, as the wind snatched her words. 'I'm only here to make sure they do it right.' The house had been left intact with every stick of rotting furniture, every cracked cup and saucer, every moulding piece of clothing inside. She watched the wrecking ball draw up to the abandoned building, as workmen paced in yellow high-vis jackets and hard hats. There was a hum in the air, faint, but she could feel it. A negative vibration that made you want to walk away. On cue, Jahmelia tugged her grandmother's hand. She felt it too.

'I wanna go home.'

'OK, Jay,' Gabby replied. 'In a second.' The clouds rolled in above them, carrying unshed December rain. Christmas was on the horizon, and a small measure of hope was in the air. The jingle of an app tinkled as Jahmelia played on her phone.

'Is any part of you sad about it?' Gabby said, her eyes trained on the house. 'I mean, there must be a reason you've left it standing for so long. Are you sure you want it flattened?'

Sarah considered the question, brushing her fringe off her face. Her scar didn't bother her as much as before. 'I left it standing because I was scared of it, not because of any loyalty to the house,' Sarah replied.

'I didn't mean loyalty, I meant . . . that's where you grew up with your family, wasn't it?'

'The place has been in the family for generations, which was why Grandad held on to it for so long. He wanted Robin to inherit it.' She broke eye contact with the house to glance at her sergeant. 'Can you imagine it? It's like an arranged marriage, tying a young boy to a future like that. When Robin died, the house fell to me.' But the farm land had gone to her uncle, and he subsequently sold it to Irving Industries to build their gated communities on. Simon Irving was a tougher nut to crack. He admitted his father had paid off John's debts but denied any knowledge of the shootings which followed. Irving's father had left John in a position that was impossible to back out of.

Gabby didn't reply. There was nothing to say. She cast her eyes to the sky as the caws of stony-eyed ravens filled the air. In the distance, Sarah saw Richie parking his motorbike. She wasn't alone. Not anymore.

'Here we go!' Sarah said, as the wrecking ball began to drive into position. She clenched her fists, her heart skipping a beat. It wouldn't surprise her if the old place refused to fall. Whatever lay in its foundations would surely not give up without a fight. As she waited for the hammer to deliver the first blow, she turned to her sergeant, voicing her concerns.

'Why did you really come here, Gabby? It wasn't just for Jahmelia, was it?'

'Anyone would think you're a detective,' she smiled. 'Actually, I wanted to let you know that I'm recommending you're taken off restricted duties. I want you full-time on the team.' Her smile faded as she caught Sarah's expression. 'I thought you'd be excited. Haven't you always wanted this?'

'I thought so,' Sarah said. 'But sometimes the things you chase aren't meant to be caught.'

Gabby looked at her quizzically. 'So, you don't want to be a detective full-time?'

'I'm not ready. Not yet. I'll keep taking statements if that's OK. I want to deal with regular people and listen . . . *really listen* to them.' She shoved her hands into her pockets. For the first time in a long time, she felt positive about the future.

'The voice of the people?' Gabby's eyebrows rose.

'Why not?' Sarah stared into the distance, waiting for the criticism to come. But Gabby wasn't Yvonne. Her words came from a place of concern, not spite. Not that Yvonne had been saying much now that Gabby had returned.

'Then I don't have a problem with it, as long as it's what you want.' She zipped up her fleece and shuddered, looking straight ahead. 'They sure are taking their time.'

The workmen *were* taking their time, but Sarah did not want to join them to see what the hold-up was. Even now, after everything, the Manor was a formidable place.

'Nanny, can we go now?' Jahmelia looked at her grandmother hopefully. Sarah had a sneaking suspicion that Jahmelia wasn't ready for the realms of her teenage years just yet.

'I thought they'd be finished by now,' Richie said, unzipping his leather jacket a couple of inches as he joined them.

'So did we.' Sarah laughed awkwardly. 'I should have sold tickets.' But the ring of her phone was about to alert her that Blackhall wasn't done with her yet. It was the builder.

'We have to hang fire,' he said. 'It's a legal issue. We're downing tools.' As the call came to an abrupt end, Sarah stood in disbelief, staring at the building which had housed so much pain.

'I can't believe it.' Exasperated, Sarah ran her fingers through her hair. 'The builders can't do it; there's some legal problem. Blackhall Manor still stands.'

Epilogue

It seemed that even prison couldn't keep the Midnight Man contained. Weeks after Lewis Carter's arrest he was still all people could talk about. Online blogs, news articles and true crime podcasts were popping up daily to discuss the mystery of the army hero turned bad. On television, political chat show hosts discussed the government's responsibility to help its fallen heroes and some enthusiastic Twitter users were campaigning to set Lewis free.

But not the townsfolk of Slayton. They couldn't bring themselves to speak his name. Each limp yellow ribbon forged a memory of Angelica's murder. Each house half-heartedly decorated for Christmas demonstrated an apathy arisen from shock. Bruised and battle-scarred, the people of Slayton had retreated into themselves, edgy and suspicious. Journalists were ignored, doorbells unanswered and curtains permanently closed.

Sarah cast her eyes to the left over Slayton's expansive lake. It seemed a monochrome version of itself – much deeper and darker than before. Further down were the outskirts of Blackhall Woods. It was a no-go area for teenagers, and it was much to Sarah's frustration that Blackhall Manor still stood. Despite locals wanting the building to be flattened, someone from out of town had kicked up a fuss. Blackhall was a listed building, and home to a colony of bats which were a species protected by law. Sarah set her gaze straight ahead. Despite the darkness surrounding Slayton, she still came back. Slayton wasn't home; without her family she wasn't sure she knew what home was, but it *was* a part of her. Checking her watch, she edged her foot on the accelerator. Maggie was waiting. She couldn't afford to be late.

Sarah had not planned on celebrating Christmas this year. Maggie, on the other hand, loved everything about it, and she wasn't letting Sarah off the hook. It was why Sarah found herself at Maggie's kitchen table, smiling at Elliott as he tucked into his turkey. Today was a day for proper napkins, for shiny candlesticks and the best plates. For the scent of cloves and oranges, of pine needles and cinnamon sticks. Maggie and Elliott had returned to Slayton having stayed with distant family after the shock of the news. But like Sarah, Maggie seemed compelled to return.

'This looks amazing,' Sarah said, enjoying the feast. But Maggie's smile was strained, and she had lost more weight than was good for her.

'How are you both?' Sarah asked in a low voice as they worked their way through dinner. Christmas carols were playing in the background and Elliott seemed a million miles away.

'Getting there,' Maggie said, softly. 'The counsellor said it's going to take time for Elliott to process it all.' Her glance fell lovingly on her son. He no longer carried his father's medal. But seeing him looking like an ordinary little boy in his bright red Benetton jumper, new shoes and jeans brought a lump to Sarah's throat. He caught Sarah staring and gave her a reassuring smile. Such a grown-up gesture brought it home what a special little boy he was.

'Finished,' Elliott said, jumping from the chair to play with the iPad Santa had brought. Sarah had furnished him with enough gift vouchers to keep him in games for a while.

'I popped in to see Elsie this morning,' Sarah said, resting her cutlery on the table. 'You should visit her, she's doing really well.'

But Maggie paled at the mention of her name. 'I can't. Not when . . .' Her words faded but the meaning was clear. Not when her husband had tried to frame Christian.

'She doesn't blame you,' Sarah said. 'Nobody does. And it's very likely Christian will get a suspended sentence for his part in things.' The more she heard about Christian's involvement, the more it was clear he had been taken advantage of.

'It's been so hard to come back and face everyone.' Maggie fingered the stem of her wine glass. 'Even Elliott said he's ashamed of what his daddy did to his friends.'

A frown creased Sarah's features. It pained her to see Maggie so upset. 'If they're real friends they won't turn their backs on either of you. None of this has anything to do with you.' But when Maggie turned to face her, she had tears in her eyes.

'But it does. If I'd been honest with Lewis about you being alive, maybe his feelings wouldn't have festered. If I'd been honest with myself . . .' She stared into her wine glass. 'When I *did* tell him the truth . . . it was the match that lit the fuse.'

'But Lewis was ill,' Sarah replied. 'Anything could have triggered him.' As Maggie sipped her wine, she did not appear convinced.

'The last night the four of us were together, I heard him say he loved you.' Maggie gazed into her wine glass as she visited the past. 'I was eaten up with jealousy. I wanted Lewis for myself.'

Sarah didn't need to be reminded of the night they'd spent in Slayton's old asylum. It was one of many memories she wanted to keep in the past. 'That was years ago, Maggie. Put it behind you and start afresh.' Her gaze went to Elliott, who was playing Teenage Mutant Ninja Turtles on his iPad. 'You've got a special little boy there. Don't torture yourself.'

'What about us?' Maggie sniffed. 'Are we OK?'

Sarah squeezed her friend's hand. 'Better than OK.' Raising her glass in the air, she proposed a toast. 'To moving on.'

'To moving on,' Maggie agreed, tinkling her glass against Sarah's. But while their friendship had survived their ordeal, something told Sarah that she would need to be strong. As Maggie downed her wine, Sarah turned to see Elliott standing next to her. Her heart skipped a beat. She had not heard him creep up on them as his game came to an end. His eyes were dark and unblinking. A sense of dread lingered, and as she heard 'Silent Night', for a moment it felt as if someone has pressed pause on the world. The haunted look on Elliott's face conveyed what she already knew. *The Midnight Game is over, but Slayton lives on.* Whatever darkness it was that inhabited the town was not finished with them yet.

Acknowledgements

Being an author is my dream job and I'm grateful each day I get to write for a living. None of this would be possible without you, my valued readers, and the teams of people who have helped me along the way. *The Midnight Man* starts an exciting new chapter in my writing, with my new publishers, Embla Books, part of Bonnier Books UK. When I got the opportunity to work with the talented Jane Snelgrove and Emilie Marneur, I jumped at the chance. Working alongside Jennifer Porter and the rest of the Embla team has been an amazing experience and I'm also grateful to the brilliant copy editors, proofreaders, cover designer, audio book producers and narrators, and all the people behind the scenes who have brought this book to fruition.

Thanks also to the bloggers and book club members who exercise such generosity of spirit when it comes to reading, reviewing, and sharing my books. They have really come on board with this book, and I enjoyed the buzz on social media when it came to meeting the Midnight Man.

Huge thanks as always to the team at the Madeleine Milburn Literary, TV and Film Agency, and to Maddy for forging this new publishing partnership – it's a privilege to work with you.

As always, a special mention to my author friends, and to Mel Sherratt and Angela Marsons for always being there for me. Crime writers are the best. A special shout out to those in a certain author

Facebook group where I spend my time. You couldn't meet a nicer group of people. Being an author can be insular at times and it's good to have a network of friends. Thanks also to all my followers on social media and now TikTok, where I've been making a fool of myself on a daily basis.

One last very special shout to my grown-up children, Paul, Aoife, Jessica and Ben. I'm so proud of each of you. To Neil, my husband, who has been my unfaltering rock from day one. I'm blessed to have such an amazing family behind me.

Thank you for reading if you've made it this far. I love hearing from my readers and you can contact me via email on hello@caroline-writes.com. You can also find me on Facebook @CMitchellauthor, on Twitter @Caroline_writes, on Instagram @Caroline_writes, and now TikTok @CarolineMitchellAuthor. Sign up to my reader's club for news, updates and a free short story here: https://caroline-writes.com

About the Author

Caroline is a *New York Times*, *USA Today*, *Washington Post* and international number one bestselling author, with over 1.5 million books sold. To date her books have been shortlisted for the International Thriller Awards, the Killer Nashville Silver Falchion Awards and the Audie Awards. Her 2018 thriller *Silent Victim* won the US Readers' Favorite Award in the 'Psychological Thriller' category.

Caroline originates from Ireland and now lives with her family in a village on the coast of Essex. A former police detective, she specialised in roles dealing with vulnerable victims, victims of domestic abuse, and serious sexual offences. The people she encountered are a huge source of inspiration for her writing today.

Caroline writes full-time.

About Embla Books

Embla Books is a digital-first publisher of standout commercial adult fiction. Passionate about storytelling, the team at Embla publish books that will make you 'laugh, love, look over your shoulder and lose sleep'. Launched by Bonnier Books UK in 2021, the imprint is named after the first woman from the creation myth in Norse mythology, who was carved by the gods from a tree trunk found on the seashore – an image of the kind of creative work and crafting that writers do, and a symbol of how stories shape our lives.

Find out about some of our other books and stay in touch:

X, Facebook, Instagram: @emblabooks
Newsletter: https://bit.ly/emblanewsletter